The Streets Bleed Murder

Jerry Jackson

Lock Down Publications
Presents
The Streets Bleed Murder
A Novel by *Jerry Jackson*

The Streets Bleed Murder

Lock Down Publications
P.O. Box 870494
Mesquite, Tx 75187

Lock Down Publications
Facebook: Author Jerry Jackson
Like our page on Facebook: Lock Down Publications @
www.facebook.com/lockdownpublications.ldp
Cover design and layout by: **Dynasty's Cover Me**
Book interior design by: **Shawn Walker**
Edited by: **Lauren Burton**

Acknowledgment

God is amazingly great!! Salute to big homie up top because without his will then it's no us.

My two beautiful daughters Jada and Kahla Jackson, you both are my reason, my motivation, my drive. I'm working strictly for y'all just know that.

To my brothers, Chan Young, Twurk, Zach, Money Mel and Q, y'all hold a nigga down how it pose to go.

To my twin, Zaraykia Jackson, thank you baby girl. You carried Bruh ten years straight. My big sister, Neisha, I love you girl. Thank you for you and your husband supporting my cause. My nephew, Rico Shawty, Wats happening, foo? To all my nephews and nieces, uncle love y'all. To my Silent Money team, here we come. Swole Shawty, you 100%. Fuck wit me. No flaw, Bruh, real shit. Silentmoney Panama, love you, foo. ONE LOVE FOR THE UNION jug what's hap, Bruh? Lonta, Lyri and Ac support team still bangers on blast fist on clash. 2luv to the mob, dat foo Bally, RIP youngin da mob got you fooly and dat boy Bril Shawty, we still gon' stick to the plan cause I know you ready. To my big homie, Da Real Big Nard East Hamp champ, I love you, foo. My brothers from another mother, Kashtor, Mj, Woolfy (big bank no one's) Zone 3 Snoop, Terio, Lil E and Trama, y'all some real official niggas, no lie. From day one it's been love. Dat boi Night, dat boi Chinese Money and my nigga Grown Man.

To my number one supporter, my day one, my true best friend, the mother of my kids, Kristy Williams (@kristybriads) I cannot thank you enough for all that you have done for me with me and for raising our kids. Dap Nick up for me and hug the family.

Mr and Mrs Williams, God knows I appreciate every lil' thing you have done to support your child through her growth.

My grandma, Mrs. Mary Ann, I love you. Aunt Pam, thank you for everything. My cousin, Tweety Bird, girl, I love you. To Marikeisha, I want you to know that I appreciate every gestur. Thank you for believing in me even when I wouldn't. I love you.

To my LDP team thanks for the support. Ca$h, I salute you for giving me direction. You saved the game for a lot of us.

Keiaundria (Tess) bunk! bunk! Kiss Alli fa me. I love y'all two lil' ladies. Tell Shag Man stay up.

Anybody I forgot, I'm sorry I hope you understand but know the love is real. I miss who miss me and I love who hate me. God bless the haters.

Dedication

RIP to Rose Mary Jackson. Mama I did it and I know you are proud.

Jerry Jackson

Chapter 1

1999

The block party was live. The whole block of Dill Avenue was packed with a slew of different cars, trucks, and bikes. Many different groups and gangs also attended the block party Big Ann threw for the south side of Atlanta every year. Big Ann always hosted Southside Day, a day everyone from the south came together to party. The loud music blasted from two six-foot-tall speakers sitting on the porch of Big Ann's house. People danced, kids played, older guys held a craps game, and the females flirted every chance they got with the dope boys and tricks of the city's wealthy men. It was a Friday night, and the atmosphere was comfortable. The scene was well flavored with over two hundred southsiders. Tonight was the night people would see guys at their best and females busting the scale with phat asses and thick thighs. Tonight was a night when the big time dealers of Atlanta showed off their success from pushing drugs through the streets through their high-priced attire and high-priced vehicles. Tonight was also the night goons, hit men, and jack bois would be waiting for any form of slip up.

Gangsta, Kash, and Dank all sat unnoticed in a Ford F150 with tinted windows, smoking blunts of loud and waiting on the correct moment to catch Danny leaving so they could tail him to either his home or hideout. Danny was nearly impossible to rob. Nobody knew where Danny laid his head. As far as the world knew, he was a ghost that supplied Atlanta's projects and ghetto streets with some of the best loud the city offered.

As the blunt of loud was being passed, Gangsta noticed three girls walking past, and one of them had been eye candy to him since middle school. Teyummie Knight was coming up to him before he knew it. He slid the chrome .45 that sat in his lap under the seat and started to get out. He was quickly stopped by his partna's raspy voice.

"Shawty, leave that ho alone. She's fucked with lame Pat Man since we were in high school. You remember, she didn't give you play back then, so why would she now?" Kash asked, laughing.

Dank joined in on the laughter, which Gangsta did not find funny, but it did stop him from opening the door.

"You dead right, so fuck that ho," Gangsta spoke and grabbed his .45, then caught the rotation of the last of the loud blunt.

Dank began to roll up a third blunt while they were still waiting.

"Dat ho is bad, though," Dank said, more to himself than to his two friends.

Out of the three guys unnoticed inside the truck, Kash was the oldest, but Gangsta had been in the streets the longest. He came from the path of his older brother, Cool, who was a major dude in the streets. Even though he followed his brother, Gangsta was very smart, humble in everything he did as he looked up to his big brother and decided to be just like Cool. Against his mother's will, Gangsta was his oldest brother's shadow. Everything Cool did, Gangsta found out how to do it. It was not until Cool died that Gangsta started getting into trouble, a trait Cool didn't possess. When Cool passed, Gangsta was devastated and lost.

Gangsta, Dank, and Kash all met up in Rydc Juveniles Detention Center, and somehow they became close. They became instant brothers through loyal actions.

Back when the boys first met, Kash was the first one to get out, and as promised, he sent both his new friends money to make store call every week. Gangsta was released, and he and Kash together made sure they sent Dank money to eat and call home. Two months passed, and then Dank was free.

They quickly came up with a plan to muscle the weak niggas in Atlanta and lots of other money figures in the game. The group rode around Atlanta and the surrounding counties applying pressure to whomever allowed. Those who didn't comply with the muscle game got the drama they brought to the table.

For a six month run, the boys had four major drug pushers paying them a cut of what they earned, but the spree didn't last long. As always, when the guys would find a sucka, they'd push up together and go directly at him. They would demand whatever price they had figured out. The guy they thought was a sucka was an undercover narcotics agent and busted them on the spot. Kash and Dank got away from the scene, but Gangsta was sent to Alto State Prison. He served 36 months on the attempt to ransom, and had been free two months. He had only hit two small licks with his partnas, who were on some armed robbery shit when he got home.

"Man, dis fool need to come da fuck on," Dank said while looking at his watch, and Gangsta agreed with a shake of his head. The block party was still alive, and they had been waiting for two hours. Gangsta only had two hours before his mother locked the doors. He was 21 years old and knew he needed to get out of his mother's crib, but first he had to get his money right. Three years in the big house had given him other sights and visions, and being broke wasn't in the plan. Another hour had passed when they finally saw Danny with one arm draped over a female they recognized as Tonya from Hollywood Courts Projects. The two of them were heading to Danny's Range Rover. Gangsta cranked up quick.

"Stay 'bout four or five cars behind dis nigga, shawty," Dank said from the back while holding a double grip pump shotgun.

As soon as Danny pulled off, Gangsta waited 15 seconds and did the same. Gangsta proceeded to follow the Range Rover onto 75 North, then onto I-20, where Danny made it to Six Flags Drive. He smoothly exited the highway with a left turn. Ten minutes into the ride and a couple of turns later, Danny pulled up to a nice-sized house. Instantly Kash knew this was the correct spot, because every car Danny owned was posted in front of the home. The three friends watched closely from three houses down as Danny stumbled out of the Range Rover. He was led by Tonya to the double doors of his beautiful home.

As soon as the couple walked into the house, the three guys made their move. Dank was first to get out, holding the pump. Gangsta quickly tucked the .45 in his waistband and followed the lead. Kash also made his way out of the car. They smoothly walked up the street unnoticed.

They were happy about that, because being in Cobb County was scary as it is. Cobb County was a higher class living, where most white people resided with good jobs, kids went to great schools, and police were overly protective and overly aggressive. If the police get called, then nine times out of ten a nigga would not make it out.

"Let's just go," Dank said once they all were in the yard of Danny's home.

They were leaning on the side of one of his many cars, hidden as best as they could be.

"Fuck, no," Gangsta said. "This nigga might freak out."

"Listen," Kash said.

That got everyone's attention. They could hear laughter and a radio, which meant Danny was inside entertaining Tonya. The guys would have to wait until Danny took her to his bedroom for sex.

"Yeah, let's wait," Kash replied.

Gangsta knew there was no going home, so he told Kash he would have to find him a place to stay. Gangsta knew by the time they were done and he made it back to the west side, his mom would for sure have the doors locked, plus she refused to give him his key back because she said he wasn't responsible enough. Kash confirmed it was all good and he could spend the night over at his girl Erica's crib with him, and Gangsta agreed.

While waiting on Danny to slow down, all kinds of thoughts ran through Gangsta's mind. He wondered if Danny really had the type of money people assumed he had. He wondered if the lick would be worth it, or was this Danny dude a fake?

This was Kash's project, and he was good at planning a lick and a getaway. He was good at coming up with a plan B, so Gangsta knew it wasn't a game, but he didn't need slip-ups, either. Bad enough the guys were barely hidden between Danny's cars. Another hour had passed them by, and now it was 3:15 a.m. and the night air was getting cool. Danny had calmed down and retired to the bedroom. Dank and Gangsta walked around the house to check for a better way to get in, but saw none. Gangsta began using the glass cutter, and took five minutes to create a hole his hand could fit through.

"Let's go," he said in a whisper when he had the window unlocked and opened.

Gangsta was the first to get inside and was met by darkness and stillness. Kash held a Mac 90 with two hands and led the way upstairs. He knew nobody else stayed with Danny, but was fully prepared for any surprises. The first room they reached was locked, the second room is where they found Danny and Tonya laid out, both dead to the world. Kash hit the lights, which made Danny open up his eyes to find three barrels in his face.

"Shhh, we gonna do this shit the right way," Gangsta was the first to speak and snatched the covers from over two naked bodies.

Tonya shot up and went into full panic mode after noticing the gunmen. She began to scream with all her might, but was silenced.

Boom!

The loud double grip pump erupted throughout the house.

Tonya's face was mashed in, and most the back of her head plastered the wall and headboard of the bed.

"Nice and easy, pimp. Get yo' bitch ass out the bed," Dank said and cocked back the pump, making the shell jump out onto the floor.

Gangsta and Kash gave Dank a crazy look before starting to look for a safe.

"Man, do y'all niggas even know who y'all fuckin' with?" Danny asked.

"Yeah, muthafucka, and dat's why we're in yo' shit. Where that money and work at?" Gangsta smacked him upside the head with the .45.

Danny closed his eyes and wished this was all a dream, but then he opened his eyes and saw the reality of things. He saw the three men with guns. He could still hear the gunshot that had Tonya laid out across his king size bed.

"I don't wanna die," was all Danny could utter out of his mouth, and that's when Kash walked over.

"Fuck dis," Dank said and aimed the pump.

Gangsta stepped in and said, "Pussy, stop playing with us before you die, too."

Gangsta acted as if he was about to hit him again with the .45.

"Okay, okay, okay. We gotta move the bed," Danny finally said.

Dank held him at gunpoint while Kash and Gangsta moved the bed. Under it they found two safes in the floor.

"The combination is 6, 21, 36."

"And da other code?" Kash demanded.

"8, 23, 37," replied Danny in a fearful voice.

"Check it," Dank said.

He had the pump aimed directly at Danny's face. It seemed like forever when it was only two minutes, and then the safes were open. Gangsta and Kash were in awe at the stacks of bills they saw.

Gangsta walked over to Danny and asked, "Now, where's the loud?"

"Dis not my stash house, folk," Danny nervously said while looking at Dank.

He could tell Dank was a man itching to kill him.

"So, if we look around and find some loud, you know you die, right?" Kash said as Gangsta went to his closet to start looking.

"Okay, okay." Danny had no notion of being killed. "It's in the deep freezer."

As soon as the words escaped his lips....

Boom!

Dank shot him in the face at point blank range with the double grip.

"Chill da fuck out, John Wayne," Gangsta said, and then proceeded to help Kash load stacks of money in a suitcase.

Dank went into the kitchen to find 12 pounds of frozen Kush and a couple of scales. After they had the money and weed secured, the three split up in the house in search of anything else of value. When they found nothing, they all fled the scene and quickly jogged down the street to their ride, pulling off from a double homicide. All three of the guys were nervous. The two gunshots for sure woke the neighbors, since one or two lights were on in different homes as the trio jogged up the street. All Gangsta did was hope they made it out.

Gangsta took direction from Kash on the route to his girlfriend's house. The clock read 4:50 a.m., and he wasn't a bit drained. He was elated because he knew from the stacks of money they had collected that he was straight. Gangsta vowed to himself to never fall off or go broke again.

They pulled up to a house in Riverdale, Georgia that was built of red clay bricks. A nice Acura truck and a 300C sat in its driveway. Gangsta pulled up next to the Acura and hit the lights. He was happy to be at a resting stop so they could split the cut.

"Y'all chill for a minute, and I'm finna get the keys to the basement," Kash said and got out of the truck.

He pulled keys from his pockets as he walked up to the door of the home and used one of them to enter.

Kash was only gone three or four minutes before he reappeared from the side of the house and waved his partnas to join him. Gangsta and Dank got out of the truck with the product and money, and then followed Kash into a well-kept basement.

The basement was wall-to-wall carpet with a mini bar and music station, and flat screen TVs lined the wall. A wraparound leather sofa and plush chairs of the same make also complimented the room.

Each of the guys took seats and started to count the money they just hit for. It didn't take them long at all to split out 33 grand each and four pounds of loud Kush.

Dank decided to take the truck and get rid of it, so he left with promises to link up with them later that day. Kash went upstairs and came back down with an exotic-looking dark-skinned female he introduced as his girlfriend, Erica. Gangsta firmly acknowledged her, and the two of them left him alone in the basement with his own thoughts walking miles throughout his mind.

***

He could hear them, but his eyes couldn't even force themselves open. He was extremely tired. His body was numb. Gangsta felt as if he had just closed his eyes two seconds ago. All he wanted was a nice rest without being interrupted in any form. Last night he fell asleep on the couch, but for some reason he did not find comfort. Thoughts of what happened crossed his mind, leaving him to toss and turn throughout the night, and rest seemed nonexistent. Thoughts of his money and drugs helped him to get up. He noticed Erica, Kash's girlfriend, and another female standing by the bar. Erica was cleaning the countertop while the other female stood off to the side, both talking in whispers until Erica saw him open his eyes

"Good Morning. Do you want anything to eat?" Erica respectfully asked him.

"Nah, I'm straight," Gangsta said and sat up to get a better look at the other female.

She kind of favored a light-skinned Halle Berry. Not the exact look, but she held that perfect pretty, the same as Halle did. She was slim with nice hips, and she was bowlegged.

"How did you rest?" Erica asked.

"It was okay. Where is Kash?"

"He's still asleep. Do you want me to wake him?"

Gangsta stood up and eyed the female again. She was also looking at him.

"Nah, let me just use yo' phone so I can call a cab."

"A cab," the girl spoke. "I can use da gas. Where are you trying to go?"

Her voice was pretty, like her face. She had a high port personality, you could tell.

"South Grand off Bankhead. Could you do dat?" Gangsta asked.

"Yeah, I can do that," the girl said and walked upstairs. "Give me three minutes," she said over her shoulder.

"That's my sister," Erica said and winked before following behind her.

Minutes later, the girl came back down to get him. They walked out the front door and climbed into the 300C.

"So, what's yo' name, Mr. South Grand?"

"Gangsta."

"Your birth name, please. I am not about to call you Gangsta." She laughed a bit.

"Gary. And what's your name?" he replied while looking over at her beauty.

"My given name is Nya. My family and friends call me NeNe."

"Okay, and where's yo' nigga?" Gangsta asked.

"Dang, you get straight to the point, huh?"

"No time to flex."

NeNe laughed and pulled her 300C into the BP gas station up the street from their home.

"How much you payin' me?" she asked when she parked next to the pump.

The Streets Bleed Murder

"Fill yo' car up," he said and watched her go inside the store.

Gangsta took that time to get out and pump the gas for her. He watched her walk back over to the car, and he fell in love with the sway of her walk and her legs. He couldn't take his eyes off the woman, and NeNe knew it, which kind of made her nervous and blush.

For a minute they rode in silence. Gangsta, being street and physically captivated, could no longer hold his tongue. He was curious and wanted to know of this female.

"I've got a question," he said out of nowhere.

"Huh?" NeNe looked from the road to him and quickly back to the road.

"I have a question," he repeated.

"Okay," she replied, eyes focused on the road ahead, but her attention was with him.

"Are you single?"

"I am, and yourself?" NeNe shot back as quick as she got it.

"I'm very single and, just being honest, I find it hard to believe you're single. Why are you single?" Gangsta asked.

"My last relationship dealt with insecure actions, and he wanted to be too hands-on, if you know what I mean," NeNe shot back.

"And how long has it been since you and him were together?"

"It's been two years and four months."

Her statement made him burst out laughing. He looked at her with a *yeah right* look before saying, "So, you ain't messed with a guy in two years and four months?"

"Yes, it's been that long, and that is nonstop," she replied.

"Damn."

"And why are you single?" Ne-Ne asked.

"'Cause I just got out from doing three years and girls ain't loyal."

"Dat's so untrue."

"Dat's real," replied Gangsta.

The rest of the ride they spoke no words. They both listened to the radio and grooved to the music until she finally made it to his mother's house. NeNe pulled her 300C into the driveway next to a Honda Accord.

"Okay, so what I owe you?" Gangsta said while opening the door to get out.

It was bright and early. The sun wasn't even out yet. The grass was misty with the morning dew.

"You gave me $50 for gas, so I'm straight," she replied.

Gangsta smiled it off while reaching into his pocket, where he pulled out a few bills. He peeled her off five twenties.

"Here, and thank you, NeNe. Now, can I call you sometime?" he nervously asked.

"If Erica says it's cool, then yup."

"Yo' sister?" he asked, confused.

She started laughing.

"Boy, I'm only joking." She wrote her number down on a piece of paper and passed it to him.

Chapter 2

"Gary, you need to come on if you want to be on time." He could hear his mother yell from her bedroom.

Gangsta grabbed his ID, phone, and a few hundreds for pocket change. He also made sure not to forget his money order for the condo he was about to lease near Buckhead Paces Ferry.

He was dressed down in simple attire consisting of Ralph Lauren with the shoes to match. He met up with his mother at the door as he was leaving the house. When she saw her son, she just shook her head because she knew he was a handful and some more. Ms. Jackson knew that no matter what, Gangsta would always be street. His actions would always show he was street. He would always get some money and did not mind a fight, rumble or war.

She was happy to not have raised a bitch boy, but she could've done without most of his street ways. Gangsta stood 5'11", 190 pounds with a light brown skin tone and wavy hair. He was cut due to working out in prison and was far from ugly.

"Let's go, Ma," he said while looking down at her 5'2" frame.

Gangsta and his mother had a beautiful relationship. He was her only living son and had never met his father. He grew up on South Grand and was raised by the west side of Atlanta. His mother loved their four-bedroom house passed down to them through generations, and over the years growing up Gangsta fell in love with the house, also.

No matter what, Gangsta knew he had a place to rest if all else failed. Since his brother was killed, he and his mother had a very close relationship. Though she could not keep him from the streets, Ms. Jackson still spoiled her only living son with attention and love.

Gangsta held a great amount of respect for his mother and always took heed to her wisdom. She was always behind him, right or wrong.

It did not take them long to do the paperwork for the condo and for him to deposit five grand into an account set up to pay the $1,600 rent every month. His mother did not understand why her son chose to live in such an expensive condo, but Gangsta reassured her.

"Ma, you raised a hustler."

Gangsta took her to a Steak 'n' Shake a few blocks away from the condo so they could eat something before he took her shopping. He wanted to show her around the area he planned to stay in so she would see he wasn't in the hood.

The food was great, the people were nice and well mannered, and the atmosphere was humbling. Gangsta and his mother laughed over dinner and spoke about her new position at her job working at Grady Memorial Hospital as head nurse.

"It's just something to keep my bills paid. I mean, don't get me wrong, when I first started my heart was in it. I was full of passion for the job back then, but over the years it has turned into just a job," his mother said over dinner, and Gangsta understood exactly what she meant.

They finished the meal and Gangsta left a nice tip as they walked side by side toward his truck, and then they headed to the jewelry store.

***

Kash

He couldn't imagine being in a better place in life as he took two big hits off the loud blunt. He inhaled deeply and held the smoke while looking around at the many pounds of midgrade weed he scored from a Mexican plug in Buford, GA.

Kash was downstairs inside his girl's basement with fifty pounds of weed — half he paid for and the other half he was given on consignment. He had plans to cop a couple times, and then he planned to wipe the Mexican's nose clean for every crumb he could get his hands on.

It'd been two weeks since the murder, and the streets were talking. Mostly the streets were pointing fingers at his group because the guys wasted no time pushing ounces of loud the very next day. Dank upgraded from a Caprice to a Range Rover super sport, Kash upgraded to a Suburban, and Gangsta was pushing a black on black Ram truck with super black tint, though nobody dared say anything out loud.

Kash finished his blunt and picked up his phone to call Dank, who picked up on the third ring.

"Yo."

"Shawty, help me jump this mid, and I got bags for 950."

"You caught a lick, fool?" Dank's deep voice boomed through the phone.

"Nah, I copped dis."

"Okay, I got a lil' ho on Simpson and we can set up at shawty spot. That's where I got off my whole network."

"Sound right to me," Kash replied.

He left the fifty pounds in the basement and walked upstairs where Erica was cooking his two kids something to eat.

"So, is you fuckin' wit' zips?" Dank wanted to know.

"I tell you what, I'ma bring you ten for seven bands. That means you will score something like five racks free money if you slang zips, right?" Kash said, walking up behind Erica at the stove.

He kissed the back of her neck and pushed up on her phat ass.

"Yeah, that's straight. I'm waiting on you," Dank replied, and they disconnected the phone call.

Kash took a seat at the table with his two kids, Charles Junior and Unique, whose mother was a police officer. Kash did not fuck with the police, so when Ebony decided she would go into law enforcement, they quickly broke up. The two of them were still cool, but they did not kick it at all.

Kash was only 23 years old. His real name was Charles McCants, the son of Susan and Jeffery McCants, two successful business owners with plenty of money. He was the only child, and as a kid he always rebelled against his parents' commands. He always strayed into trouble for all types of reasons, and his parents couldn't understand what was going on with their child.

His parents placed him in the best schools, spoiled him with anything he wanted, and took him any place he wanted to go, and still Kash found trouble. He seemed to get a rush from the drama of being a badass kid. It had gotten so out of control that Kash's mother and father sent him to doctors and schools for kids who are overly hyper and need special attention. Nothing seemed to work for Kash, and with every day that passed his attitude got worse and his parent's couldn't deal with it any longer.

They kicked Kash out of their home when he was arrested for burning a cat alive. He was sentenced to five years, but only served two years on good behavior. He was released to the streets because his parents refused to open their home to him again. His mother went as far as renting him an apartment and kept his bills paid until it got raided for drugs.

It had been six years since he'd reached out to them for any type of help. All Kash did was drop his kids off to his parents when they had time to watch them. His relationship with his parents was rocky, but still on okay terms.

Erica sat a plate down in front of him and a plate for both of his kids. She joined him at the table.

***

Gangsta

Gangsta was at the four-way red light of Bankhead and Hightower in his black Ram truck beating Monsta Swole, a zone four west side cat who was hot in the city. He was feeling great as he nodded his head to the music. He made a left on Hightower and then quickly turned into the gas station for some blunt wraps.

The Texaco Gas Station was crowded, though he managed to find a spot to park and quickly jumped out. Gangsta was draped down in a blue and lemon-colored Duckhead shirt and the heavy-duty Duckhead jeans with the duck face on the pockets. He wore all white Mari tennis shoes and an Eso Movado watch. He got all types of strange looks from people because Duckhead had long ago played out, though his clothes were fresh off wax. Gangsta made it his business to wear all throwback clothing, no matter what the day.

Out of all the looks and whispers Gangsta saw and heard, he noticed a familiar face of a known hitman out of Atlanta named Glock. Gangsta saw him from a distance watching him, but Glock tried to play it off as if he wasn't looking. Gangsta played his role also, but silently wished he had the .45 on him instead of in his truck. He paid for the blunt wrap and a can of soda, and then walked out of the gas station. He saw Glock pulling up when he made an exit. Gangsta eyed the money green Crown Victoria and watched for any type of movement from Glock. He didn't see any, and Glock pulled off into the streets as he blasted his music.

Gangsta was elated that no drama unfolded on Bankhead, but was still fairly paranoid. Gangsta jumped in his truck and smashed off in a different direction. Glock did not like Gangsta, and his feelings were the same. Glock was a older head in the streets, a hired hitman. Word was that Glock was paid to kill Cool to get him out of the way. Gangsta was only a kid back then, so he never really gave it thought, plus he asked his mother one day and she said it was all rumors. Even though Gangsta just got out of prison, he knew to be on point, 'cause when someone saw Glock's face, someone would unfortunately die soon.

It took him fifteen minutes to pull up into Hollywood Courts Projects on Hollywood Road where Dank stayed with his oldest son's mother. Gangsta also knew a couple dudes from the projects that he dealt with on different occasions.

The projects was full of its daily activities: grownups on their porches having beer and playing spades, kids running around playing or riding their bikes, the older crew playing basketball while the girls their age flirted every chance they got.

He pulled up next to Dank's whip and noticed Kash's car out there as well. Gangsta parked and got out. He saw both his partnas and showed them love.

"What's up?" Gangsta spoke.

"Shit, fool, we were 'bout to smash to yo' spot. We thought you were scared to come outside," Kash said, laughing.

"Nah, nigga, I just been coolin'. What's up, though? What da play is?" Gangsta replied.

They all walked to the Range Rover and got in. Gangsta began to roll a blunt in the backseat as Dank informed them of his newfound trap spot on Simpson. He quickly painted a beautiful picture and threw extreme numbers out that sounded good to his two partnas. Even though it sounded nice, Gangsta still liked taking money better than hustling.

They smoked two Kush blunts and went over plans to rob Cris and Dinky, two of Bowen Homes Projects' weight men with powder and weed. Kash was super cool with Cris through doing business. He could see in Cris' eyes he wasn't built to control the type of money he had. Dinky had to be pussy as well, because two birds of a feather flock together.

Dank agreed to the plot as well as Gangsta. Dank wanted to kidnap Cris or Dinky and ransom the other. It seemed crazy at first, but Gangsta was down, so Kash set a date to strike.

After leaving Kash and Dank, Gangsta decided to ride to his first cousin's house on Johnson Road. It was a major drug spot in Atlanta's zone one area. Johnson Road was a family hood, a rough place to live, but those that lived there adapted to the ins and outs of how it rolled. Everybody knew everybody. Most of the people who stayed on Johnson Road were either family or childhood friends.

Everybody was in the yard like always when he pulled his truck up behind his cousin's Impala. Nobody knew it was Gangsta until he jumped out super clean in his throwback gear. The first person to spot him was his long ago ex-girlfriend Terry, whom he heard was messing with Zay, a weed and crack slinger with a mean hustle game.

"Hey, Gary, come here," Terry said, standing next to her two friends, Nikki and Roxanne.

Terry was light skinned like Lisa Raye with that same player's club shape. She was considered one of the baddest females on the Westside. All types of dudes tried to get with her, but failed. She just had a thing for west side cats, and that's why she was in love with Gangsta.

The two of them broke up when he did his first bid, and they never got back together. He was her first love and her first sex partna, and that had a big hold on her. She didn't stay down the few months they were together, and she knew Gangsta didn't respect that.

Gangsta acted as if he didn't hear her as he walked up to where his cousin was seated. He was on the porch with a few goons on call. He gave everybody dap, then took a seat.

"What's up, boy?" Gangsta spoke to his cousin and pulled out a blunt wrap as Terry strolled over.

"Nigga, I know you heard me," she said with one hand on her hip.

She wore a pair of jeans that looked like they were painted on her slim waist.

"What's up, shawty?" Gangsta acted surprised to see her.

He poured a gram of Kush into a wrap.

"Come here," she demanded, looking at him with her grey eyes looking good as ever, but he wouldn't let her know that.

His cousin Eric jumped in and said, "Man, get out my yard with that ghetto shit."

Everybody knew Terry would get stupid if she didn't get her way, so Gangsta got up to see what she wanted.

Gangsta stood up to walk down the steps toward her.

"What's up, shawty?" he asked, and she grabbed one of his hands and pulled him away from his friends and family.

"I know your mother told you I called," Terry said and looked him directly in his eyes, waiting on him to lie.

She was practically daring him to lie in her face when he knew she could read him well.

"Nah, she ain't said nothing," Gangsta lied, because his mother did tell him every time Terry called.

His mother was a big fan of Terry. She loved her like her own daughter. She talked to her all the time and always said at any given moment Terry could pull up to her house and get a bed.

"Why is your ass lying, Gary?" She playfully pushed a finger in his face before asking, "Who's truck you driving?"

"It's mines, and where is Zay at? Ain't y'all fuckin' around?" he decided to ask.

"And?" Terry shot back.

"Shid, I don't want shawty to ride up da block and see me in your face. He might get the wrong idea." Gangsta spoke through a smile, which made Terry roll her sexy eyes.

"Zay do not own me, honey. I am grown. Zay knows how I feel 'bout you. Won't nothing or no nigga change that," she replied.

"Oh, really?"

"Yes, really, nigga. Anyhow, drop me off when you leave. I gotta go to work tomorrow, and I do not feel like waiting on Nikki."

She rolled her eyes as always.

"Oh, Terry got a job?" Gangsta laughed. "I know it's gonna snow."

"Gary, I'm for real. Will you take me home?"

"You going to Bankhead Court?" he asked and hit the fresh blunt he just lit up.

"Yes."

Gangsta had wild thoughts in his head of him and Terry making rough love in a nice suite and blowing on loud. He kind of missed seeing her sexy body and that lustful look she held when in the heat of the moment.

"We need to hit da hotel, and then I'll drop you to work from the room. I'm try'na taste you."

"Honey, please, I'm for real man. Take me home, boy."

Terry stomped her feet and tried to snatch the blunt from his hand, but failed.

"Why don't you ask Zay?"

Terry took a slow step back.

"Don't play," Terry replied and walked away to rejoin her two friends as Gangsta rejoined his cousin Eric on the porch.

Minutes after he talked with Terry, Gangsta noticed a money green Impala on big rims with loud music pull into the yard next to his whip. Zay jumped out with two of his shooters. Gangsta knew them both, and he knew that the both of them were about that life. Gangsta watched Zay call Terry over and speak a few words to her. Then he reached into his pocket to produce a wad of cash. He peeled her off some money, and Terry jumped into the Impala with her friends and they pulled off.

"What's up, boy?" Zay asked as he walked up the steps toward Gangsta, followed by his shooters.

Gangsta passed him the still-lit blunt he had been smoking.

"Shawty, what's happenin'?" Gangsta asked.

Zay hit the blunt and took a seat on the steps. Gangsta knew deep down that Zay enjoyed the fact he had Terry. Every slick chance he got he would throw it or rub it in Gangsta's face.

One thing Gangsta knew was that, no matter what, he could take Terry back any day because Zay caught her on the rebound. He caught her when she was single and started to shower her with gifts and money. Zay wasn't the best looking guy on the streets and he knew it. It was no shock when word hit that Zay was near rich in the game and had a major connection for the work.

"How long you been out, bruh?" Zay asked.

"'Bout two months."

"You try'na get some money? You know I fucks wit'cha."

"Dat's all that's ever on my mind, shawty."

"We gonna link up. I got my swagger in these streets going hard," Zay shot back.

"Shid, that's the move. I'm with that."

After they smoked the blunt, Gangsta decided to leave. He gave all his partnas dap and then exchanged phone numbers with Zay. Gangsta stood up and jumped down the three steps into the yard where his truck was parked. He got in, cranked it up, and Monsta Swole boomed through the speakers.

Gangsta's mother only stayed a fifteen-minute walk or a five-minute drive away on South Grand, so Gangsta rode up Johnson Road. He made a right and then a left on Gun Club. He came out to the flashing light on Hollywood Road, where he made another right and punched the gas, making the truck fishtail a bit. Gangsta looked both ways to make sure it was clear to cross over to South Grand. As soon as he turned on his mother's street, he saw Glock coming out. Glock threw up the deuces, and then he hit Bankhead, smashing the gas up the street.

Gangsta instantly got heated, because now he knew this nigga was on some more shit. Gangsta vowed to handle it, because being this close to his mother was no excuse, no exceptions.

Gangsta finally made it to his mother's house and pulled into the driveway. He quickly got out and used his keys to enter the house. He found his mother in the kitchen. Gangsta's heart went back to its normal pace, elated to the highest degree to see his mother was safe.

Gangsta kissed his mother's jaw.

"What's up, Ma?" he asked with a smile on his face.

Then he grabbed one of the pork chops she had cooked and took a seat at the kitchen table. He pulled his phone out and texted Kash.

Chapter 3

Five Hours Later

The sun was slowly dropping in the cool of the night and giving the sky a pink and purple glow. It was a beautiful sight. It was a sight that let people know their day was about over and the darkness would soon embrace. Gangsta was inside his room, seated on his bed with two rubber-banded bankrolls of four grand each. A Glock .40 with four clips was also on the bed, sprawled out next to his phone and a bomb of one thousand pills. His small safe was opened and nested neatly in the closet.

Gangsta grabbed the phone and read its message from Kash. It was the address to Glock's baby mama's crib. After he read the message, Gangsta tossed his life savings into the safe along with three clips from the Glock .40. He didn't plan a war with this nigga. *It could be only one thing,* Gangsta thought. *A hit.* Someone must have put a hit on him, but *who* was the question.

The phone lit up again with a message, and this time it was Terry. The message read:

Come get me.

Gangsta paid the text no attention as he got his keys to leave. He was on a mission to figure out what was up with this dude Glock.

Gangsta heard the horn blow and proceeded to go outside to find Dank in a Cutlass waiting on him. He made his way downstairs and out the door after giving his mother a kiss and firm hug.

"What's up, fool?" Gangsta said as he climbed inside the Cutlass.

"What's happenin'?" Dank asked.

Gangsta noticed a .357 long barrel handgun lying across Dank's lap. They pulled off from South Grand and onto Bankhead, then headed to Fair Street Bottom where Glock's baby mama stayed. It was a place Glock was almost always posted.

It didn't take but twenty minutes to make it to the University Homes Projects on Fair Street Bottom. Dank found a good place to park in view of the baby mama's apartment to watch Glock's comings and goings.

"What's up with dis fool?" Dank asked while he began to roll up a blunt of loud.

"Shawty, I don't even know, but he fucking with the right one," Gangsta replied and tightly clutched the Glock .40. He was ready to light University Homes Projects up. Gangsta heard his phone start to ring and saw on the caller ID that it was Terry. At first he wasn't going to answer, but decided to go ahead.

"Hello," he said.

"I like how you stood me up, nigga," her voice humbly said through the phone.

"Shit, I saw you driving that nigga shit."

"And?"

"And I knew you was straight then," Gangsta shot back, and then he noticed a car pull into the parking lot.

He focused on the ride as it parked and two females got out with a kid.

"It's 8:30, so come out here and see me," Terry said.

"I'm handling something right now."

"Well, come by when you're done. I don't know why you acting crazy."

"Yeah, I can do that," Gangsta replied and kind of smiled it off.

Just like Terry was crazy about him, he was as crazy about her. He made a mental note to swing by when things were handled with Glock.

Fifteen minutes after he hung up the phone with Terry, he saw Glock pull up with his music blasting, without a care in the world. Gangsta made sure not to take his eyes off Glock as he parked his car. It was fully dark, but kids were still out and about running around, and older folks acted as if the sun was still out as they mingled through the projects.

"His ho stays on the end, shawty. I'm finna pull around on Fair Street and you can handle yo' bizness and come down the steps," Dank said as Gangsta opened the door to get out.

He did not want to miss the right moment and slip up. He got out and slid the Glock .40 in his back pocket. He still had his eyes locked on Glock as he was going to his trunk.

Gangsta walked unnoticed toward the side of the building. He went in the same direction Glock would to enter his baby mama's apartment.

Gangsta saw two young females walking toward him, so he stopped them because they would make him fit in.

He asked them if they knew where he could find some weed. They pointed him to an apartment and gave him a name, then walked off. That's when he saw Glock getting closer, so he tightly gripped the Glock .40 in his back pocket. Once Glock was only a few feet away from his baby mama's door, Gangsta lifted the Glock .40 to his face and let off two shots.

Boom! Boom!

The shots snapped Glock's head back and made his fitted cap fall off. Glock stumbled a bit and began to reach for his face. His hands failed to make it as his body hit the ground. Gangsta saw Glock's body jump a couple times as life left it. He stood over his lifeless body and shot him again in the face.

Boom!

Gangsta still didn't have a good reason to just take Glock out, but it was better to be safe than sorry, so whoever was at him would get a clear picture to fall back and stay safe.

He tucked the Glock .40 and ran back around the corner and down the steps to the waiting Cutlass.

***

Kash

Kash held his sleeping son in his arms as he made his way to his Range Rover followed by his daughter. She was carrying her small overnight bag. Kash unlocked and opened the truck's doors with the remote. He pulled back the door, placed his son in the car seat, and buckled him up. Then he helped his daughter climb inside and buckled her up, too. He looked up before getting in the driver's seat and noticed Erica standing in the doorway. Kash threw up deuces and jumped in the truck.

He needed to drop his kids off to their mother. Erica and he stayed in Riverdale while his babies' mother stayed on Six Flags Drive, so he made a quick stop to get gas and then hit the highway.

It took him thirty-eight minutes to pull into the driveway of Ebony's house. Sitting in her driveway was her BMW truck and Cobb County squad car. Kash hated to see that car. He saw the front door open and out came Ebony's husband, another police officer. Even though Ebony was on the police force, she did not sweat him or his ways because she met Kash that way. Indeed, she wanted him to change, and she could not wait for him to do it. She changed herself and prayed he'd follow.

Kash reached over and unbuckled his daughter, then gave her a kiss as she jumped out. Ebony's husband opened the back door to get Charles Junior.

"What's up, Kash? Are you good?" he asked while unbuckling Charles Junior.

Charles Junior got out of the car seat and climbed into the front seat to give his daddy some dap and a hug.

"Bye, Daddy," he said and climbed out through the driver's side door.

Kash threw one of his hands back over his head to give Ebony's husband some dap.

"What's up, Greg?" Kash spoke back as they dapped each other up.

Ebony appeared out of the house. She was a pretty, jet-black female with long hair. She had the build of a runner, the ass of a stripper, and a face of someone exotic. She walked over and picked up her daughter, then waved to Kash, who in return waved back. Both of them held a full respect for the other and remained cool for the kids' sake. It seemed to work out well.

Kash backed out of the driveway and pulled off to head back to his girl's house in Riverdale. He decided to ride the street way to make a stop on the west side. He wanted to holla at Dank again about the lick in Bowens Homes.

Before Kash made it to Hollywood Courts, he saw Dinky's gray pickup truck at Do Drop In, a hood store on Hollywood Road. Kash quickly pulled over and looked at the time. It was almost 10 p.m. and the only thing he had on him was a .357 and some chloroform gas. This wasn't in the plan, but the opportunity had presented itself. Hollywood Road at night was a dark hell, so hardly anyone walked these streets at night. If he was going to make a move, now was better than anything he would come up with later.

Kash pulled up a few feet from Dinky's ride and saw it was empty. He parked beside it quickly and cut the truck off. He stuffed the keys inside his pockets and jumped out, his eyes watching the door to the store. He went to the back of the truck, which was automatically opening after he had pressed the button. He found the small can of gas and held his breath as he twisted the cap off, then poured some onto a rag he found.

Kash quickly closed the back to his Range Rover and looked around at his surroundings. Nothing was out of place, and the coast was clear. He walked toward the store and stood next to the icebox. Dinky stepped out with a soda in one hand, and he was fumbling with his keys with the other hand.

Kash quickly crept up behind Dinky and placed the rag over his mouth and nose. He held the fighting Dinky in a tight grip while talking in his ear.

"Fuck, nigga, go to sleep!"

Kash held Dinky for a few minutes, then finally his body went limp and he was out cold.

Kash looked behind himself while holding Dinky's limp body. The few occupants inside the store didn't notice him, so he started to drag Dinky's body toward his own pickup truck. He tossed him inside and laid him across the seat. Kash hurried around to the driver's side and climbed in. He went through Dinky's pockets for the keys and came up empty. A quick search around the truck found nothing. He looked outside by the door of the store and saw the keys on the ground. He wasted no time in getting out and going to retrieve them. He jumped back into the truck, started it up, and drove up Gun Club.

***

Jerry Jackson

Gangsta

He was flipping through the TV channels when Terry walked into her room from a shower wearing only a t-shirt and some panties. She reached for the covers, but Gangsta was lying across the bed, so he got up to allow her to pull them back.

"Hey, you need to take dis down, and them," Gangsta said, pointing to the many pictures of Zay and her.

"You take 'em down if you don't wanna see 'em."

Terry climbed into bed to get comfortable and Gangsta got back on the bed, but this time he laid across her thighs.

"Man—"

"Man, my ass," Terry said.

After he couldn't find anything on TV, Gangsta decided to take off his shoes.

"What are you doing?" Terry asked.

"I'm spending da night, partna," he replied while taking off his pants and shirt.

That left him naked except his boxer shorts. He pulled the covers back and slid into the bed beside her warm body.

"You're crazy," she said with a smile.

"Yeah, but just 'bout you."

Gangsta pulled her small frame into his arms and held her until she fell asleep. He went to sleep himself minutes later, mind spinning with thoughts of what went down tonight and hopes that the girls he spoke to did not stick around long enough for the police to get there. If they did, it would be a long day in hell for him. Gangsta knew he was treading on thin ice and had to tighten up or go down big.

Something made Gangsta wake up out of a beautiful sleep to the still of the night. Darkness met his eyes when they fluttered open, though light peeked through the cracked door of the bathroom. The TV was off and the entire house was quiet. Gangsta reached for his phone and saw he had four missed calls, all from Kash. He also noticed the time was 5:46 a.m. He put the phone back, and the first thing he did was reach for Terry's small frame. She was lying on her back wildly with one arm thrown over her pretty face and the other over her flat stomach.

Gangsta slid his hand on top of the hand she had on her stomach. He moved it down around her navel until he reached the elastic of her white sheer panties. He pressed down with two fingers to dip under and continue his journey down and felt her pubic hairs. Gangsta didn't stop there and kept going until he reached her pussy lips and felt the warm wetness. He knew from past experience that she was awake, and nine times out of ten she would wait for him to make his move

Gangsta could not help but push a finger into her pussy to feel her tight walls. He leaned up and kissed her lips. She kissed him back while rolling her hips to his finger, fucking her pussy.

He stopped his thrusts, pulled his hand back, and began to take off her panties. Terry lifted her hips up to help him remove them, and then she took off her shirt. He slid his boxer shorts off and positioned himself between her legs while they tongue kissed each other. Terry moaned his name and arched her back when she felt him enter her.

"Oh, Gary," she moaned.

"Yes," Gangsta said back.

He went deep inside her. She almost panicked at how he filled her up. It hurt, but also felt great.

It had been nearly six years since they'd had sex. To be honest, the both of them were still kids at the time, and now they were both grown. Terry felt so good wrapped around his dick. She was warm and tight like she hadn't been fucked in a very long time. Her body was soft and warm, and the way she was fucking him back and moaning was driving him insane.

Gangsta thrust in and out of her and had both his hands under the arch of her back. He felt his balls soaked from her wetness. Terry continued to roll her hips harder.

"I'm 'bout to cum. Oh, *Gary*," she yelled.

She bit down on his shoulder and her body shook uncontrollably. After she calmed down a bit, Gangsta pulled out of her.

"Turn ova," Gangsta ordered. "Lay on yo' stomach."

Terry obliged him by lying face down with her ass up. He entered her and she slowly laid flat on her stomach. That allowed Gangsta to get in the push up position and beat her pussy up good. He went fast, and then slow. On those slow moments, he would kiss the top of her back and shoulder blades. He also placed kisses on her neck.

Terry put her face in the pillow and screamed as Gangsta deep stroked her hard. Terry gripped the sheets.

"You finna cut dat nigga off?" he asked while continuing to enter her deep.

He felt himself in power and about to cum — two of the best feelings in the world.

"Okay," Terry wasted no time replying, because she cared more for Gangsta than she did for Zay. Within seconds he shot his load inside her and jerked a few times while sucking on her neck. He rolled from on top of her onto his back.

"What time you gotta work?" he asked.

"I have to be there at 11 a.m."

Terry moved closer to him, placing one of her legs over his and resting her head on his chest to listen to his rapid heartbeat.

"Well, I'm finna dip, shawty." He kissed the top of her head.

Terry sat up and looked at the clock. She removed the wild hair that was in her face, and then found her t-shirt that had tangled up in the sheet and put it on. After she found her panties, she spoke while putting them on.

"I get off at 8 o'clock, so are you coming to get me?"

Gangsta stood his naked body up and found his boxer shorts, then got his jeans.

"I guess I am," Gangsta replied.

"Zay usually picks me up, but he is history, am I correct?" Terry asked.

She held his shirt out to him and then looked at him for some form of confirmation.

"Don't be flexin', 'cause if you fuckin' wit' me, then Zay is out da picture. I'm not sharing," Gangsta replied.

"You said what you said, and I said what I said, so fuck Zay. I'm wit' you now."

That was all Terry had to say.

Chapter 4

Kash

When Kash woke from his slumber, the first thing he did was look next to him to find Erica was gone. The wall clock read 11:47 a.m. He reached for his phone on the nightstand and saw Gangsta had texted him.

What's the haps, fool?

Kash got up and headed toward the bathroom. He washed his face and brushed his teeth, then stared at himself in the mirror to make sure he was straight. Kash took a brief shower and put on some fresh gear Erica had laid out for him.

Kash walked into the living room and saw NeNe, his girlfriend's sister, seated on the sofa watching a movie on their sixty-four inch TV.

"What's up, sis? Do you know where Erica put my sack at?" he asked about his personal stash of purple haze he smoked faithfully every morning.

"Yeah," NeNe replied, and then pointed to the bowl under the coffee table with almost twenty-eight grams in it.

"Bet dat," he said as he proceeded to get his product.

He paid NeNe no more attention as he took the entire bowl, walked back into the bedroom, and closed the door. He got the phone and called Gangsta, who picked up on the third ring.

"Whoa," Gangsta answered.

"What's up, shawty? I been try'na link up wit' you all night," Kash said as he began to roll up a blunt wrap.

"I was tired as fuck last night, boy. What da play is, though?" Gangsta shot back.

"I got Dinky," Kash said.

"You did? Okay, so what you got 'im for?"

Gangsta was kind of surprised that Kash hit the lick alone.

"Naw, I just kidnapped the sucka. He on Ruth Street at Pat's crib, duct taped down," Kash replied. Pat was one of the weed men in the hood and a known spot where people could find some of the best dogfights.

Kash explained how he pulled the kidnapping off, then how he wanted the ransom to go down. He told Gangsta that Dank already knew and was gonna be the one who applied the pressure to Dinky for information in two more days. Kash wanted panic to set into Cris and Dinky before he approached the situation.

"Okay, well, I'm in da streets now, shawty. We'll link up in Hollywood Courts a lil' later," Gangsta replied, and minutes later they hung up the phone with each other.

Kash put fire to the blunt wrap stuffed with purp. The next phone call he made was to his mother.

"Hello," his mother stated in a joyful tone.

"Ma, what's up? What y'all doing? Where's dad?"

"Hey, baby," his mother greeted him before paying attention to his questions.

He could hear in his mother's voice she was happy to hear from him. She thought any day Kash missed going to jail was a blessing in her eyes.

"Where's dad?" he asked again.

"In the yard messing with the help. You know he can't stand to sit back. He's too much of a boss to not give orders," his mother said, laughing.

Kash sure did miss his mother and made a mental note to go see his parents soon.

Kash talked with his mother a few more minutes, and then he ended the call with a promise to ride down with the kids and Erica. After he hung up, he checked around the house, making sure all was good, and then rolled over to Hollywood Road.

***

Gangsta

Gangsta saw Terry standing outside of her job by the pay phone. He pulled up beating Velt, a new rapper out of Atlanta who signed with P. Diddy and was hot in the game.

Terry got in and closed the door. She rolled the window down to let most of the weed smoke out.

"Gary, put dat shit out. You smoke too much," Terry said with a frown.

He pulled away from her job and tossed the small blunt out the window.

"Where you going? Home or Jay Road?"

"I'm going home."

"How was work?" he asked, punching the gas to the Ram and making it fly up the street.

"It was okay until Zay came up there try'na start shit."

"What'd he do?" Gangsta asked as he laughed a bit.

"They were 'bout to lock his ass up. I guess he couldn't take the truth."

"So, you straighten that out?"

He looked to her, then to the streets. She had his full attention.

"Yes, I told him it was over with and he snapped. I have never seen him that mad. I was all type of bitches and hos," Terry said, shaking her head.

"Dat's what's up."

Gangsta liked what he heard and turned the music back up. Within minutes he was pulling up to her apartment in Bankhead Courts.

Gangsta still held love for her, and it was again growing inside him, but this time it was a bit faster than the first time. This time he wanted their relationship to last and make it through the hard times. He knew he was in the streets and anything could happen. He could go to jail any day, and that would leave her lost and confused. It bothered him so much that he turned the radio down and looked at her as he parked in front of her apartment building.

"Terry," he started to say.

She looked over to him and answered, "Yes?"

"What happened? What went wrong to make you not stay down when I caught that case and did those nine months?"

Gangsta needed to know, and he had never asked her.

Terry looked away from that question because she instantly felt bad and couldn't look into his eyes at all. After a few seconds, she decided to still give him an answer.

"Gary, we were kids back then. I listened to the wrong people — my mom, my aunt, my friends — and I thought you would never get out."

"You thought I'd never get out?" Gangsta asked, confused.

"Yes, you killed somebody, Gary. What did you expect me to think?" Terry asked with teary eyes, which made Gangsta shake his head.

"Dat man was already dead when I broke into his house."

"That's not what I heard."

"Okay, so what about the now, though? What if I get knocked now that we're together again, what will you do?" Gangsta asked because he needed to know the truth.

"We're not kids anymore, and I promise not to ever let another person dictate my life or my relationship again," Terry said, and then grabbed one of his hands. "I have your back, and I promise to keep you. I know I messed up, Gary, but I will not mess up again."

"And what's up between you and Zay, for real for real?"

"I promise you, Gary, it's a wrap. Here you go. You can call him and ask him."

She reached in her bag, pulled out her phone, and passed it to him.

"I believe you, shawty. I was just asking," he said while waving his hands.

They talked a couple more minutes before Gangsta decided to leave. They shared a quick kiss and Terry got out. At the same moment, a black dude approached the driver's side window of the Ram truck. He tapped the window to get Gangsta's attention while looking in Terry's direction. Gangsta turned to find Veedo, whom he did time with in Alto. He rolled his window down.

"What's up, Vee?" he asked.

"Man, I'm cool, bruh. What's good wit' you, though?"

He leaned in so he could feel the air conditioner blowing.

"Ain't too much going on. I'm just glad to be home."

"Hell, yeah, I'm so fucked up out here though, bruh. It's been super ugly," Veedo stressed, and Gangsta could see it in his eyes.

"You workin' or you slangin'? What you got goin' on?"

"Shit, bruh, but you know I'm a go-getter," Veedo boasted, because when the both of them were in Alto, Veedo was the weed and cocaine man.

Gangsta wrote his number down and told Veedo to call him later. He said he had something for him. They gave each other dap and Gangsta pulled off.

***

Dank
Two Days Later

It was a gray, cool, and misty morning with no clue of sunshine, just a rush of humble winds here and there. The clock read 8:15 a.m., and Dank was awake and had money on his mind.

He cranked his trunk up from the living room window with his remote and smiled to himself at the new toy. It was something he'd never had, but always wanted, and now he'd gotten it. He couldn't be happier.

Dank took a seat on the sofa and picked up his phone. Kash had just texted him an address. He then proceeded to roll up something to smoke and decided to give Gangsta a call to make sure he was en route to the spot on Ruth Street.

"Whoa," Gangsta answered.

"Shawty, what's up?" Dank said.

"Shit, bruh, finna get dressed. Just got done eating," Gangsta replied.

"Okay, well, I'm on da way to meet Kash."

"Bet dat. I'ma see ya there in a few."

Dank sat his phone down and found his lighter on the table. He lit the blunt and hit it twice. He inhaled a cloud of smoke, but couldn't hold it in, so he choked.

Jerry Jackson

Donte Colman was twenty-two years of age and vicious. In the streets he was a natural-born killer with not an ounce of heart or pity. He was born and raised in Perry Homes, but moved to Simpson when the apartments were torn down, and that's where he developed his status in the streets. That's when he killed his first person and made his first buck.

He was good with applying pressure to niggas in the streets. It was said that he should've stayed in school and played ball because of his size. Dank had always been the biggest kid around. At the tender age of thirteen, he was 6'0" and weighed almost two hundred pounds. Now he stood 6'3" and was solid muscle. He was a beast with what he did.

Dank was well respected on the west side, east side, and south side. He was feared the most in the areas he posted up in, and with every chance he got he took advantage of that fear he bestowed upon those around him. The only time the streets rested was when he went to jail or prison, because then the inmates had to deal with him and his ways.

Dank finished his blunt, grabbed his 9mm from beside him on the sofa, and walked into Tiffany's room. His girl was weighing up ounces of mid-grade weed. He kissed her.

"Love ya," he said.

"I love you, too," she replied, and then watched him leave.

Dank walked out to the gloomy morning and felt the misty rain attack his face. There was hardly anybody outside. As he jumped in his truck, his ears were filled with music from T.I.

When he pulled out of Hollywood Court Apartments, he made a right turn and rode down Hollywood Road and passed Do Drop In. He went around a sharp curve where there were graveyards on both sides of the street. A white hooker was out and about trying to find her a trick. Dank rode past her without a second thought.

Dank pulled up to the fence and was let in by two of Pat's workers. The yard looked to be a mechanic's shop with the many cars scattered about with hoods up and wheels off. Pat's yard was also filled with pitbulls on no chain. He parked the truck and got out to be met by Kash.

"Let's go inside," Kash suggested.

Dank followed his partna into Pat's basement, where he found Dinky tied up and duct taped to a chair. Dank walked straight over and snatched the tape off Dinky's mouth. He took a deep breath of air into his lungs and exhaled harshly.

"Man—" Dinky started to say before he was cut off.

"Shut da fuck up," Dank yelled, cutting him off. "Listen up, nigga. What's Cris' number, fool? Dis a robbery."

"Man, what the fuck? I don't go—"

"Pussy, stop playin' before I leave yo' ass down here for two more days," Dank said, because he knew that type of pressure would break Dinky.

It had already been two and a half days since he'd been kidnapped, and this was the first time anybody had said something to him. Dank knew his body had to be sore and he must be starving. From the harsh smell, Dank could tell Dinky had already used the bathroom on himself.

"What you want, man?" Dinky's weak voice cracked.

"All the money you worth, nigga," Dank said, and then smacked him upside the head with his Glock .40. "What's yo' boy's number?"

Dinky winced in pain as the side of his face opened up and started to bleed.

"What's up, bruh? I ain't got shit, man," Dinky pleaded, but his voice fell on deaf ears.

Kash texted the number Dinky gave him from a prepaid phone.

This Dinky, so call me back.

"I know you and Cris run Bowen Homes with loud and pills, and I want in, nigga. I want my cut," Dank said. "I want every penny in yo' safe."

The prepaid phone started to ring in Kash's hand, and it showed Cris was the person calling. Kash passed the phone to Dank, who quickly flipped it open.

"Pussy-ass nigga, you next," Dank said when he answered the phone.

"Hello?" Cris said, confused.

"I got Dinky, nigga, and you next." Dank hung up the phone and walked back over to Dinky. "I want a million for yo' life."

"Man, I don't have that type of cheddar."

"Man, stop," Dank said, and then kind of laughed as he heard the phone ring again. "What's up?"

He pointed the gun at Dinky's face and pretended to shoot him.

"Who dis is?" Cris asked, still confused.

"Where's Cris at?" Dank asked, ignoring his question.

"Dis Cris, so what's up? Where is Dinky?" Cris asked, nearly panicking.

"How many pounds of loud y'all niggas worth?"

"Huh?" The question confused Cris, and that's when Dank hung up the phone again.

"Okay, so I'ma ask you da same question, and I'm gonna see who lying," Dank said.

"Please, man, I swear—" Dinky again started to speak, but again was cutoff.

"Shut da fuck up," Dank yelled in Dinky's ear and almost burst his eardrum. He pushed his head before he finished his statement. "As I was saying, my nigga, if you lie, then you die. So, how many pounds is y'all worth?"

Dank smiled over at Kash, who was silently laughing at the performance his partna was putting on. It took Dinky almost two minutes to answer, even though Dank knew ninety percent of the time the truth would come out at this point.

"We just got a fifty pound bail," Dinky said humbly, feeling broken down.

The phone started to ring again, but he ignored it and continued questioning Dinky.

"How much paper y'all make a week?" he asked him.

"I don't really know, bruh. Somethin' like five racks."

"Bitch, stop lyin'," Dank shouted and picked up the ringing phone. "Hello."

"Who dis?" Cris asked again.

"Where's Cris?" Dank asked back, again ignoring his question.

"Dis Cris, who you?"

"So, y'all niggas worth fifty pounds?"

"Huh?"

"Pussy-ass nigga, don't *huh* me. It's a ransom, nigga."

"A who?" Cris had anger in his voice, but Dank could also hear panic.

"Listen, fuck-nigga. Only one option, homeboy, and dat's to comply. If not, the bitch-ass Dinky die," Dank forcefully stated.

"Every real nigga in the city is looking for shawty. Do you know what the fuck you getting into before you go too far?" Cris replied through clenched teeth

"Fuck you and every nigga wit' y'all. I want one hundred grand and 50 pounds of that loud y'all got at the stash. You got one hour, and if you do not comply, if you alert the cops or run to get every fuck-nigga in Atlanta, then Dinky die and I will personally pick you off later in life. I will text yo' bitch-ass the address to bring the product and money. Oh, and come alone, fuck-nigga," Dank spoke, then hung up on Cris.

Jerry Jackson

Chapter 5

NeNe
Two Months Later

Her wet body emerged from the shower and she wrapped a beach towel around her frame. Her long hair was dripping wet as she stepped in front of the full-length mirror to get a good look at her baby face.

NeNe had full lips, a small, cute nose, and a beauty mark on her chin. She had naturally long eyelashes with sexy honey-hazel eyes. NeNe wondered why so many guys failed at making her happy. She wondered why she wasn't married with kids or even just had a man to run home to like her sister did. NeNe had a near perfect body, a flat stomach with nice C-cup breasts. She had a small waist, nice hips, and a round, juicy ass just right for her body. One of her best assets was her stance. She was bowlegged, stood 5'2", and only weighed 125 pounds soaking wet.

She entered her bedroom and music could be heard blasting from the living room. The clock read 10:30 p.m., so she only had fifteen minutes to get dressed. She first put baby lotion all over her body, and then slipped into her lace panties and bra set. Tonight she decided to wear her jean skirt outfit by Allure with the Allure sandals to match.

NeNe quickly turned when her bedroom door flew open to find Erica all jazzed up and ready to leave.

"Girl, come the fuck on," Erica said. "It's my nigga's birthday, and you want me to be late?"

"Here I come," NeNe replied, combing her long curly hair down.

She wanted it to hang loose tonight. She grabbed her lipgloss and Allure pocketbook.

Tonight was Kash's birthday party, hosted at Club 321 on Martin Luther King Drive. She knew it would be a wild night out and vowed to not let anyone get under her skin with the unwanted attention she got.

NeNe and Erica climbed into Kash's Range Rover. Erica cranked it up and blasted the music, which NeNe quickly turned down with the remote. She never understood why people rode around with such loud music in their ears.

"Bitch, I'm balling tonight," Erica boasted. "I might smoke me a blunt."

NeNe shook her head at her older sister. Erica was the type of female who always attracted street dudes even though she was a bookworm. She had never dated the hard-working type, unlike NeNe, who had tried all flavors of men, yet nothing seemed to work for her.

Erica used to say NeNe wanted too much from the guys she dated and intimidated them with her stubborn ways and beauty. She was almost always demanding. NeNe wasn't always the mean girlfriend. At one point in her life she was innocent. Her very first boyfriend played her so bad that she wanted to kill herself. She caught him going out with her best friend. Her second boyfriend popped her cherry and in the end broke her heart. Her third boyfriend was killed, so before she jumped into relationships, she dated and demanded. She was also very picky about whom she dated.

Plus school was a help to her, because her main focus was on obtaining her degree. She loved the job she had, so it kept her busy. Mostly she chatted on MySpace or talked over the phone with guys until she felt comfortable, then they'd date. Dating wasn't so important to her. She was twenty-three years of age and had one year remaining in school with no kids. She wasn't happy, but she was content.

It took them almost an hour to get to the club. The parking lot was jam-packed with cars and filled with people coming and going. It was a Saturday night, and it was about to be a long one.

Erica drove the Range Rover around to where the V.I.P. parking was located and showed the parking attendant her pass. Both the girls jumped out and strolled past the line heading toward the door. NeNe could hear the remarks from the guys in the line. Erica gave the bouncer at the door the pass and she and NeNe were led inside the crowded club.

As they made their way toward the V.I.P. section, a guy grabbed NeNe's arm and pulled her to a stop. She turned around to find this young dude with dirty dreads and brown golds in his mouth, holding a bottle of Hennessy.

"What's happenin'? You fuckin' wit' da mob?" the guy asked her.

She took in his attire. He wore black pants and a black shirt with the letters GF on the front.

"No," she directly stated, pulled her arm from his grip, and then walked off.

She found her sister at the entrance to the V.I.P. section, so she quickly followed. The room was well placed. It was easy to spot Kash and his crew, who were at least twenty deep with just as many bottles of all types of liquor.

NeNe saw Kash stand up with a blunt hanging from his lips and a bottle in one hand. He reached out to Erica with his free hand and snatched her into his embrace.

"Happy birthday, Kash," NeNe said loud enough for him to hear.

She waved and he nodded his head to assure her his thanks.

***

Gangsta

When NeNe first walked through the door of the V.I.P. area behind Erica, he did not recognize her until he noticed that stance when she stopped moving. Gangsta was instantly captivated once again, and then he vividly remembered she gave him a ride home some months ago. He forgot to get at her, and him seeing her in that jean skirt made him hate himself for slipping on this beautiful lady.

When she stopped at the table and spoke to Kash, her honey-hazel eyes somehow met his own, but she did not smile and she did not speak. She just politely waved her hand to indicate she remembered him. Again, he hated himself because she gave him the phone number and he didn't use it.

"What's up, Erica sister? Ahh..." Gangsta spoke as he was trying to think of her name, but couldn't get it right.

"My name is NeNe, honey," she stated and took a seat next to her sister who was nestled under Kash.

Gangsta could tell by his crew that he had to make a move on her before anybody else. All eyes were on her, and even though she waved to him, he knew to move in for the kill.

"Wat'cha been up too?" he asked, clearing the air after a minute of thought.

"Nothing much, just school."

"You gave me da wrong number, you know."

Gangsta sat up from the leather seat and leaned over so she could hear him better. NeNe looked at him a second and shook her head.

"I did not. You just never called," she spoke and took a sip of the drink she had.

"I did hit yo' line. I promise."

"Don't lie."

"Give me yo' number so I can lock it in," Gangsta said.

"What happened to the first number I gave you? It's still the same."

"Man, I called and it was the wrong number." He smiled because he couldn't believe how she was acting.

NeNe turned toward Kash and her sister to ask them a question.

"Does your friend always lie?" NeNe asked.

"He's solid," Kash defended his partna as the entire group of people agreed.

"I should have known," she stated.

She rolled her eyes and blushed just a bit.

"Come here," Gangsta said, and then waved her over to the spot he patted next to himself. "Come sit by me."

"Ha ha," NeNe said to let him know she thought he must be trying to be funny.

Gangsta stood up from his spot and looked to Veedo, who was next to her and draped down in Polo gear with the big horse and man on it. He got the picture and stood so that he could trade places with Gangsta.

"Can I please call you tonight?" he asked as he sat beside her and passed her his phone.

She pushed it back to him.

"Yes, but you should have the number already."

She was being stubborn.

"Man, I'm tellin' you I called a couple times," Gangsta protested.

"A couple time, huh?" NeNe turned to ask.

"Hell, yes."

"What's my area code?" she demanded to know.

"Man—" he started to say, but was stuck because when she wrote her number down he never even glanced at it. Gangsta had moved from his mother's crib a long time ago, so knew he couldn't and wouldn't find it. "Man, I think it's 678."

"Wrong," she said and tried to get up from sitting by him, but Gangsta took hold of her arm and prevented her from leaving.

"Look, what's up? I'm try'na get at you when I finish up my nigga's party. How about that?"

"What's yo' number, honey?" NeNe asked in reply.

"Where's yo' phone?" he asked her back.

She passed him a Blackberry. It took him a quick second to get to her contacts and program in his number, then text himself so he would have her info. He passed it back, and at the same time he saw some commotion in the rear part of the V.I.P. section. Dank was involved. Everybody moved when Gangsta excused himself to moved toward the back. Two dudes were holding Dank, and a girl was being helped up by two more guys.

"Man, we don't want no problems," one of the guys said. "Everythang straight," he assured, and they led the girl out of V.I.P. Gangsta and Kash got on either side of their partna and pulled him away from the drama.

After they calmed down Dank, they lit up more blunts. Gangsta put his attention back on NeNe. She was still acting stubborn, but he kind of adored that.

Gangsta almost had his shit together. He wasn't near where he wanted to be, but he indeed was on his way. The ransom with Dinky got them seventy pounds of loud and a 138 grand in cash. Cris had sold Dinky out and left him for dead. He bailed out on poor Dinky, leaving him no choice but to give up his address. Gangsta, Kash, and Dank all took the chance and went to Dinky's mother's house. Dinky had promised them his personal stash for his life.

"Please don't kill me, my nigga. It's yours," Dinky said while he pointed to his stash in the basement of his mother's house. The crew

had everybody in the house tied up except Dinky. Dank wasted no time killing him with a headshot. Kash and Gangsta had to stop Dank from going up the stairs to kill Dinky's mother and younger sister.

"We got on masks, shawty, and they tied up. Let's just get this shit and go," Gangsta said.

He was smart enough not to sell his product. What he did was lay his half on Veedo, and he went to the country parts of Georgia to slang. They had a trap apartment in Bankhead Courts where he sold x-pills and lean. He had a major plug with Pat Man, who was a guy from Perry Homes, so Gangsta was doing okay for himself.

They enjoyed the rest of the party, and everybody left the club in peace. Gangsta even was successful at getting a quick hug from NeNe.

***

Dank

It was a gloomy Sunday morning, and he could still feel the effects of the party from last night. The many drinks, blunts, and pills had given him a major hangover.

He was sitting at the red light on Bankhead in front of Overlook Atlanta. He had his girl with him, who was asleep on the passenger's side after getting off of work, but she still looked as beautiful as ever.

Dank was content now more than he had ever been in life, and he had her to thank for it. She was a true rider and loyal. Even when she knew Dank was up to no good, she stayed down and faithful. Tiffany was one girl that didn't cross him.

Time and time again she had held him down, so now that he had money he spared no expense when she wanted something. Things were looking good for him and his team. He put up a weed trap in Hollywood Court and West Chester off Simpson with nothing but loud. The spots were doing numbers, and Dank had the pressure down on a lot of niggas. Nobody dared to try him, so he had hos selling the loud while he ran the streets with his partnas taking money from pussies. He reached over and touched Tiffany's leg as he was about to pull off from the light.

Dank did not notice the red van that pulled up beside them, and he did not notice the gun until it was too late.

The sounds from a chopper and semi-automatic machine gun filled the air.

Boom! Boom! Bhhalac! Bhhalac! Boom! Boom! Boom! Bhhalac!

Dank smashed his foot on the gas. He ran the red light and a truck hit him, then the truck hit a pole. The red van pulled up beside him again.

Boom! Boom! Bhhalac! Bhhalac! Boom! Boom! Boom!

Shots fired, the van peeled off down Bankhead.

As the shots rang out, Dank could feel his side go numb with pain. He saw his girl was hit — she was leaning over the console with blood pouring out of the top of her head. When he tried to pull himself up by the steering wheel, a sharp pain ran up his neck. Blood fell from his head and filled his eyes. He heard people screaming, horns blowing, cars speeding away, and people stopping to be nosy. The crazy thing is, no one tried to help.

Dank reached for the door, but as soon as he did, his chest felt like it exploded. He couldn't breathe any longer, and his eyes were getting heavy. He started to hear bells in his ears. He couldn't bear the pain anymore, so he passed out completely.

***

Kash

"Say what? When? What happened?"

"He in Grady Hospital, and the girl is dead." The caller told Kash she saw everything when it happened because she was at the gas station across the street.

Kash was hungover from last night, but quickly jumped up when he hung up the phone. He stumbled to his pants, and the movement made Erica lift her head from the pillow.

"What's wrong, babe?"

"Dank got shot a few minutes ago," Kash said as he put on his shoes.

Erica sat up with a shocked look on her face.

"Is he okay?" she asked.

"I don't know, but his girl was killed," Kash replied, and then rushed to get his gun, car keys, and some small bills.

His mind was moving a million miles per hour. He left the room and found NeNe on the sofa eating Golden Grahams and watching Cartoon Network. He did not bother to speak and simply walked out the door.

Inside the Range Rover, he dialed Gangsta's phone number and wondered where this sudden beef came from.

"Whoa," Gangsta said when he picked up.

"Shawty, Dank just got gunned down. He at Grady. His ho is dead. I'm on my way to his momma's house now," Kash said.

"Okay, I'll meet you there," Gangsta replied, and he hung up.

Kash wondered how he was gonna walk into Ms. Smith's house and tell her Dank got shot. She would instantly assume he and Gangsta were the reason because she always did.

It was times like those when Gangsta and Kash questioned each other about the things she would say concerning Dank and their relationship. It was as if she thought the two were bad influences on Dank, but when Kash and Gangsta met Dank, he was six months in on an 18-month sentence already.

Dank's mother stayed in Fairburn, GA, so it took longer than he cared to drive there, but he made it, and moments later was met by Gangsta. Kash was the first out of the ride, followed by Gangsta. They both dapped each other, holding looks of concern on their faces. Ms. Smith's home was well built and kept up. It was a nice area with very beautiful surroundings. Kash knocked on the door once on the porch. It took a minute for the door to finally crack open, and Ms. Smith peeked her head out. She looked both the boys over and spoke.

"Where is my son?"

Suddenly Kash's mouth went dry, not knowing what to say. Gangsta stepped in.

"We just got a call, Ms. Smith, saying someone shot Dank and he is at Grady. We came to tell you to get down there and let us know what's going on so we can help him out. Dank got caught with a lot of drugs, also, and some guns. We just wanna help."

"So, this is about drugs?" Ms. Smith asked. Now panic was clearly in her voice. She fully opened the door.

"We don't know, Ms. Smith," Kash added.

"Oh, my god," she shook her head. "Ok, where is he again?"

"Grady," Gangsta answered.

"Ok, I'm heading there now," Ms. Smith replied. Kash and Gangsta left after telling her to call as soon as she knew something.

***

NeNe

Erica walked into the living room with a robe wrapped around her body. Her hair was wild from a long night of sex, and her face was swollen from sleeping with it smashed into the pillow. NeNe looked at her sister and shook her head at the sight.

Erica took a seat in the recliner. She ran her fingers through her hair before saying, "Kash's homeboy got shot last night. I mean, this morning."

NeNe's heart dropped to her stomach.

"So, that's why Kash was in a rush," she said out loud to herself.

She remembered she was just with his friend. She was waiting for his call, and now she gets this news.

"Is he okay?" she asked.

"The girl he was with got killed," Erica replied. "You know the big dude who got into it last night?"

Erica grabbed a bag of weed off her table while shaking her head. She placed it in a glass bowl and placed a top on it.

"Oh, okay, I know who you talking about."

NeNe remembered and was kind of happy it wasn't Gangsta, because he seemed cool. Even though she was picky, she chose him and his swagger, so she was back to waiting on his phone call.

"Yeah, I wonder was it 'bout last night?" Erica wanted to know.

She sat the bowl under the table, knowing Kash would be soon looking for it.

"Girl, I hope not," NeNe replied.

She would hate to be a part of that type of drama. That's why she rarely did clubs, and last night was all Erica's idea. NeNe would rather sit home and watch movies versus hanging out and spending money she truly didn't have.

NeNe and her sister sat around while they talked and watched TV. Erica was so sprung on Kash that she couldn't stop bringing him up in conversation. NeNe just laughed, but she listened. Her mind was also consumed with Kash's friend Gangsta. She liked how he had pushed up on her yesterday at the club. She liked how aggressive he became and how he would not give up until he got what he wanted. NeNe still played hard to get, but gave in at the last minute. She was glad she did, because he most definitely was her type.

Chapter 6

Gangsta

Gangsta met up with Kash at his girlfriend Erica's crib. When he entered the crib behind Kash, he saw NeNe on the sofa in a pair of light blue cotton shorts, a tank top, and some hot pink socks. They made eye contact, but neither one spoke a word. Kash and he went straight down to the basement. Word got back that it was about last night at Club 321 when Dank knocked Mickey down for frontin' on him. Her brother was a major cocaine pusher named Grich. When Gangsta heard the name, he knew Grich was the type of guy who would pull a stunt like this. Most niggas in East Hamp were about the trigger play, and East Hamp is where Grich rolled at daily.

"Veedo says he mounted up," Gangsta said as he looked and saw four guns laid out on the floor and some clips.

"Okay, cool," Kash replied while placing bullets in the clips.

Kash wanted to strike back fast and hit Grich where it hurt. He wanted to shoot up Grich's mom's crib in Riverdale, Georgia because his crew wouldn't make it out alive if they pulled up in East Hamp.

Gangsta really didn't agree with Kash's way of thinking. He was waiting on a phone call to get the exact spot where he could find Grich when he wasn't in East Hamp. He kicked it with Kash until Veedo made it over. He had some information about what went down, and he knew where Mickey stayed. That's when the three guys came up with a plan to kidnap Mickey and kill her.

Gangsta left them in Riverdale and then made it to Newport Street on Simpson. He pulled his Ram up in the yard of a house on a hill surrounded by a black iron gate that was open. Over eight different cars were parked out front. Gangsta parked behind Pat Man's Benz and climbed out wearing Rocawear pants and a shirt with some white Air Force Ones. He also wore a clear pair of Gucci frames and an Atlanta Braves fitted cap that was all white with the white A.

He walked up nine steps that led to the door. He knocked twice before Teyummie snatched the door open and instantly got his attention. It had been months since he has seen her. It seemed like she had gotten finer, especially with the Prada dress she wore that stopped mid thigh.

"Pat Man is in the back," she spoke and closed the door when he passed her.

Gangsta followed her lead and was elated he did, because with every step she took, her ass bounced. Teyummie reminded him of Chilli from TLC. She was taller and lighter, but with that same swagger and happy face. Ever since middle school Pat Man had her, and Gangsta always wanted to have her, but he never got the chance.

She led him to the back of the house where Gangsta saw Pat Man and his boys weighing and sacking up pills. Pat Man smiled a mouthful of gold teeth at him when he walked through the door.

"What's up, boy?" Pat Man greeted him.

"Whoa, what's happenin'?" Gangsta replied as Pat Man gave him a pink pill.

"These the pink ladies. They some new shit, but same price. They just a different flavor," Pat Man boasted, which made Gangsta give the pill back.

He reached into his pocket and produced a wad of cash. He counted off three grand for a seven grand profit.

"Just give me a few bags of those shits?" Gangsta asked.

"Okay, so do yo' people still got loud?" Pat Man asked.

"Hell, yeah," Gangsta answered quickly.

Gangsta got served and linked Pat Man with Veedo, because that's who held his weed. Teyummie walked him to the door, and once he stepped out, she followed.

"I see you coming up," Teyummie told him.

"Hardly," Gangsta replied and started to walk down the steps.

"Damn, you just gonna walk off like dat?"

"Like what?" he shot back.

She walked down the steps and stood beside him. She took his phone and programmed her number into it. She gave it back, blew him a kiss, and walked off with her ass bouncing in that Prada dress.

Two Hours Later

"I think I'm pregnant," Terry said when Gangsta walked into her apartment.

She was sitting on the sofa with Nikki.

"Huh?" He was baffled at her statement, though he knew he heard correct.

He knew it was a great possibility she really could be pregnant.

"Huh, my ass," Terry stated.

Terry got up to follow him to the chair he sat in after removing the gun from his waistband.

"You must be late, huh?" that was his next question.

"Yes, I'm late. Plus, I'm throwing up too much. I'll find out for sure tomorrow, though."

"Okay, and if so, are you gonna be mad or happy?"

"Confused, and you?" she asked.

"Happy!"

"Told you," Nikki added.

His reply put a smile upon her face, and Gangsta adored the sight. He was happy with the relationship they shared. Terry fell into his arms and they kissed long and deep.

Gangsta already had a plan for them to become roommates in an apartment. He still hadn't let anybody know of his condo but his two partners and in the few months he'd owned it he had only spent four nights. Gangsta used it to stash his work and his safe. He needed somewhere other than his mother's house. Terry would be okay to live with because he could handle her quick temper and fly mouth. Plus, she had the perfect girlfriend role down, and he liked that the most about her. It made the situation much better with her being pregnant with his seed.

As Gangsta was talking with Terry, Kash called, so he excused himself and stepped into the kitchen.

"Whoa," he answered.

"Dank got hit seven times from the neck down, but he is still alive. Police got 'im in custody because dis nigga had nine pounds on him that I just gave 'im yesterday. He had a vest and like twenty racks in his pocket, plus he had two pistols."

"Shit, Dank," Gangsta said as he shook his head.

He knew Dank was going to jail unless he put everything on the bitch, then it would be up to Kash and him to get him a lawyer, which would be no problem.

Gangsta agreed to mount up and get at Grich as soon as possible, so they made all the correct calls, because this business had to be handled, regardless.

Exactly two hours later, Gangsta, Kash, and Veedo sat in a black Tahoe outside of Grich's mother's house. The crew followed Mickey and her brother there, and they were waiting on them or Grich to leave. They wanted him the most, since he was the man behind the shooting.

"Dis pussy need to let us get it and come out," Kash said while holding two Glock .40s.

Grich's mother stayed on a peaceful block in Riverdale a few blocks away from Kash's girlfriend.

"He coming, bruh, just chill," Gangsta spoke while his eyes stayed on the house.

"Man, we should just rush up in dat bitch and murk everybody," Kash said out of nowhere, and Gangsta knew he was for real.

He knew payback was something that had to be done. It was the code of the streets. *You shoot, and then I shoot. You kill, and then I kill.* Their partna was almost murdered and now had a fresh case under his belt because Grich pulled a stunt like this. Grich was a dead man walking, along with Mickey, but they just didn't know it yet.

Just as Gangsta was about to reply to what Kash said, they saw the door to Grich's mother's house open, and out walked Mickey. She was followed by her brother, who had the body of a pro football player, the height of a basketball player, and the blackness of the rapper B.I.G. He also had the mug of a killer, which is exactly what he was.

The brother and sister headed to the pickup truck parked in the driveway. Mickey was the first to climb inside the truck. She was smiling from ear to ear without a care in the world, and Grich followed.

Kash was the first to open the door, and then Gangsta and Veedo followed. Quickly, the three ran across the street with guns out and started shooting when they were only a few feet away.

Boom! Boom! Boom! Boom! Boom!

The guys fired repeatedly. Grich's body twisted and turned inside the truck as he tried with great effort to get away from the bullets. Kash ran over when the shots stopped. He snatched the door open to find Mickey hit, but still alive. They made eye contact as he pointed at her face.

Pop! Pop! Pop! Pop! Pop!

All the guys ran back to the Tahoe, which was already cranked, and pulled off as they heard the mother scream.

***

Dank
Four Days Later

"You're well aware that you're in deep shit, correct?" the detective asked as soon as he opened his eyes. "I will give you only one chance."

"Man, I haven't done nothing," Dank said with a weak voice.

"The guns and dope alone will send you to prison, so play stupid if you wish," the detective said loudly.

"That was Tiffany's shit, man, not mines."

As soon as the words left Dank's lips, the detective got up off the chair and towered over the bed.

"Well, guess what? She's dead, and the truck is in your name."

"Man—" Dank started to speak, but was cut off.

"As soon as the prints come back from the gun, you better hope it don't link to no open cases, because you'll be in prison for a long, long time."

That statement made Dank's heart drop into the pit of his stomach. He most definitely had the double grip pump in the truck with him when he was gunned down. Dank closed his eyes and wished this was a dream. He thought there was no way karma had gotten him this fast. He wasn't able to enjoy all the good money he was taking and making.

"Man, I ain't done shit," he tried to say convincingly.

"Suit yourself, or help yo'self," the detective said and walked out of the room, leaving Dank to his own thoughts.

Mentally, he was breaking down and unable to do anything about it. Dank knew the gun used to kill Danny was still in the truck with his prints all over it. He wanted to scream and snatch the IV out of his arm, but he couldn't. He was cuffed to the bed, which meant he was already in police custody.

The room door opened, and it surprised Dank when two more detectives — one male, one female — walked in. The woman held a folder in her hand. The guy pulled out a small writing pad and read it before he spoke.

"Sir, I'm Detective Paul and this is Detective Gray," Detective Paul introduced them both as the woman opened the folder, and then she pulled out a sheet and tossed it across Dank's lap.

"Do you know him?" she asked.

Dank looked at it and saw it was Danny. His heart dropped, he felt lumps in his throat, and his mouth went dry.

"We think you do," Detective Gray said.

***

NeNe

"Hello."

"'Sup, Miss Lady, you busy?" Gangsta asked.

A smile came to her face at the sound of his voice. She already knew who it was because he was the only guy she had given her number too.

"Nope," she replied.

"Oh, cool. Well, I told you I was gonna call."

"I see."

"Yeah, 'cause I miss that smile."

"Is that right?"

"I'm for real. I'm being honest."

"I hear ya."

NeNe loved his voice. Plus, he was extra cute in her eyes and had swagger. She wouldn't let him know all these things because guys have a tendency to get a big head. That's the last thing she needed from a guy right now.

"So, since the first day I met you, has your status changed?" he asked.

"No, and why?"

"Just wanted to know, 'cause I got plans."

"Plans?" NeNe laughed a bit, then added, "So, has your status changed?"

"I'm like a dollar bill, still."

NeNe enjoyed his conversation. She was able to be herself. She laughed how she wanted to laugh, joked around, and their conversation was smooth and interesting. She liked his smile, which was rare. She also liked his down south slang, and he made it seem like everything was under control at all times.

While talking on the phone with Gangsta, she walked into the bathroom to look at her hair in the mirror as if he was actually on his way over.

"So, is your friend okay?" she asked while leaving the bathroom, going back to her room.

She saw her sister and Kash talking in the living room. She continued to her room because it seemed as if they were arguing.

"Who?" Gangsta shot back to her question.

"The one who got shot?"

"Oh, yeah, he good. But what do you got on?" Gangsta switched subjects, and the question confused her.

"Huh?"

"You heard me," he laughed.

"Clothes and?" NeNe wanted to know.

"Can I come kick it wit'cha?"

"Boy, you crazy, huh? You sound like you got one thing on your mind. Who do you think I am?"

NeNe was feeling some type of way.

"That's the last thing on my mind. I'd rather visit your past and learn your future."

"I hear ya."

NeNe lay across her bed.

"So, can I?"

"Now?"

"Yeah," Gangsta replied.

"Well, if anything I will come to you, because it's too many people at my house."

Gangsta gave her directions to his condo. She was the first person other than his mother to know he had a spot. they hung up with each other. She laid there with the phone still to her ear and a slick blush on her face. She liked Gangsta. It was something about him.

***

Kash

Something did not feel right. Something was wrong, and he could feel it, but he didn't want to say anything. He thought maybe he was tripping or thinking too much about the same situation. He tried to think of other things, but his mind would not allow it. *Stay on track*, he told himself over and over again. He was confused as to why his thoughts were negative. Maybe it was the death of Dank's girlfriend, or maybe it was Grich and Mickey's mother. They had made eye contact as he ran around the truck to kill her daughter. Kash had been killing since childhood, and not once had he held remorse or regret behind his actions. Kash was on the sofa seated next to his girl and having a dispute he cared not to have about what happened with Grich and Mickey. The murders were all over the news.

He saw his girl's sister, NeNe, come out of her room, and then go back in after going inside the bathroom. Minutes later she reappeared, but this time she was dressed and heading for the door.

"And where you heading?" Kash joked, because it seemed as if she was rushing.

"Going to meet someone, why?"

"Who?" Erica demanded to know.

She got up and stood in her sister's way.

"Girl, move. It's none of yo' bizness who. Yo' man is right there," NeNe said as she pointed toward Kash.

"You're my sister, and I have the right to be nosey."

Erica put her hands on her hips, and then Kash cut back into the conversation.

"I'ma tell my folks."

"Who?" NeNe wanted to know.

"Gangsta," Kash said.

"And just maybe when you call to tell 'im I'll answer the call."

"Oh, shit," Kash said as he laughed, and so did her sister as she got out of her way.

NeNe smiled on her way out of the door.

As soon as the door closed, Kash fixed his attention back on Erica.

"Go lock the door," he said, and she did as she was told.

Erica stood 5'3" and was a shade darker than her sister. She was the same kind of pretty with the same hazel eyes. She was thicker than NeNe and had a bigger butt, too. Erica was tatted and pierced, and NeNe had neither. Erica was the bad one out of the two, and that's what attracted Kash to her when they met.

"Come here," Kash said as he pulled her down on him.

They shared a kiss. She straddled his lap, pulled his shirt over his head, and then tossed it on the floor.

"I love you, bad boy," Erica moaned in his ear as he caressed her back and booty.

"I adore that," Kash replied as he stood, and she stood, too. He peeled her pants and panties down and then removed her shirt before laying her back down, but this time completely naked.

Jerry Jackson

Chapter 7

Gangsta

His heart pounded away in his chest when he heard the knock. It was a soft knock, which he knew could only be one person. He slowly made his way to the door, because he didn't want to seem as if he was rushing.

When Gangsta opened the door, NeNe was standing there looking as beautiful as ever.

"What's up?" he asked and moved to the side.

She stepped in and walked past him, smelling good.

"Hey," she spoke back.

She smelled like strawberries or something of that nature. It made him want to bite her as he closed the door.

Inside the living room of the condo there was a seventy-inch TV and a stereo with speakers. He had black wood and glass end tables, a sofa table, a black futon, and two leather sofas. He had pictures of his mother, his brother, and one of his father. A father he hasn't met yet. He kept it simple and neat. NeNe took a seat on the futon. He grabbed the remote and walked toward her.

"Here, make yo'self at home."

"Thank you."

She took the remote and their hands touched. It sent chills through his body. It wasn't his first time touching her, but this time it was different. This time the two of them were alone in his space. Gangsta walked into the kitchen and watched her play with the TV.

"You hungry?" he asked.

"A little," she replied.

"We can do one of two things. We can order in or cook," he said.

"It don't matter," she said and made eye contact with him.

"Well, pick one," he shot back.

"Okay, go ahead and cook," NeNe replied.

"I said we," Gangsta said, laughing.

Just like the first time they ever spoke, the conversation was good, and this time he was able to find out more about her. While they were cooking the meal, Gangsta found out she only had one year of college left and was twenty-three

The two of them shared a lot in common. They liked most of the same music and movies and almost the same types of food. Gangsta shared with her about his brother's death, growing up on Bankhead, and how he met Dank and Kash in Rydc. He informed her about his three-year bid in Alto and how he really never had room for a relationship. He told her how he'd never been in love and how he couldn't even distinguish the signs.

"You'll just feel it," NeNe said while lying back on the sofa wrapped in his arms.

"Feel what? I mean, I feel shit now,"

"It's when someone is always on your mind. You're always happy to see them and happy to hear their voice. Your heart seems as if it skips a beat when the two of you embrace. It's a lot more, but those are some of the signs."

"That's how I feel right now. So, what does that mean?" Gangsta replied.

"Boy, hush wit' da games," NeNe laughed.

"I'm being honest, though." Gangsta looked at his watch and it read 1:08 a.m.

They had been talking for over two hours.

"You got game, huh?"

She sat up, turned and looked at him, and then she got up. He reached out and grabbed her hand.

"You leaving?"

"Yeah, it's getting late."

"And—"

"And I do not want to be driving in the streets all night." She found her flip-flops, slid her feet into them, and grabbed her phone.

"Then don't. Just leave after we cook breakfast in the morning."

Gangsta stood up this time. He removed the phone from her hand, pushed her shoulder to make her sit down, and then pulled her flip-flops off.

"Boy…"

"Boy, what?"

66

"You moving a lil' too fast, ain't cha?"

"Nah, da speed's just right."

He sat down beside her.

"Well, I'm not that easy. Sorry, but I gotta—"

"Like I said, we'll cook breakfast in the morning. I just wanna hold you and tell you a bedtime story. I don't expect you to be that easy," Gangsta replied.

***

NeNe

She felt his arms wrapped around her waist, and it didn't feel right to her. She was not used to this type of feeling. She was accustomed to having her own space, though at the same time it felt great to be held by a man. His body pressing to her body was warm, and feeling his semi-erect penis up against her backside had her wet from thoughts of them making love.

It had been three long years since a man had been inside of her, and just thoughts of it scared her. She knew it would hurt, and she knew she would be lost. Plus, she did not want to seem as if she was a freak or just so easy to get in bed. She turned inside his arms so they would be face-to-face in the darkness. She wanted to lean over to kiss his lips, but decided against it. She was confused and frozen. She was frozen until sleep found her once again.

***

Gangsta

He felt NeNe turn inside his arms. Gangsta thought he saw NeNe looking at him, but wasn't sure because it was too dark. He knew her beautiful face was inches away from his own because he could feel her breathing.

Her cold feet rested on his ankle, and her thighs were sandwiched between his thighs. He pulled her closer to where he felt their noses touch. They touched in a soft manner that made Gangsta humbly kiss her lips as his heart rate sped up from being nervous.

He waited a second and kissed her again. Just as he was about to kiss her once more, she surprised him with the return gesture and kissed him back. They kissed each other as their bodies moved closer than just friends. He could feel the heat between her thighs and his hardness he could no longer hide. Gangsta pulled her close while running his hand down her back. He gripped a handful of her soft booty and broke away from their kiss. He proceeded to suck on her neck.

Gangsta sucked NeNe's neck lightly. He then went lower to her shoulders, and then to her breast, where he pulled her bra down to free her nice-sized titties. He began to suck one of her hardened nipples.

"Umm, uhh, stop," she moaned and pulled away.

Without a fight, Gangsta came back face-to-face with her and kissed her again.

"Damn, yo' lips soft," Gangsta told her.

"Yours, too," she replied. "Now, go to sleep."

Gangsta wanted to protest, but did not want to seem pressed, even though he was horny beyond words. He liked the girl more than he wanted the sex.

He knew waiting would be worthwhile, so he kissed her again and said, "Good morning and good night."

Then he pulled her close so the two of them could rest once again.

"Gangsta," NeNe said as she shook him until his eyes opened. "Gangsta."

"Yeah," he said into the pillow. He had fallen asleep again.

For some strange reason he was more tired than ever.

"Your phone," she told him.

Without even looking, he reached for his phone.

"Yeah," he grumbled as he answered it.

"Baby, the police wants to talk to you," his mother told him.

He rose up fast and his heart dropped into the pit of his stomach. The tone of his mother's voice made him extremely nervous.

"Where they at, Ma?"

"One is right here, so hold on."

"Ma," he yelled into the phone as he tried to stop her so he could question her on what the police wanted.

She moved too quickly, and seconds later a male voice came through the phone.

"Gary?" the male voice asked to make sure he had the right person.

Gangsta motioned for NeNe to get dressed. He saw the clock read 5:40 a.m.

"Yeah, what's up?"

He did not want to speak, but he did because his mom put him on the spot. Gangsta wondered why she chose to do that.

"This is Detective Brooks. I need to see you. Is it possible we meet?"

"Ah yeah, but when?" Gangsta asked while getting out of the bed.

"Now, if possible. Can you come down to the station?"

"Yup, give me 15 minutes. I'll be there."

"Okay, see you soon," Detective Brooks said, and then they both hung up.

"Is everything okay?" NeNe asked nervously as she pulled up her pants.

She looked at Gangsta for a yes or no answer.

"Hell, naw. That was the cops."

Gangsta picked his cell phone up and dialed Kash's number. He picked up on the first ring.

"Yeah," Kash said.

"Shawty, the police—"

Bam! Bam! Bam!

The loud banging on the door made Gangsta stop moving.

"This is the police! Open up the door," Gangsta heard them yelling through the door loud and clear.

By the way Kash hung up the phone, he had to have heard them, too.

Thinking as fast as he could, Gangsta gave NeNe six grams of Kush to flush, and then he rushed to hide his .45 Ruger as the banging on the door continued.

"We know you're inside," he heard one of them say.

"What's going on?" NeNe asked in a panic.

Gangsta shook his head and headed to the door. The banging grew louder and louder as he entered the living room. He had sweat on his palm as he reached for the doorknob.

"Chill da fuck out," Gangsta yelled as he snatched the door open and was instantly pushed to the ground.

"Get down and don't move! This is the APD!"

They cuffed him up quickly, and minutes later the detectives also had NeNe in cuffs, and then the officers started going through the condo. They found an empty safe, a .45 Ruger, and $800 in cash.

The police took Gangsta outside to a waiting squad car. Gangsta watched them release NeNe, which made him feel a little bit better. Gangsta had already gone through this before, so it was kid's play to him.

When the police got him to the station, they left him in a cold room by himself. There was one table, three chairs, and a clock on the wall, which most likely held video recorders inside it. Gangsta sat calm and cool, because he already knew the game.

Two detectives walked into the room. Both were in their forties, and both took a seat across from him. They just stared at him, and he stared back until one of them spoke.

"Damn, Gary, you in deep shit," one of them stated, and then introduced himself. "I'm Detective Paul, and this is Detective Gray."

"What's up with y'all got me up in here? I haven't done shit," Gangsta said.

"We got you on kidnapping, robbery, and murder, so you tell me."

The other detective tossed a folder on the table and opened it. The first thing he saw was Danny's face, and he wondered how this case came about.

"I can't tell you shit, homes," Gangsta said as he looked the detective right in his eyes.

"That's not what, ahh," the detective paused as he read from the paperwork, "Dank said."

"Dank? I don't know anybody named Dank."

Gangsta's heart dropped at the sound of his partna's name, but he couldn't show the detectives his sweat.

"We got his statement and your prints. Help yo'self out, son," the other detective spoke. Dank had written the statement to lessen the prison time he knew he would receive.

"Man, either let me go or lock me up. I don't know what the fuck y'all talkin' 'bout."

"Fine, hang yourself. And by the way, we got the gun," the first detective said and closed the folder.

Gangsta knew they didn't have a murder weapon on him, so he decided not to say anything. The two detectives left him, and minutes later two police officers entered the room and charged him with two counts of murder, cuffed him, and took him to the county jail to be booked.

He couldn't believe for one second that Dank rolled over to the cops. He knew it had to be true, because nobody but Kash, Dank, and him knew. When he arrived at Rice Street County Jail, he was booked and sent to 6 south 400. He was cellmates with a dude from the Bluff who also had a murder charge. The guy's name was Tevine, a cool cat with a humble demeanor. After Gangsta got situated, he decided to step out to see if he knew anybody. Gangsta saw Steve Mack, an old school crackhead from Bankhead. He got word that Kash was also locked up on the north side, and Dank was in protective custody, which confirmed he was the rat that ate the cheese.

It took Gangsta three weeks to get a visit from Michael Swinn, one of the best lawyers money could buy. He was a young white dude who knew his stuff. He was friends with most of the district attorneys and ate dinner with most of the judges. Gangsta was glad he had a stash at his mom's house. It was money to pay for the lawyer he knew he would need one day.

Gangsta was led to the booth where the white man was seated. He had on a nice three-piece suit, his long hair was pulled back in a ponytail, and he had glasses on his face.

"How are you feeling today, Mr. Jackson?" he asked Gangsta.

"Ready to get out."

"And that's the plan," he stated as he looked over the paperwork. "From the looks of things, all the state has is one statement, which could convict you, but it won't. I will not let that happen." He paused for a moment as he continued to read. "Yes, they do have your prints from a safe, along with Danny's prints, his wife's prints, and a host of other prints. Anyway, what I will do is go for a bond tomorrow, and then after that a dismissal. The only problem is that Dank has told the detectives of other homicides."

"So, this nigga is just snitching his ass off," Gangsta said, starting to get heated.

"Very much so," the lawyer replied.

"What about Charles?" Gangsta asked.

"They have him charged with Danny and Tonya's murders, plus two other murders. A mother pointed him out in a line up," Michael Swinn said, reading from the paperwork.

"So, you gonna get me a bond tomorrow?"

"Tomorrow you'll go to court, and do not talk to anybody of your case. Just let me handle everything."

"Yeah, I am," Gangsta replied.

The lawyer gave him all the hope he needed, though he still couldn't believe Dank snitched on them. He had broken their childhood pact. He would die for that, because there was no crossing that line. Gangsta still wondered what made Dank break like glass. He had watched Dank kill people a number of times, and he had seen him stand firm under all types of pressure, so why fold now? He never saw this coming.

He called his mother just as soon as he made it back into the pod. She picked up and accepted his call.

"Hey, baby," his mother said into the phone.

"What's up, Ma? The lawyer came by today talking good."

"Yeah, he said he would."

"How much did you give him?" he asked.

"Twenty five thousand." It was money from his stash.

"Ok, cool. I love you, Ma. You gonna be in court tomorrow?"

"You know I am."

"Call Terry for me, Ma," Gangsta said, and told his mother the number.

She dialed it and clicked over when Terry was on the line. Gangsta had to blow into the phone, because inmates weren't allowed three-way calling, but niggas found a way around it. If they blew into the phone while the other person dialed a number on the other line, it would work.

"Hello," Terry answered.

"What's up, boo?"

"Gary, Gary, are you still in jail, and for murder?" she asked.

"Terry, don't start going by everything you hear and just do as I ask you, okay?" Gangsta asked as he started to get heated, because he knew that's exactly what she did the first time he got locked up.

"Okay, and I'm sorry. I'm just worried," Terry replied.

"Don't be. Everything is good. I love you, shawty."

"I love you, too."

Gangsta talked with her briefly, because inmates were only given fifteen minutes on the phone before it automatically hung up. He just encouraged her to stay down and not stress. She promised she would and told him, "Just pray, baby."

"Alright, bye, girl. I'ma call you tomorrow," Gangsta said, and then the phone hung up. "Ma, call another number."

"Hell no, Gary. You need to worry about getting out. I am not about to run my phone bill up calling all over town for you. Anyway, I thought you and that girl were done," his mother said.

"Nah, we good, and she pregnant, too, Ma."

"Pregnant," his mother yelled in shock.

For the next four minutes, Gangsta heard it all from his mother. She called him every name under the sun. He just stood there and listened to every last word spoken to him until the phone went dead, and he was glad that it did.

Jerry Jackson

Chapter 8

NeNe

"Ms. Robertson," Professor Victor Gresham called out to her as all the other students walked out of the classroom.

NeNe turned around at the door with her book pressed to her chest and her book bag tossed over her shoulder. She had to face the man who has helped her overcome several obstacles along the way concerning schoolwork during this final year. This was a class she needed to ace badly, and a class she was working hard to pass.

"Yes, sir," she finally spoke.

"Today you weren't with the class. You didn't write a single note down. You did not have a single question, as you always do. Is everything okay?" her professor asked as he walked toward her with a fatherly look of concern on his face.

"Yes, sir, I'm ok. I'm just tired."

"Well, you know finals are in three weeks," He said as he stopped inches away from her.

He took her by the shoulders and forced her to make eye contact.

"Yeah, I know," NeNe replied.

She broke free from his hold and left the class. She walked down the hall at a fast pace, because she had to work today and refused to be late again.

Outside, NeNe unlocked her car door, got in, and cranked up her car. Her cell phone read that she had four missed calls. All the calls came from her sister. She pulled off into traffic.

The past three weeks had been a mess. Erica informed her that Gangsta and Kash both were charged with murder, and neither one of them had a bond as of yet. Erica also told her that Kash's parents got him a good lawyer. She said that Dank snitched the guys out. NeNe couldn't understand that because she thought the three of them were tight.

When she finally made it to her job's parking lot, her phone started blowing up from her sister's number. At first she wasn't about to answer, but Erica would not stop calling.

"Hello," she finally answered.

"I just left court, and they will not give Kash a bond. Those crackers got him charged with four murders and all types of other shit. He got twenty-three charges in all. Girl, you should've seen how he snapped."

"Dang, girl, for real?" she asked, shocked.

"Yes," Erica replied and began to explain in detail. "Girl, he got four murder charges, but on each one they give him two. That don't make no fucking sense. He have all type of gun charges, and some kidnapping charges, armed robbery, aggravated assault, all kinds of shit, honey. My baby just snapped, girl."

"So, what's the next step?" NeNe asked while parking her car.

"More money," Erica quickly stated.

"Damn."

"Yeah, I know. Girl, I'm so pissed off," Erica said.

"Well, I'm at work. I'll call you when I get off," NeNe stated, and they hung up the phone.

***

Gangsta

They had already called his name to pack up his things, and now he sat downstairs awaiting the bonding company to come get him. The judge gave him a bond in the amount of a hundred grand. With the help of his mother and aunt, he was able to post a property bond. The added condition of house arrest was the main reason he was able to get a bond.

Gangsta vowed he wouldn't be convicted on the murder charges, even if it took him spending every last drop of money he had to pay lawyers.

"Jackson," the female officer called his name.

Gangsta hated the smell of the holding cell. It made him sick to his stomach, so he moved fast to get to the door as it was opened.

He walked over to the glass window, and he was greeted by another young female officer. The woman passed him $800 in cash and his belt. They gave him his clothes and then directed him through another door.

He did as he was told, and then he saw his lawyer, his mother, and the bonding lady.

The district attorney had an officer put a black box around his ankle, and then he was released into his lawyer's custody. His mother's car was waiting outside.

Gangsta held a quick conversation with his lawyer, took a picture for the bondsman, and then jumped in the car with his mother.

"Gary, how did you get into this mess?" his mother asked when they pulled off.

"I haven't did a thing. One of my supposed-to-be friends just said I did."

"I told yo' ass you do not have any friends," his mother said as she drove.

"Ma, let me see your phone," Gangsta said as he ignored her comment.

"Hell no. Now sit back and put on your seatbelt." Gangsta just shook his head and enjoyed the drive home.

The first person he called when he got to his mother's house was NeNe, and she did not answer. He decided not to leave a message, but to call back later. He then called Veedo, who picked up.

"Yo," Veedo said when he answered.

"Shawty, what's happenin'?"

"What up, bruh? Where you at?" he asked before getting too deep into the conversation.

"Shit, I'm out, but I'm on house arrest, though," Gangsta said.

"Oh, okay. Well, I got that check for ya," Veedo said, talking of the money he owed.

"Ok, cool. I'll send my lil' ho your way in a bit. Just got home, and I'll let you know what's up in the next hour or so."

"Alright, dawg. I'm waiting on you," Veedo replied, and they hung up.

***

NeNe

NeNe saw the missed call, but did not recognize the number when she got into her car after work. The call was made over an hour ago. She pressed redial while pulling away. She was tired, stressed out, and wanted nothing more than a nice, hot shower and some much-needed rest. NeNe knew it would be impossible, because Erica needed a shoulder and NeNe had promised she would be there to console her.

"Hello," a sleepy voice picked up.

She was baffled at first because it was a male voice.

"Ah, yeah, someone called me from your number."

"What's up, this Gangsta."

She heard what he said, then recognized him instantly and almost missed her turn. She was happy to finally hear his voice, but at the same time shocked.

"Thank God."

"Where you at?"

"I'm headed home from work. Where are you?" NeNe asked as she turned her car onto the highway.

"At my mama's crib. The place you took me the first day we met."

"Ok, well, that's good."

"You coming over? I cannot leave 'cause I'm on house arrest."

He sounded so good, and at that second she realized she missed him and how sweet he was with her. He was nice and humble as he could be. She liked Gangsta for some strange reason.

"I can, but where is your mom? Is it gonna be ok?"

"I sure miss you, Miss Lady."

"Boy, hush," she said and laughed.

She indeed did miss him and his swagger. She enjoyed the small time they spent together, and most of all she enjoyed their conversations.

"So, are you on your way?" he asked.

"Yeah, I guess so."

"Okay, do you know the directions?" Gangsta asked.

She could hear the joy in his voice.

"I do," NeNe laughed at bit, and then they hung up with each other.

She tossed her phone into the passenger's seat and pushed the pedal a bit more. *He's home, and that's good*, she thought to herself. She also wondered how he got out if Kash didn't. It was strange, but she enjoyed the thought of being around him one more time.

It didn't take her long to find his mother's house. The time read 8:10 p.m. when she finally pulled into the driveway. She became nervous all of a sudden as she sat in the car, looking to the nice home painted white and blue. The front yard was large with fresh green grass. A nice flowerbed trimming the walkway to the steps, and old but neat chairs sat on the front porch. She noticed the living room lights were on, and she saw movement on the inside.

NeNe got out of her car, and she was still fairly shaken by her nerves. She made her way to the front door. She was dressed in jeans, a nice shirt, a small jacket, and boots. Her long hair was in a simple ponytail. NeNe started to ring the doorbell, but she heard the door already being opened. In a few seconds, Gangsta was standing face-to-face with her with a bright smile on his handsome face. He only wore some Nike gym shorts and a tank top. He had a box on his ankle, and he was wearing a pair of socks. He stepped to the side to allow her in.

"What's up?" he asked as she entered.

"How are you?" she asked in return with a smile.

He pulled her arm when she walked past him, making her come back toward him in a humble manner.

"I missed this," he said.

He touched her face and pulled her into his arms. They shared a much-needed hug, one she did not want to let go of, and then he kissed her softly. She lost herself and gave him her tongue. She couldn't help it.

After the kiss, Gangsta closed the door and led her to the sofa. She felt so good just being in his presence. NeNe wanted that feeling to last forever.

"Are you okay?" he asked.

"Yes, I'm fine, but what about you? What's going on with you? Are you okay? Is everything fine?" She asked questions a million miles a minute.

"Yeah, I'm Gucci. I just got to beat this case."

"What happened? I heard yo' friend told on you and Kash," NeNe said.

"He did, and for what I don't know."

"How did you get out?" she wanted to know.

"I bonded out," Gangsta said and touched her face again.

"I know that, but why isn't Kash out, too?"

"He got extra charges, I heard." He leaned over and kissed her again, and she kissed him back. "So what's up wit' me and you?" he asked.

"What do you mean?" NeNe asked in reply.

Gangsta pulled her toward him.

"I want to know, are we gonna be more than just friends?"

"I don't know. Are we?"

She pulled away from his embrace to look him in the face.

"Man, you's mines," Gangsta answered.

"How are you so sure?"

She laughed, because she enjoyed being near him and in his arms. She wanted to be with him more than anything, but at the same time she did not want to rush things.

***

Kash

"Man, can't you get that statement Dank wrote tossed out?" Kash asked his lawyer while sitting in the lawyer's booth.

He was beyond mad. Dank snitched on Gangsta and him because he was afraid to take a fall. What made him even madder was the fact he killed the people who shot Dank.

He was only acting in the solid form he would want his friends to do for him if the shoe was on the other foot, and being that Dank ate the cheese, it crushed him badly.

"I'm pretty sure we could get this case beat, but it's the mother on the stand that's the cause of you not getting a bond," his lawyer, James Pennet, said.

He was a high-priced lawyer out of New York that Kash's parents paid for to help their only child.

"Yeah, I know, so what's up now?"

"Well, you'll have to appear in court in the next three weeks. I'll be working day and night to come up with a defense against Dank's statements and the mother being the eyewitness to her children being killed."

"Ok, cool," Kash said, and then stood up to leave.

"Have a seat, Charles," the lawyer said with a look of concern on his face.

"What's up?" Kash asked while sitting back down.

"The district attorney is bringing up another murder charge on you."

The lawyer began to tell Kash that Dank wrote another statement about a murder committed years ago that Kash was well aware of, but acted oblivious.

"Man, that dude just making shit up."

"Charles, I'm going to need you to be honest with me if you expect my best help," the lawyer stated.

"I'm telling you the honest God's truth," Kash stressed, looking his lawyer square in the eyes. After they talked a bit more, Kash was led back to his pod, where he walked directly to his room.

"What yo' lawyer talkin' 'bout, shawty?" his cellie, Dread, asked.

"Same shit. Oh, listen, I need to get a jive to this sucka on protective custody. Shawty, can you handle that?" Kash asked as he took a seat on his bunk.

He had put his head in his hands and attempted to rub away the stress that was building up. He was in shock at all the shit Dank was telling about Gangsta and him. Kash remembered the day he killed that witness like it was yesterday.

He was fresh out of juvenile after serving thirty-two days for violating probation. He made a promise to Gangsta, who was on lockdown for murder with only one witness against him. He promised to rid the problem that held his partna.

Kash was picked up by Dank in a gray Honda Accord with black tinted windows from Bankhead Train Station minutes after he got off the train. He jumped in and gave his brother from another mother a pound.

"What's up, bruh?" Kash asked.

"You," Dank said, and then pulled off onto Bankhead.

"Who's ride?" Kash asked, but truly didn't care.

"My old ho."

The two boys ended up on Hollywood Road in some apartments called Hollywood Brooks. That's where Dank had an older female. They chilled at the crib until nightfall, then Kash decided to make his move, being that the girl stayed on Center Hill.

Dank was in the bedroom with his girl when Kash knocked on the door. To his surprise, Dank's girl opened the door in a long t-shirt and walked past him, so he entered the room. Dank was laid out under a sheet.

"Shawty, you strapped?" Kash asked.

"Yeah, why?"

"I need a tone to get bruh free," Kash said.

"Ok, grab that Glock. It's in the closet," Dank said, and pointed to an open closet.

"Bet, shawty, I'm gone get at you later. Give me a flathead."

Fifteen minutes after he left the apartment, he had stolen a car from Hollywood Manor Apartments across from Hollywood Brooks. It took him less than ten minutes to find Center Hill Church Street. He knew the area well because Gangsta stayed over on South Grand.

Kash parked the stolen car on Baker Road and started walking toward Star's house. She was the girl who was the witness set to take the stand against his second brother from another mother. He did not have a plan. He just knew she needed to go.

When he finally made it to Church Street, he pulled the paper out and read the address Gangsta had written down. He saw the house, and the lights were on, which meant somebody was there. He kept walking past the house until he reached the end of Church Street.

Kash started back in the direction he came from, and when he got to the house he walked into the yard. He walked on the porch as if he was about to knock, but he slick-peeped in. He noticed Star on the sofa talking on the phone. Her little brother was playing a video game, which meant her parents were probably asleep. Kash softly knocked on the door and looked in the window again as Star got up to see who was *at the door. Kash had never met her, so he knew she wouldn't know who he was. She opened the curtain to have a look and stared at him for a minute. He gave her a phony smile and a wave to make her feel comfortable, and then mouthed the words 'Let me holla at you.'*

The curtain closed, and seconds later Kash heard the clicking of the door unlocking. That's when he eased the Glock out from his back pocket. The door cracked open. He saw Star's face peek from behind it, and Kash raised the Glock in one instant motion. He let off three shots.

Pop! Pop! Pop!

Three shells hit the porch as Star's body tumbled back, and then the phone fell out of her hand. Two of the bullets tore through her cheek and jaw, and the other bullet missed her. She was dead before her body crashed to the ground. Kash jumped down the few steps and ran from the scene as fast as possible. He made it back onto Baker Road and to the stolen car. He cranked it and pulled off.

"Just write the letter. I can get it to the kitchen dudes when they run trays this evening," his cellie said, breaking his train of thought and bringing him back to reality.

Kash shook it off and got hold of a pen and some paper, still with a confused mindset. *What is Dank getting out of all this snitching?* he wondered as he began writing.

Pussy,

What you doing isn't cool, my nigga. Da game god gonna spank you one day, homie. I promise, boy, I wish you to be dead on arrival, nigga. I wonder what yo' momma and yo' kids gonna think 'bout you, huh? You pussy, bruh. You lying to them folks to save yo'self. The streets gone eat you alive, nigga.

Kash knew not to write too much, but he did want to get his point across.

Jerry Jackson

Chapter 9

Gangsta

The next morning, Gangsta was seated at the kitchen table in his mother's house while Terry prepared him breakfast. NeNe had left last night with promises to come over the next day, so early this morning he called Terry over. His mother was at work, which gave him rights to smoke a blunt and look at Terry's sexy ass in lust.

He heard the doorbell and wondered who it could be at an early time such as this. Gangsta got up with the blunt in hand. He put it out as a form of respect and walked down the hall toward the front door. He peeped out the window and saw his lawyer, Michael Swinn. He instantly knew something wasn't right, so he opened the door.

"How are you, Mr. Jackson?" Michael Swinn asked and walked in holding a folder.

Gangsta closed the door behind him and then asked, "What's going on?"

"We need to talk, so have a seat."

Michael Swinn sat in Gangsta's mother's favorite chair. He was lucky she wasn't home.

"What's up?" Gangsta asked.

The lawyer opened the folder and took a deep breath.

"The district attorney is about to bring up more charges on you that date back to 1994. Dank is stating that you killed a guy called BL. Bobby Loon is his given name."

"That's a lie," Gangsta stated immediately.

"Dank is willing to get on the stand and say that he witnessed the shooting."

Gangsta stood to his feet from the sofa. His heart dropped in his stomach because he knew Dank was the only dude who could rat him out on the case with BL. He could not believe Dank was going this far with the snitching.

"Man, that's bullshit all around."

Jerry Jackson

"Maybe so, but that won't stop a district attorney who thinks he has a strong case against you. He's giving me three weeks to return you back to the county jail for a new bond hearing."

"Man, fuck naw, I ain't doing that. I don't even know no muthafuckin' BL," Gangsta stated, and he knew he was lying.

By now Terry was standing in the doorway to the living room.

"Listen, Gary, I'll eat this case alive. I just may not be able to get you a bond this time, and if so, you would have to sit it out. Your parole hold will pop up this time around, too," the lawyer said, which made Gangsta shake his head.

"What about this shit I'm on bond for now? Can you beat that case, too?"

"I'm sure I can. I'm 100% positive if your friend doesn't take the stand I can put you there as Danny's tight man for the prints found on the safe. If he says different, then it's another ball game."

"Man, this some bullshit, real talk."

Gangsta couldn't remember a time he was madder than at that moment. He wanted to kill the world to show his anger. He could not believe all this was crashing down around his feet. He reflected back on the day it all went down with BL.

Dank and he went to West Fulton Middle School. Gangsta had only been out of juvenile two weeks and wanted to fly straight for a moment. They were walking down Bankhead when they made a stop at the gas station. All the afterschool students hung around at the store, so it was crowded with badass boys and fast ass girls. It was Gangsta's third day at school, so most people didn't know him, but they knew who Dank was.

Gangsta walked through a crowd of guys and into the store, where he got two blunts from the clerk. Gangsta noticed three females looking in his direction, so he decided to holla at the baddest one, who was a slim redbone named Star. She was a known freak from the Grove Park Center Hill area. As he got his mack on, BL and two other dudes entered the store. BL was a known bully who had a major reputation in the streets and the school for being the best fighter out of young

86

niggas. He stood 5'9" and weighed a solid 190 pounds at the age of fourteen.

"Yo, nigga, get out my girl's face! Bitch, get over here," BL demanded with a mean look upon his face.

Star quickly ran to his side out of fear.

Gangsta just looked at the guy who was a few inches taller than him and shook his head. He walked out of the store after getting his two blunts and was met by another crowd of dudes. Dank was across the parking lot on the payphone. Gangsta said nothing to their slick comments and remarks as he made his way to his partna.

"Let's go, shawty," he said to Dank, never looking back to the guys who began to follow them.

Gangsta opened the blunt and starting busting it while crossing the street to Hollywood Road. Dank noticed six dudes following them.

"Man, hol' up," Dank said and waited for the crowd.

"What's up, Dank?" one of the guys asked.

"Shit, try'na figure out do y'all niggas got beef wit' my brother?" Dank asked and looked everybody in the eyes.

"Naw, bruh, naw," the six guys spoke.

That's when Gangsta saw BL coming toward them with two dudes his size and no Star.

"What's up, nigga? You got a problem?" BL asked as he walked up.

The other six dudes walked off in fear of BL, who was looking at Gangsta.

"This ain't what you want, pimp," Gangsta said, low and humble.

"What the fuck you mean?" BL asked, and he started to step toward Gangsta, but Dank got in between them.

"Hold up, BL, don't make no scene. Just walk past the fire station. Y'all niggas can get a head up, but ain't no jumpin', though."

"That's what's up," BL said with a smile and began walking in the direction Dank was talking about.

It took them five minutes to make it to the plaza on Hollywood Road. They all stepped behind the building, and that's when Gangsta pulled out his .38. He pointed it at BL's face and pulled the trigger.

Boom!

His two friends struck out running as BL's body hit the ground.
"Shawty," Dank yelled out in shock.
He didn't even suspect his partna was strapped or would even pull
a stunt such as this. Gangsta stood over BL's body and shot him two
more times.
Boom! Boom!
"Let's dip, shawty!" Gangsta said, and then took off running in the
opposite direction the two other guys ran in, and Dank followed.

"Well, Mr. Jackson, I want you to know that I will try extra hard. The case was dead docked because the witness died, but now they have Dank willing to talk, so they will try to reopen this case.

"Man, it's too much going on, and it makes no sense," Gangsta said out loud. "So, listen, if I so happen to leave the house—"

"They will revoke your bond," Michael Swinn cut him off.

"And then what?" Gangsta asked as his lawyer started gathering the paperwork.

"You'll get locked up."

"Which they gonna do anyway."

"Probably," Michael Swinn stated as he stood up, and Gangsta stood up also.

"Okay, I'll give you a call if anything changes or I have any more questions," Gangsta said as he walked his lawyer to the door.

When he returned, Terry was seated at the kitchen table.

"So, you going back to jail again?" she asked.

"Listen," Gangsta said as he grabbed a paper and pen. "Go to this address and get all my clothes."

He gave her a key.

"But—" she started to say, but he interrupted her.

"Don't question me, Terry. Just do as I ask, baby."

"Okay," she said while shaking her head.

Gangsta knew he could only run for three weeks, and then he would be forced to turn himself in because his mother and aunt put up their homes for his bail. Within those three weeks he needed to get shit together on the outside, because he knew if the probation hold popped up, he was sure to be sent down the road again.

***

NeNe

As soon as she climbed into the car, she reached for her cellphone. NeNe could not go another second without hearing Gary's voice.

"Whoa," he answered.

"How are you?" she asked nervously when his voice embraced her ears.

"I'm good. So, are you coming over here?"

"I'm on my way as we speak," she said with a smile.

"Okay, 'cause I wanna go somewhere. I'm tired of this house," Gangsta replied.

"I thought you were on house arrest."

If she could remember correctly, that was what the black box taped on his leg meant.

"It don't mean I can't leave out wit' my girl," he said with a slight chuckle that made her smile.

So he considers me his girl, she thought to herself as she drove, and she liked the sound of it.

"Well, I am on my way over, so I guess you'll be ready to leave when I pull up?"

"Right."

"Bye."

She smiled, bit her bottom lip, and ended their conversation.

She could not ever remember feeling like this about a guy. This thing just happened so fast and felt so pure. It was as if the both of them belonged together.

All her life she'd never believed in love at first sight — up until now. She remembered the first time she ever laid eyes on him when he was asleep on her sister's sofa.

He had a rich brown skin tone, a nice solid frame, and with his ripped muscles she knew he worked out. He wore waves in his jet-black hair with only a few strings under his chin. She watched him for only a minute and wondered who this man was. Her sister joined her in the basement and informed her the guy sleeping was Kash's friend. Them talking had woken him up. He slowly sat up with bloodshot red eyes that locked in on her own. When he spoke and asked for Kash, she felt chills run up her spine. He had a deep voice and used a lot of slang, so she could tell he was from the city. He had two gold teeth at the top on either side of his middle teeth and two at the bottom.

NeNe was glad to take him home. Even though their conversation was small, it was good, and just being in the same car as him did something to her that felt wonderful.

Their very next encounter was the one that did it for her. She knew that what she felt the first time was real and she had fallen in love with a guy she did not know. She tried her best to play hard that night in the club, but in reality NeNe knew what she wanted. She just needed to see if he would put up a fight. Her question was, did he truly want her as she did him.

He quickly proved that night that he wouldn't give up until he had her attention. Now here she was on her way to pick him up, yet she couldn't reveal exactly how she felt, not just yet, because it would be too soon. Maybe he'd think she was a freak or something, so she had to hold it in.

NeNe spotted him before she even pulled into the driveway of his mother's house. He stood on the porch decked out in Guess shorts and a tank top. She looked on with lust in her eyes at his 5'10" frame as he walked down the steps toward her car.

She couldn't help but smile from ear to ear as he opened her door. She placed her car in park, unbuckled her seatbelt, and he pulled her out. NeNe wrapped her arms around his neck. She was standing on the tips of her toes. They shared a kiss, a very warm kiss.

"What's up, sexy?" he asked once they stopped kissing.

"Nothing," she said as she blushed and he let her loose. Then she asked, "Are you ready?"

"Yeah, just let me lock the door."

NeNe watched him run inside the house and quickly back out. He jumped down the steps and ran across the yard. Her passenger's side door opened and she saw a chrome handgun. He slid it under the seat, and then got in himself. He leaned over her console for another kiss, which she gave him. She wanted to protest herself from riding around with guns in her car, but said nothing. She just pulled off.

"Where are we heading?" she decided to ask when coming to the end of South Grand onto Bankhead.

"Make a right, and then a left," he replied while pulling out a pocket knife.

He reached down with the blade and started to cut on the strap of the black box.

"Boy what are you doing?" NeNe asked as she made the two turns he told her to make.

She kept watching him closely.

"I'm taking this shit off," he said.

"Why? Didn't the courts give you that?"

Now she was confused about what was going on.

"Yeah, but they finna lock me back up. Just keep driving and I'll explain what's going on," Gangsta said and tossed the box out of the window when they reached Hollywood Road.

They ended up on Johnson Road. He didn't get out of the car. He just waved somebody over to the car from a porch.

"Say, Eric," he called out.

The dude was sitting on the porch with a couple more guys. He came toward her car with a smile on his face from ear to ear.

"What's up, nigga? I thought yo' ass couldn't come out?" the guy asked when he got to the car.

They gave each other dap.

"Shit, when did you know me to follow the law?" Gangsta asked and took the blunt Eric was smoking out of his hand.

He hit it and passed it back.

"What's good, though?"

"This," Gangsta said and reached up to Eric's neck and touched a chain with a chicken foot hanging as a charm. "I need to holla at dem people."

Gangsta was speaking of a root doctor, better known as voodoo.

***

Gangsta was lying back on NeNe's bed watching TV while she took a shower. He had just recently gotten off the phone with Ms. Doc. She was a root doctor, and she agreed to meet him the next day.

The wall clock read 10:30 p.m., and he wondered how mad his mother and aunt were about what he did. He badly wanted to call, but decided against it. He did leave his mother a letter explaining that he was gonna turn himself in once the three weeks were up. He told her he had a lot of business to handle. He said not to worry about him and that he was sorry.

Gangsta said he would also give his lawyer a call to inform him that he would be turning himself in after three weeks were up and he was not going on the run. Gangsta had plans to run his money up as fast as possible, because he knew deep down he would need it, and most of all Kash would also need his help.

When NeNe entered the room, she killed his train of thought. She was wearing some baby blue boy shorts and a yellow tank top. She smiled at the way he stared her down.

"What?" she asked while climbing into bed under the covers.

"You and, umm—" he started to say, but didn't. He was eyeing her up and down and let his eyes do the talking.

"Boy, hush," she shot back, and Gangsta leaned over to kiss her.

Just as they began to kiss, her phone started ringing.

Gangsta tried to stop her from answering, but she did anyway. She found out it was Kash calling collect, so she accepted it.

"Hello," she said once the call was connected.

"What's up, sis? Where is my wife?" Kash asked.

"She not here, but yo' buddy is. Hold on."

NeNe passed Gangsta the phone as he pulled at the covers, trying to get a good look at her half-naked body, but he failed due to her holding the covers tight.

"'Sup, boy?" he asked when he took the phone.

"Shit, you, man. Bruh, Dank playing some fucked up games," Kash stated.

"Tell me 'bout it."

"Yeah, well, I need a favor, shawty. Send Erica down here and I'ma tell her to tell you. I can't talk over the phone like this. Ya feel me?" Kash asked, and from the tone of his voice, Gangsta knew what he was trying to say.

"Yeah, I'll do that."

"Why you not at the house though, fool. I thought you been on house arrest."

"I cut dat shit off. Pussy-ass Dank got these folks opening up another case, bruh."

"Pussy-ass nigga trippin'," Kash said into the phone.

"You got money on da books?"

"Yeah, I'm straight. So, you going on the run?"

"Nah, I just needed a few weeks to hit these streets before trial starts. In three weeks I'ma turn myself in," Gangsta replied.

The two friends talked the entire fifteen minutes nonstop, and then they got off the phone. NeNe took that time to lay her head on his shoulder.

"Want something to eat?" she asked.

"I'm straight."

"Wanna talk about it?"

"Nah."

"Oh, okay. Well, are you gonna get in this bed and hold me?"

She raised her head from his shoulder and looked into his eyes. This was one of the very first times they ever really locked eyes. He saw pure intentions in her. He saw that she wanted to be there. She felt for him what he felt for her. He saw it clear as day. Gangsta was 100% positive, and he realized at that moment he was in love.

Gangsta pulled her up to him and their lips met. Their tongues touched and spoke to each other. He slid his hand under her tank top to pull it off. NeNe pulled away and looked at him a moment, and then she pulled the tank top over her head herself. He exposed a nice set of firm breasts with brown nipples that stood at attention. She helped him out of his shirt, unbuckled his belt, unzipped his Guess shorts, and pulled his shorts down. Gangsta stood up and kicked off his shoes. NeNe took the free time to lay back herself and pull her shorts off to reveal a pretty pussy. As Gangsta moved between her legs, she spread them. They kissed once more, and then he moved down to her neck. She moaned when his tongue embraced her flesh.

"Gary," she whispered as he went to her breasts and sucked each nipple with great passion.

She held his head as Gangsta made love to her chest.

"Gary," she moaned again as he slid down her flat stomach, planting wet kisses all over her.

He moved down to her pussy, which, due to the foreplay, was soaking wet. He kissed NeNe there once, twice, and then he drove his tongue into her.

"Shit," NeNe said as she rolled her hips at the feeling she'd never felt before.

No man had been there in that way before. Gangsta stopped and kissed her inner thigh and down to the back of her knee. Then he moved to her small, pretty toes. He sucked each toe into his mouth. She gripped the sheets as her body shook. After making love to both feet, Gangsta moved back to her pussy. He stuck two fingers into her tightness and sucked her clit into his mouth. He moved his tongue from side to side.

"Gary, Gary," she yelled as she rolled her hips. "Oh, my good God."

She tried to roll from under him, but he had her locked as the orgasm burst through her entire body. She held his head with both hands and shook until she thought she had died. Gangsta, now fully between her legs, pressed his hardness into her center and started to slide inside her warmth. It hurt her a bit, though she arched her back.

They kissed, and she sucked her own juices off his tongue. He went in, out, in, out, deeper and deeper until she tried to run from the pain.

"NeNe."

"Yes."

"I'm in love," Gangsta admitted and went to work on her.

They made love for an hour straight, then he came with loud moans and jerks inside her.

He was woken even before his eyes opened. A slight smile painted his face as he thought of last night. Even with his eyelids closed, he felt the sun embrace the room. It was bouncing through the window, off the walls, and down to both of their naked bodies. He could feel NeNe pressed against him. It gave him a major hard on. He turned his head slightly to see her sleeping peacefully with her back to him and hair all over her beautiful face.

Gangsta rubbed his hardness between her warm thighs. She did not move, so he positioned himself and started to move his dick up and down between her pussy lips. He felt her wetness, heard her breathing get heavy, and then he entered her. NeNe arched her back and turned her head to look at him. She took hold of his hand on her hip. She squeezed it, then pulled it around to her stomach. She rested her head on the pillow as Gangsta moved in and out of her wetness. She was so warm on the inside, and so tight around him that it felt like heaven. He kissed the back of her neck, then bit down on her shoulder. He pushed deep into her, and with one motion he rolled her onto her stomach while still inside her. He placed either hand on the outside of her shoulders and went deep into her.

"Shit, baby," she said as she pulled at the sheets she had gripped in her hand with her face deep into the pillow.

Gangsta found a motion and kept a steady pace. He hit a corner wall every now and then, which made her moan a little louder.

After she came with a loud scream into the pillow, Gangsta sped up until his cum poured out. He pushed as far as he could go and laid there, tired from a morning round one.

***

NeNe

She woke for the second time of the morning, but this time Gangsta was not in the comfort of her bed. Something also told her she was extra late for school. She got out of the bed naked to find her panties and tank top. She put them both on, then her robe, and proceeded to the living room to find there was no Gangsta. NeNe walked to the front window and pulled the blinds back to see her car also missing.

She headed back to retrieve her cell phone to call him, but quickly noticed his keys and money was on her coffee table. As she began to get upset, she walked back into her bedroom. She began to wonder if he would be back in time for her to go to work. She also wondered where he was and what he was doing in her car. She sat on the bed and noticed that there was a note and some money by the clock on her nightstand. She picked the note up and read:

Hey, beautiful, I had to run out for a minute and did not wanna wake the peace I saw upon you. I left some money for Kash, so give it to his girl. I'll be back.

Gary

P.S. Breakfast is on me.

Chapter 10

Gangsta

"You must turn yourself in, Mr. Jackson. This is not good," Michael Swinn said.

"Man, I told you I am not running. I ain't going nowhere. I just got bizness to handle before I get tied down. Niggas owe me, and dats money I'ma need to pay yo' firm with," Gangsta stressed through the phone.

"Listen, I'm tell—"

"No, you look," Gangsta cut him off, "I hear what you saying, but hear me. I am not about to turn myself in until three weeks is up, point blank."

"Mr. Jackson, just let me do my job."

"Yeah, do what I paid you to do."

Gangsta hung up the phone.

He needed to get back to NeNe. He cranked up the car and looked at the bag on the passenger's seat. Everything he needed from Ms. Doc was in that brown paper bag, so now all he had to do was put his plan into motion. He mashed the gas and pulled off into traffic.

A person will never know the outcome of the next person until the heat is on. No matter what type of reputation a nigga's got in the streets, how much money he gets, what kind of crew he runs with, or what he did in the past, when it's just him in that tiny room and he is alone with the police, somehow, someway all that solid shit flies out the door. All that shit gets broken down and peeled to the true surface of a snitch.

Gangsta wanted badly to hit Dank where it hurt, but that would involve his mother, and she was like Gangsta's mom. She must not be held to blame for her son's actions.

It wasn't long before he made it back into the city limits. He headed straight to College Park and to Terry's apartment that she'd recently moved into. She wasn't home when he got there, so he took a quick shower.

After the shower, Gangsta called Teyummie, who answered her phone in a sexy tone.

"Hello?"

"Teyummie, what's up wit'cha?"

"Oh, hey, boo. What's up?" she asked with a sense of excitement.

"Coolin', so I just thought I'd hit ya up. Where y'all at on Simpson?" Gangsta asked while leaving the apartment and heading back to the car.

"Nah, I'm at our house, 'bout to bathe."

When she spoke those words, it gave him visions of her naked, and her sexy body matching her beautiful face made him brick up.

"Damn, that sounds good."

"Would be even better if you came over. Maybe you can help me and wash my back," Teyummie said and started laughing. "I'm just playin'."

"Don't get scared now," Gangsta replied.

"Never dat. I'm just chilling, though."

"Let me come chill wit'cha, though."

"Um—"

"You can let me kiss on the other lips for 'bout twenty minutes," Gangsta pressed.

"Boy, hush, you crazy."

"I'm for real, though. I just wanna cuddle for an hour or so."

"Yeah right, Gangsta. I don't know."

"Girl, just text me the address. Don't get scared now, and I can keep a secret," Gangsta said.

"I swear, if this comes back to—"

"Real niggas don't talk," he said, cutting her off.

Gangsta's mind drifted back to the seventh grade during the first day of school when he first tried to get with her.

He was walking down the hallway with his cousin, Eric, when he noticed her walking alone and looking lost.

Teyummie was fresher than most girls in the school and was hands down prettier, so she had caught Gangsta's attention. He noticed her hands filled with rings and her neck had two chains around it. Her hairdo was priceless and nails were well done, so he couldn't help but to speak.

"Excuse me. What's up?" he asked and stepped toward her.

"You're excused," Teyummie said with a voice matching her beauty.

"I'm Gangsta. What's yo' name?"

"I'm late for class, and my boyfriend is walking up behind you," she shot back with a smirk on her face.

Gangsta turned around and saw Pat Man walking up, so he walked away. He saw her walk into Pat Man's arms, and then she kissed him. Gangsta went on about his business, because he wasn't a hater.

Later that day, he caught her in the hallway and asked her name again.

"Teyummie," she spoke.

"Okay, I'm Gangsta," he shot back, looking directly in her eyes to let her know he was choosin'.

"Ok, cool, so I'll see you around," Teyummie said as the bell sounded off.

Gangsta decided to leave school early that day and never returned that year due to being arrested. When he did finally get out, Teyummie and Pat Man were in an even deeper relationship than before, and she was looking even better. Bad as Gangsta wanted to fuck her, his focus was his comeuppance, so he quickly forgot about her when his feet hit the ground until recently seeing her.

Pat Man and Teyummie had a nice home in Forest Park, a very low-key area with beautiful houses and big yards. He was amazed at the sight he saw as he pulled up to the address given.

The house was surrounded by an iron gate. Three cars lined the circle driveway, and Teyummie stood on the porch holding a remote to open the gate. Gangsta parked beside a Range Rover and watched Teyummie watch him. He climbed out of the car with eyes filled with lust. He wanted nothing more in the world than to fuck this woman.

She was standing on the porch in a pink robe, and her hair hung loose. He could see the nice figure she had under the silk robe, and could tell she wasn't wearing a bra by the way her nipples poked out.

"Thought you stood me up," she spoke once he made it on the porch and walked into the house. "Close and lock the door," she said over her shoulder.

Gangsta kicked the door closed, but didn't lock it while looking around the spacious living room. He knew Pat Man was straight, but he didn't realize he was doing it as big as he truly was. Now he saw and knew he had to play it cool like it wasn't nothing to his eyes.

Teyummie walked to the wet bar.

"Want something to drink?" she asked while mixing herself a drink and looking more beautiful than ever.

Gangsta took a seat on the plush sofa and said, "Yeah, pussy juice if it's any over there."

"Boy," she laughed and tossed back a shot. "It's plenty of that, though."

"I hope it's sweet as it looks," he shot back as Teyummie walked from behind the bar and untied her robe.

It fell open to reveal she was naked. She had beautiful breasts, a navel ring, a trim pussy, and thick thighs. Gangsta just stared, and his dick was getting harder by the second. Gangsta's mind drifted a few summers back when he almost had a chance to fuck Teyummie.

It was a hot summer day and everybody could be found at the pool at Gun Club Park. Gangsta and Kash had got there late and were told it was packed.

Kash wanted to argue with the park patrol, but Gangsta stopped him by placing a hand on his shoulder and pulling him away. Gangsta knew they both had guns and drugs on them, and neither could afford a slip up. He decided to park the bikes they rode on Ruth Street. It was indeed overcrowded, but they didn't care as long as they were in the midst.

Gangsta saw all of his schoolmates. He saw the entire Johnson Road clique and his girlfriend, Terry. This was somebody he did not want to be bothered with, so he made sure to stay his distance. He knew if she saw him it would be a problem at the park today.

Gangsta and Kash posted up in the corner of the park to roll up blunts and watch who watched them. He noticed Teyummie getting out of the pool. She grabbed a towel from one of her friends, wrapping it around her waist, and then headed to the shower room and restroom.

Gangsta made his move and headed in that direction as slick as he could without being seen. He walked unnoticed inside the girls' restroom, where he saw Teyummie standing in the mirror.

"What yo' butt doing in here?" she asked, surprised.

"I saw you and I miss you."

"Where you been? It's been a minute, huh?"

"Yup, now lemme get a hug." Gangsta walked into the bathroom toward her.

"You crazy," Teyummie said nervously.

"'Bout you. Where yo' nigga at?"

Gangsta pulled her into his arms. She had no time to reply as Gangsta's lips met her own. She wrapped her arms around his neck. While in his embrace, she felt Gangsta's hand brush between her thighs.

"Un huh, nah, no," Teyummie softly moaned, but she didn't stop him from pulling her panties to the side.

"What? Shh, and just let me—"

He pushed a finger into her wetness, and she moaned louder.

"Stop, Gary," she said.

As soon as she said those words, somebody else walked into the bathroom and caused them to break from their embrace while Teyummie fixed her clothes.

"Oh, wee, look a here, look a here," one of Terry's friends from Johnson Road named Nikki said.

Nikki laughed as Teyummie quickly left. Gangsta just looked and then walked off, shaking his head.

"You just gonna stare me down or come get ya drink?" Teyummie asked, breaking his train of thought.

Gangsta then realized she had allowed her robe to fall to the floor around her ankles. She was fine like frog hair, and he wanted some. All the years of pent up lust and now here was his chance to finally enter her. The moment he has dreamt about was finally about to happen.

Teyummie walked toward Gangsta. She walked into his arms, and with one smooth motion the Glock was in Gangsta's hand and pressed to her side.

"Bitch, take me to the safe."

He pushed her out of his arms hard and her back crashed against the wet bar. She screamed out in pain as she hit the floor. She looked up with fear in her eyes.

"Gary, baby, wh—"

"Bitch," Gangsta cut her off and slapped her so hard with the Glock that it cracked her jaw. "Take me to da safe."

Teyummie balled up from the blow as blood poured from her mouth to the floor.

"Please, I thought we were cool. Please don't do me like dis, Gary, please."

Gangsta kicked her naked side and knew he cracked her ribs from the way she yelped out in pain.

He grabbed a handful of her hair and said, "I'm not gonna ask yo' ass no more."

"Upstairs, it's upstairs. Please, Gary. Pat Man's gonna kill me. I thought it was 'bout us," she begged as he pulled her up the steps while still holding her by her hair.

"Bitch, fuck you, now let's go!"

She showed him where the master bedroom was, and then pointed to the bed.

"It's under it."

"Bitch, get it." He snatched a pillowcase off a pillow and tossed it in her face. "Hurry da fuck up."

Teyummie staggered over and shoved the bed out of the way to reveal an in-ground safe. She punched a code in and pulled it open.

"Fill it up. Empty the safe," Gangsta demanded and loved the sight he saw.

"Gary, please—" she started to plead again.

"Bitch," Gangsta shouted, and then he raised the gun.

Pow!

He shot through the wall. Teyummie jumped and began to start pulling stacks from the safe while cryin'. After she was done, she handed over the pillowcase.

"Thanks," Gangsta said with a smile and shot her three times in the face at point blank range.

Pow! Pow! Pow!

He knocked half of her face off with the bullets. Blood and brain matter went everywhere, even on Gangsta's pants leg and shoes. He didn't sweat it as he loaded the money and drugs up. Gangsta made sure not to touch anything. While searching for the stash of drugs, he ran across a bulletproof vest and some more cash.

Gangsta found a book bag full of pills and two drink bottles full. After he secured everything, Gangsta got up out of there.

***

Kash

"Damn," Kash said out loud at the thought of Dank. Kash jumped off of his bunk and stormed out of the cell. He needed to workout and get the stress off his mind. It was killing him to know his so-called friend dropped a dime on him. A group of guys were doing pull-ups in the corner of the pod. Another group of guys were under the steps working out with a water bag. He pulled off his shirt and walked to where the bag was being lifted.

"How many sets y'all doing?" he asked while watching one of the guys strain from the weight of the bag.

Kash thought he knew the guy, but he wasn't sure.

"This seven, but we doing twenty, though."

"Let me get last down," Kash replied and watched the two guys switch spots so the one he was speaking to could get his turn on the bag.

Breathing heavy, the other guy, who was light skinned with freckles in his face, gave Kash a long look before he spoke.

"Where you from, folks?" the freckle-faced guy asked.

"Simpson," Kash quickly replied and took his turn.

"Ok, yeah, you got into it at the Tasty Dog, huh? You ran wit' Dro, Slim, and them," the guy said with a smile of admiration on his face.

It was a smile that put Kash at ease, because at first he thought it was some beef.

"Hell, yeah," Kash said. Now Kash remembered his face.

"Boy, I been gone ever since back then."

"Damn, that's been like two years ago," Kash said and put the bag on the ground so the next guy could get his reps in.

"Hell yeah, bruh. I'm in here on a fucking body. Folks got me with felony murder and malice. That's crazy."

"Damn, sho' is."

"What you in for?" the freckle-faced guy asked.

"Nothin' major like you, bruh. A lil' weed case and fightin' the police," Kash lied, because he didn't need anybody in his business like that.

He ended up doing seventeen reps with the guys and talking and kicking the shit until it was time to eat.

Kash still didn't have an appetite for some odd reason. Usually when he went to jail he knew how to adapt to the situation, but for some reason he couldn't get into his mojo.

Out of all the trouble he went through, he never felt so stuck, so held down, so defeated. He knew of all the crimes he had committed, this was the one that would keep him locked up for a while. That was something he did not want to face, but was forced to deal with. Kash wished like hell he could change the hands of time, because he would've left Dank in the hospital to deal with the issue himself. He wished he could have seen Dank's disloyal ways in another form. Then his mind drifted to his kids and how they would be without him for years. He really wasn't concerned about a female, because he knew they would come and go. He knew they would be there. He also knew they would play games, but his kids were a different story. Kash shook his head at the thought and gave the tray he just received to the person next to him, and then he walked to the phones. He called his lawyer, who accepted the collect call.

"Charles, how are you?" James Pennet asked.

"Looking for a miracle," Kash replied.

"I agree. Well, right now nothing has changed for the good."

"And for the bad?" Kash pressed.

"Nothing has changed for the bad, either, so that gives me time to work out what little kinks I can," he replied.

"Ok, cool."

"I will be to see you in two weeks. We will work out some things. I have some ideas."

"Ok, bet that," Kash replied and hung up the phone.

He then dialed his baby's mother, and the call was accepted.

"Hello," his daughter said into the phone.

Her voice made him smile and gave him sense of life.

"Hey, baby, what's up?"

"I love you. I wanna come see you, Daddy. You wanna talk to my brother?" she asked, sounding so excited.

"Yup, where he at?"

***

NeNe

She was elated to see her car pull up an hour before it was time for her to go to work. She was even more elated because she got to see Gangsta again. NeNe never knew when he would go to jail or how long he would be in there when he did go.

NeNe met him at the door. He had pizza in his hand and a slick smirk on his face. She moved to the side, matching his smirk, but held a blush on her face as he passed her.

"Sorry I'm late, so I did lunch instead of breakfast."

Gangsta placed the pizza on the table. He had a book bag tossed over his shoulder. He pulled it off and put it on the sofa.

"I'm just glad I won't be late for work."

"Who says you not gonna be late?" Gangsta shot back and pulled her into his embrace.

He stared into her pretty eyes and kissed her soft lips.

"I can't be," she said, and then kissed him back.

"Every time I touch you, I wanna—" Gangsta bit his lip before he could finish his sentence.

He kissed her neck and inhaled her smell.

"You should've done like your letter said," NeNe shot back, even though she would so love to feel him inside her.

She knew she had to be at work, so she pushed softly out of his arms and sat on the sofa.

"Money calls, babe."

He also took a seat on the sofa and grabbed the book bag. He began to open it, but stopped short. He looked at her hard and long before he spoke another word.

"NeNe, check this out. I know it may seem as if I'm rushing or pressed, but I'm in love with you. I trust you heavy even though we just met. I'm taking a big chance, but fuck it. If it kills me, then so be it."

NeNe was caught off guard with that statement. She was shocked, and it showed on her face even though she was flattered. She trusted him, too, and her feelings for him were deep. She wanted him just as much as he wanted her.

"Gary, I, um, I—" She stopped her statement and swallowed hard. "Whew, well, I—"

"Are you here with me because you wanna be?" he asked, cutting her off.

"I am. Yes, I so wanna be," she replied.

"Cool, me too," Gangsta smiled.

NeNe watched him pull stacks of money out of the book bag and bundles of colorful pills. He put everything on the table beside the pizza box.

"And what's all this?" NeNe asked as she found herself picking up the pills.

"Shit I'm 'bout to bless my people with. Here put these up." He gave her two knots of money. "And then go wash yo' hands. Let's eat," he said.

NeNe did as she was told. She stashed the money in her shoebox and hid it in her closet. She washed her hands and joined him at the sofa. They both ate two slices of pizza, then she dropped him off in Bankhead Courts Projects before she went to work.

NeNe knew she was truly feeling Gangsta and wanted what they both had started to continue to grow because it felt good to feel like this. She accepted him as a blessing because of his good looks and great charm. She adored how he treated her, how he looked at her, how he talked to her, and how he kissed and hugged her. NeNe crossed her fingers and hoped to God that Gangsta did not change up. She vowed to be loyal and upfront and honest with him. She vowed not to cheat or betray him in any form or fashion. She was finally happy and did not want to lose what she had.

Jerry Jackson

Chapter 11

Two Weeks Later

"Jackson!" the female officer who ran intake at the county jail called his name.

Gangsta got up from the steel bench and headed for the iron door while another officer used his keys to open the door. Gangsta walked out and was led to the windows.

"Empty all your pockets. Place all devices, rings, watches, chains, and money in the tray," the woman spoke while showing a mouthful of gold teeth.

Gangsta could tell she was ghetto to death by her long, colorful fingernails and colorful hairdo.

He reached into his pocket and pulled a bankroll while looking at her. He noticed greed. Gangsta tossed the money on the table along with his watch and chain.

"That's it," he said.

"They must've got you straight out the trap. How much is this?" she asked while pickin' up the money.

"Think ten racks," he said, and then moved closer to the window. "Keep a band, but just put me in the pod wit' my partna."

"And what pod is that?" she looked at him as if he was crazy.

"6 north 400."

She made eye contact with him. She made the kind of eye contact that said she was down, and he understood. She typed him up an account and passed him a paper with the amount of $8,766. Gangsta was led back into the holding cell as another dude's name was called. He took a seat and waited. He was ready to get upstairs so he could kick it with his partna. He wanted to talk with Kash and see what was on his mind. He also wanted to smoke with him, because he knew Kash needed it.

NeNe also crossed his mind, and her wellbeing. *How will she handle this journey so early in the relationship?* He knew his parole would violate, so he'd end up going back to prison with the open murder cases. He held strong faith she would hold him down. Gangsta explained everything to her one week before turning himself in. She cried like a baby, but promised to hold him down because she was truly in love, just as he was.

Gangsta and NeNe were inseparable the last two weeks. All they did was have fun spending time with each other, getting to know each other, and growing a bond as one. He enjoyed every second of being with that woman.

Terry was another issue. She was pregnant, and he was confused. He wanted to tell NeNe about Terry and her being pregnant, though he wasn't really sure about Terry. Was she game playing? Was she for real? If so, then would she really go through with the pregnancy? He was pretty sure she would not hold him down, and in the long run she would get back with Zay. All these things made it easy for him to choose NeNe and put his faith into her, even though in the two weeks he had left before he turned himself in he did spend a few days with Terry and had sex with her. He also had a long talk with her about what was going on with him and what he expected to happen. She also promised to hold him down. Gangsta decided to inform NeNe of Terry only if she indeed was pregnant, because that was fair.

Gangsta truly disliked the fact he had to turn himself in, but he could not and would not allow his mother or aunt's property to be taken on his account. He had all his business handled. He got a chance to bless Veedo with ninety thousand pills, to break bread with his mother and his lawyer, and to make sure Kash's lawyer was on his job. He took Kash's kids shopping before turning himself in and put most of his things into storage. Gangsta let his truck go back to the lot. He also stashed his bulletproof vest, six guns, and seventy-five grand in cash deep in the woods behind his mother's house. He was prepared.

After another two hours had passed, Gangsta and six more guys were given county jail stripes and shower shoes and were led to the sixth floor. Some guys went north, some guys went south. Gangsta went to 6 north 400 as he requested. The pod smelled like a workout gym and looked like a jungle when he walked in. At that very moment, it seemed as if everyone stopped whatever it was they were doing.

He saw guys hung over the rail looking down, guys watching TV, guys on the phones, and guys at card tables and checker matches. He noticed different sets of guys working out. All this time he was looking for Kash. Gangsta found an empty bunk in the back of the pod. He decided to place his mat before he looked again. Again he looked around for Kash, but he still did not see him.

"Say, folk, you wanna sell those?" some random dude asked Gangsta.

Before he could reply, he noticed Kash coming out of the shower. Kash saw him, too, and smiled.

"What's up, boy?" Kash asked.

"What's up, nigga?" Gangsta asked and smiled back.

He walked around the dude and his questions about buying the all-black Jordan number eight's off his feet.

"Where yo' shit, boy? I ain't got no cellie, so bring it up," Kash said, elated, and then walked into his cell. Dread had went down the road the last shipping day.

Gangsta got help from a dude and took his things to the cell. He slid the door closed and put a flap up after the guy who helped him had left. He pulled off his shirt.

"Watch the door, bruh." Gangsta stood over the toilet and stuck a finger down his throat. His stomach jumped twice before he vomited everywhere. Gangsta did it three more times, and each time he filled the toilet with balloons. He stood straight up, and his eyes were bloodshot red. He reached down and pulling out handfulls of balloons, then tossed them into the sink.

"Let's blow, shawty," Gangsta said, while cleaning himself up.

After Gangsta washed all the balloons, he counted out fifty-six, each one with a gram of purple haze in it. He let Kash break the purple down while he peeled away the shoe pad to one of his Jordans to reveal two ounces of mid-grade weed. His other Jordan revealed rolling papers and a lighter.

It felt good to be around his partna. The both of them were locked inside the cell and smoked out. They discussed how Dank surprised them with the shit he was pulling. Gangsta explained to Kash what his lawyer was saying and how the case with Danny was weak and both of them had a fighting chance to beat it. Kash showed him the statements from Grich's mother and told him it was nearly impossibly to beat with her pointing the finger.

There was a knock at the door. A tall, skinny guy with no shirt walked into the cell. Kash sat up on his bunk and reached out to dap him up.

"Shawty, this Moncho. Moncho, this my nigga Gangsta," Kash introduced them.

"What's up wit'cha?" Gangsta asked.

"Coolin', young blood. Y'all got this bitch stank up in here," Moncho stated.

"You blow?" Gangsta asked.

"Hell, yeah, that old nigga go in," Kash cut in, and the three of them shared a quick laugh. Gangsta tossed him a balloon. "Roll dat up."

A smile painted Moncho's face as he closed the door and sat on the toilet to begin breaking the purple haze down. Kash and Gangsta continued to talk about their old days in the streets and told tales of Rydc. All three of the guys laughed, joked, and smoked.

The traffic in his room was niggas in and out, everybody trying to get in where they fit in at. Some walked in to spend money, most walked in for handouts and left with nothing. Before lockdown and lights out rolled around, Moncho had made a few plays and sold an ounce in sacks.

Even after lights out, the inmates were able to move from cell to cell, so Kash and Gangsta were up in the wee hours of the night sacking up and kickin' it.

At 4:00 a.m. Gangsta was finally able to lay down on the top bunk bolted to the wall. Every now and then he'd take a glance out of the window and wish he would've went on the run instead of turning himself in. Every time he thought like that, he thought of a million reasons why he did turn himself in.

His mind drifted to NeNe, and he wondered what she was doing, what she was up to, how she was sleeping, and what she was sleeping in. He wondered how long would he be locked down. Would he beat the case or not? All Gangsta did was wonder, wonder, wonder.

"Shawty, get up," Kash said.

When Gangsta heard Kash's voice, he knew he wasn't dreaming and he was in the county.

"Yo' parole officer down here," Kash said while standing in front of the sink brushing his teeth.

Gangsta finally opened his eyes to the sunlit room, and then he slowly sat up. He was kind of hungry, still high, and could use a few more hours of sleep.

"What's up, boy?" Gangsta was able to ask.

"Shit, they called yo' name for parole hearing."

"Ok, bet."

Gangsta didn't think his parole officer would be here so fast. He was not expecting the sudden visit, but jumped down from the top bunk to the floor. He found his toothpaste and toothbrush. Gangsta quickly brushed his teeth and washed his face. He decided to smoke when he got back from his visit. After leaving the cell, he saw it was still early at just 10:15 a.m. Most inmates were still in their beds asleep as he made his way to the door to go out.

Three minutes later, Gangsta was seated in the lawyer booth in front of his parole officer. He was a hard-nose white man who loved to send people back to prison. He loved when you slipped up and got caught. He spared no one.

"Murder?" That was the first word spoken as he opened the folder that sat in front of him. "You just love violence, huh?"

The parole officer shook his head and finally looked up at Gangsta for an answer.

"They got the wrong guy, Mr. Mann," Gangsta said.

He did not want to overplay himself even though he knew the verdict already. He thought anything was possible, and Mr. Mann could be in a good mood.

"To hell with what you say. Them folks will not say two different murders if the truth wasn't in it. I'm revoking the remainder of your five years. Do you wanna go to court, or do you wanna sign?"

"I'm sayin', Mr. Mann, how can you just convict me like dis?"

"If you beat ya charge, you make parole, but if you don't, then oh well. You signing or going to court? It don't matter to me," the parole officer said.

Gangsta knew he wasn't playing. He wasted no time because he was ready to get this show on the road. He signed the paperwork and couldn't believe he was on his way back to prison. Gangsta was truly hating Dank, because he was the reason behind all this bullshit.

Mr. Mann held a smirk on his face as he gathered the paperwork and stood to leave. Gangsta felt so defeated with his back against the wall. He did not like this feeling. Quickly, Gangsta made his way back to the pod. He needed to smoke one badly.

Both Gangsta and Kash hated that they made the mistake of embracing Dank.

After smoking three phat sticks, Gangsta made his way downstairs to the phones. It wasn't so crowded this morning, so he found an empty phone and dialed up Terry's number, who picked up and accepted after a couple rings.

"Hello," Terry said into the phone.

"What's up, baby?" Gangsta asked.

"Why is you just now calling me, Gangsta?"

"Been stressing, sleeping, and working on my case."

"Oh." She sounded down. She had been missing him like crazy and crying herself to sleep at night. She was scared he would never get out of prison. "Baby, just pray and everything will be okay," she told him.

"Yeah, I am, but I gotta go down the road."

"Where?"

"To prison."

"For what, murder?" Terry asked.

She sounded as if she panicked quicker than his words.

Gangsta kind of laughed, but quickly reassured her.

"Yes to prison, and no to murder. I'm on parole, baby, and that's why, but when I beat this charge they gonna let me out."

Gangsta hoped that was enough understanding for her. They talked the entire fifteen minutes, mostly about his case and about them some, and then they said their goodbyes.

The very next day Kash and Gangsta both were called to visitation because both Erica and NeNe came. They got as clean as possible and headed to 700, another part of the jail where they held visits. Gangsta, followed by Kash, walked up the steps and looked through the booths until he spotted Erica, and in the very next booth sat his love.

"'Sup, girl?" he asked, and then took his seat.

"Hey," NeNe replied with a nervous smile.

"Stand up, step back so I can look at you," Gangsta spoke, and NeNe did as he said.

Gangsta loved the way she stood back on her bowed legs. Her hips and small waist were perfect on her slim frame. She wore capri pants, a sheer blouse top, and sandals with her hair pulled back in a ponytail.

"Babe—" she started to say.

"Turn around, boo, I need all dis."

Gangsta got closer to the window so he could see.

"Baby, I miss you," NeNe said, and then took her seat.

"I miss you, too, baby. Just hold me down, 'cause this ride ain't gonna be long."

"I pray not, 'cause I hardly sleep at night."

"I hardly sleep, too."

"I love you, Gary. I hope you know this. No matter what happens, I'ma be right by your side."

Tears started to form and fall from her eyes.

"I love you, too."

Gangsta wanted badly to hold his woman. It hurt him to see her hurt like this, and it made him want to snap for some reason.

**

Kash

"I miss you, honey," Erica said when he took his seat.

He looked her in the eyes hard and wanted to blow up on her, but he bit his tongue and spoke.

"What's up? What them lawyers talking 'bout?"

"Trial, baby."

"Yeah, well, they need to come on with it, then."

He shook his head.

"They talking good about the case with Danny, but not so good with the mother going on stand," Erica shot in.

"How much money in the stash?" he asked.

"I don't know."

"Count it up, 'cause I need ten bands." Kash decided to play mind games with her because it was showing to him her true side.

It was becoming clear what type of female he had in his corner.

"Ok," was all Erica said.

"Well, I'm gone," Kash started to get up.

"What's wrong wit' you, Kash?" she asked.

"Nothing."

"You sho' acting funny. You acting different."

"Nah, everything straight," Kash replied.

He got up and gave her a disgusted look before he walked away. He made it back to the pod before Gangsta, so he waited until he came back before he smoked. It didn't take Gangsta long at all to make it back, being that Kash just walked off leaving Erica crying, which messed up his visit.

"Shawty, why you do Erica like that today?"

"What, bruh?" Kash asked Gangsta while eating a honey bun spread with peanut butter.

Gangsta laughed.

"Man, you just walked out on the girl. Her ass was cryin' and shit to NeNe. You fucked up my visit."

"Shawty, fuck that ho, bruh. I'm not finna let that bitch handle me like I'm some peon."

"I feel that."

Gangsta started to roll up a blunt of purple haze. It was time to talk some more about their case and how it could be beat.

Chapter 12

Veedo

The sunlight peeked through the blinds and caressed his face. The radio played low overhead, and his wall clock read 9:35 a.m. Boy, was he tired from hanging at the strip club all night with a couple partnas. Veedo turned to the side and saw April, then behind him was her best friend Balinda. A slick smile crept to his face as memories of last night played in his head. April was his baby's mother. She was highly jealous, insecure, and extra ghetto, so it surprised him when he got home and she had her best friend willing to comply with a threesome. Veedo got out of the bed, crawling over Balinda's good-pussy self. He was completely naked as he made his way to the bathroom to piss.

Veedo was twenty-nine and raised in Atlanta's Bankhead Courts Projects. He was the only son to a known stripper named Goldie and a mack for a father, whom Veedo still hadn't met. He grew up hard like most people in his hood, so by the age of thirteen he was a drug pusher and slanging nickel bags of weed. He was spoiled due to his mother's success in Atlanta's best strip joints. Growing up, Veedo always wore the best clothes and shoes, and he was always known to keep money in his pocket. By the time he turned fifteen, he was caught and convicted of drug charges and received five years probation. For the next two years he hustled on the low and stayed far away from slangin' on the block. He sold out of his girlfriend's mother's apartment, and fate landed him on Rice Street when the police raided the apartment. Veedo got sent to prison for the next seven years of his life.

When he was released, he worked different jobs, but nothing seemed to sit right with him. Nothing seemed to work in his favor. He continued to try to walk straight because his third strike was sure to land him in prison for life, and that was a pill he wasn't willing to swallow.

For the next seven years, Veedo busted his ass for the white man and got his record cleared. He was struggling, but he no longer had probation or parole on his backbone. He had two children by April. She didn't have a job, so that made life a bit harder for him, but with every ounce of him he tried and tried to stay focused — until he saw Gangsta a few months back.

Veedo knew Gangsta from doing time in Alto. He knew Gangsta was solid, so he swallowed his pride and asked for help, and he got it. Gangsta hit him off with four pounds of purple haze and blew Veedo's mind.

The day he received the four pounds, Veedo swore his loyalty to Gangsta. He promised not to look back, not to break stride, and not to fall short. Veedo hit the streets serving ounce after ounce of purp to the strip club people and the hip-hop club jumpers.

By the time Veedo was ready to pay Gangsta for the love he showed, he was shocked when Gangsta dumped ninety thousand pills on him. He told him, *Don't slang these in the A*. He left, and Veedo understood. What truly confirmed that he shouldn't slang the pills in the city is when word travelled through the street that Pat Man got took off and his bitch was murked in their home. Veedo always admired Teyummie.

After Veedo pissed, washed his face, and brushed his mouthful of gold teeth, he walked naked back into the room.

Atlanta was turning into a war zone because Pat Man was out for answers and killing anybody he thought was capable of such an act. Since Veedo was out of weed, he decided he had sat on the pills long enough, and it was time to find a spot in the country to push the pills.

He found his Joe Boxer briefs and put them on, then took a seat at the end of the bed to roll up a blunt of Kush.

After rolling and putting fire to his blunt, he picked up his phone to check the messages and missed calls. *I need a weed connect*, he calmly thought to himself while scrolling through his contents.

"Daddy, I'm hungry."

Veedo looked up to see his youngest daughter standing in the doorway. With a smile on his face, he tossed the phone to the side and looked at his pride and joy. He was happy to be able to take care of his seed.

"Go get yo' brother up and y'all get dressed."

***

Kash

"Man, ain't no muthafuckin' way," Kash shouted and punched the hard plastic window in the holding cell. He had to be removed from the courtroom because he snapped when the district attorney brought up another charge on him. They had the body he buried with Dank. *Dank is a low-down, dirty mutha'fucka*, Kash thought as he fumed in the holding cell. He couldn't believe the shit that was going on around him.

Gangsta had just gone down the road the night before, so he wasn't around to let his partna lay the drama down to him. Kash was madder than he'd ever been in his life. He wanted to break Dank's neck for the sucka shit he was pulling.

Thirty minutes later, the officers came to his holding cell and cuffed him up. They escorted him to another empty holding cell where a team of lawyers awaited him. The officers stepped out of the holding cell to give him some privacy.

"Man, what da fuck is going on?" Kash asked, still in handcuffs.

"Your co-defendant has worked a deal with the D.A."

"Man, he lying!"

"Yes, we are sure he is, and we are working extremely hard to prove this to the courts. We know for sure two of the five murders will get thrown out, and if they can't connect you to this recent charge physically, you will also get out, because Dank's word alone will not convict you," the lawyer said, and that statement alone made Kash calm down.

"Ok, so when do we start knocking this shit off?"

"We start today. When we walk back into the courtroom, please hold your quick temper and let us do all the talking. Do not butt in or stand up and shout what you think or what you see fit, ok?"

"Alright, let's do it," Kash replied.

Kash knew he had just showed out in the courtroom minutes ago, but he was shocked about a new murder charge that was years old. He saw his mother breakdown and cry. He saw his kids' mother holding them as they cried their eyes out. He even saw Erica in an emotional state of shock. He just snapped and let his anger override his intellect.

"Okay, give us a minute to speak to the judge and the D.A. so we can proceed with the hearing."

***

Gangsta
One Month Later

He heard her pick up the phone and accept the call. He missed everything about this woman.

"Hello," NeNe said.

"'Sup, baby?"

"Nothing much, just missing you, that's all. I heard the good news," she replied.

"Yeah, I know my ma told you," Gangsta shot back.

Last week his charges concerning the Danny case were dropped. Kash's case was also thrown out, but now Gangsta had a fresh murder charge and witnesses saying it was him. This news he didn't share with NeNe just yet.

He'd been at Calhoun State Prison for a month, and he was truly homesick. He was missing his family and friends like crazy and wanted to be free. He could nearly taste freedom on the tip of his tongue.

"Did you get the pictures?" she asked.

"I did, and as a matter of fact I'm holding them right now." They were pictures of her and Erica at different places.

"Okay, well, Kash's trial is over already."

"Fo' real?" he asked with shock.

Kash's trial had only been going on for six days.

"Yeah, it over, and he got life."

"Why?"

Gangsta was confused and hurt behind the news.

"They stopped the trial and asked him if he would plead out to life, and he did."

"Damn."

"I know, baby. So, will your parole officer let you out now that you have beat the case?" she asked with excitement in her voice.

120

"Hell yeah. I've gotta talk to my lawyer, and hopefully he can get my parole officer to release me."

Gangsta wasn't ready to break the heartbreaking news to NeNe, so he lied with regret.

After hanging up the phone, Gangsta walked down the hall to the TV room where a couple of guys were seated around a table playing a game of chess. A fair crowd of inmates sat in front of the TV while one dude was off by himself in the corner shining his state-issued prison boots. All this reminded Gangsta that he was indeed in the system again, so he might as well get used to it until his fate was passed down. He calmly walked out and back to his assigned cell. Most guys inside his pod were returning from the yard, and then lunch was being called for their entire pod.

Inmates were instructed to walk in a single file line, and they were not supposed to talk, although most guys did. Some didn't, and Gangsta wasn't among most. Dank had already proven that he couldn't trust no man. From the day Dank betrayed him forward, Gangsta stuck with that code.

They only had five minutes to eat, and the food was not good at all, but he forced every spoonful down because he couldn't make store call until next week. He vowed to never eat out of the chow hall again once he did make store call.

Gangsta ate as fast as he could and then put the tray through a tray room flap. Then he stepped into the line that led back to the pod. Some dudes went straight to the TV room, some went to get cards for a game of spades, and some went to take a shower. Gangsta went to the phone.

He called his lawyer to see if there were any new updates about his case. He got no answer when he called, so he dialed his mother's number. He waited for her to accept the call, and then he heard her laughing with somebody in the background.

"Ma?"

"Hey, baby, what's the name of that prison again?" she asked.

"Calhoun," Gangsta replied.

"Okay, Terry and me want to get down there, and this girl is stressing bad. I told her to stop before she lost that baby."

"I know, right. Have you talked to my lawyer yet?"

"Yes, the D.A. wants you to stand trial."

Gangsta did not want to hear his mother say those words, but he embraced the fact.

"Man—"

"Your lawyer said he will be to see you first thing tomorrow because he has to discuss some of this stuff with you personally. He said you're lucky, boy, and Gary, I truly hope you have learned your lesson."

"I have, Ma."

The next day, Gangsta was led to the warden's office to sit down with Michael Swinn, who was dressed to impress and awaiting him with a firm handshake and big smile on his face. He passed Gangsta a thick folder, so he took it and sat down.

"What's this?" Gangsta asked.

"It's a case dismissal. The '94 case from middle school was dropped because there was no evidence to link you to it, but if you turn the page, you will see two witnesses. The first one is Kia Knight, A.K.A. Kay Kay, and the second one is Amanda Brown, A.K.A. Slim. Both of the females said they talked with you minutes before you shot and killed Gerald Blackshift, and the district attorney wants a trial."

Gangsta took in all he had just heard and sat there in thought. If Dank didn't open his mouth, then he was safe on home plate, but this pussy nigga had snitched his way to a manslaughter charge.

"So, when does the trial start?" he asked.

***

NeNe

The room was cold, but crowded. It was very loud in there with so many different people talking at one time. She noticed the floors were shined and clean. She could look down and see her own reflection in the floor. A small table sat in front of her, and on the other side of the table was an empty chair. NeNe was excited, but also nervous. She held herself and bounced her knees up and down, while she continued to wait. She noticed that guys who were locked up wore white pants with blue stripes, and some wore black boots and others white shoes. She saw kids playing and crying while mothers attended to them. NeNe's eyes wouldn't stay away from the door. She saw where the inmates entered. She saw them pass their I.D. card to the officer who sat at a wooden table, and then the inmates would proceed to find their appointed table where they would embrace their family.

NeNe was elated that she would finally be able to hold her man after almost four months. In the county jail visitors and inmates were separated by glass, so she had to wait until he got to prison and got her approved on his visitor list before she had a chance to touch him. The letters he wrote were always nice to read. The phone conversations they held always consoled her for the moment, but there wasn't anything better than physical contact. She wanted to be able to kiss him like she's saw so many inmates kiss and hug their girlfriends, baby's mothers, or wives.

Today she wore jeans by Apple Bottom, the shirt to match, and a pair of flats on her small feet. Her hair was in micro braids with just a touch of lipgloss. She was holding a clear bag filled with change, which is something Gangsta constantly told her to bring if she visited him so she could buy him food and drinks.

Nervous, she sat there and wondered how the visit would go. Would he be nervous as she was? Would he be happy to see her? Would he be too nervous to hold her or to kiss her? All these thoughts ran through her mind while sitting there, and even while she was driving down the road that early morning.

Gangsta entered the room, and when NeNe saw him, her heart skipped a beat. He didn't notice NeNe seated in the back. He looked so good to her. She wanted to get up and run into his arms badly. She saw him looking to find her, so she raised her hand up high and waved him over. NeNe saw his smile. She loved his smile, and she loved how he walked toward her. She stood up, and all of a sudden she was scared for some reason, but she didn't know why. When only inches away from her, Gangsta pulled NeNe into his embrace. She wrapped her arms around his neck and he grabbed a handful of booty. He kissed her neck, her jaw, and then her lips.

His lips were ever so soft, and their tongues found one another for a brief moment, then they both broke away.

He stared into her eyes and then kissed her again and again before saying, "Damn, I missed you."

"I missed you, too!" NeNe smiled, and goosebumps covered her entire body for a strange reason as they both took their seats.

Damn, he looks great, she thought to herself.

"How was the ride?"

"Long, and I got lost twice. It's almost four hours, baby."

"I know." Gangsta reached across the table to take hold of her hands. "I love you."

"I love you, too. I got that money from Veedo."

"Okay, cool," Gangsta replied, and picked up the clear bag full of change. "Go get something to drink and some chips real fast."

"What do you want?" NeNe asked.

"Whatever you want your nigga to eat," he shot back, and that got a smile out of her.

She stood up to do as he asked. When she walked past him, Gangsta lightly slapped her booty. NeNe had on a thong, and when he did that it made her ass bounce. NeNe hated the fact that other dudes stared her down as if she was fresh meat or something. It made her think they could attack her at any time. She grabbed two sodas, a burger, two hot wing plates, a bag of chips, and a pack of Starburst candy. She walked back to the table and placed everything down, and then she took the wings to warm them up. Minutes later, after NeNe came back with the food, Gangsta wasted no time eating while looking across the table at her.

"What's up with yo' sister? Has she holla'd at Kash yet?"

"Yeah, he called last night. He's in Smith State Prison. He told Erica he does not like it there, and I gave him your address to write you."

"A'ight."

NeNe looked at her man for a moment. She was happy to see him, and she was happy she got the chance to touch him. She clasped her hands together and locked in on his features, and then she let what she was holding in out.

"Baby," she paused, took a deep breath. "I'm pregnant."

Gangsta looked up and dropped his burger on the table.

"Fo' real?"

She saw he was happy, which made her smile, because ever since she found out she was pregnant, NeNe had been going crazy about telling him. She was going crazy even though during the lovemaking he said he wanted her to have his baby. She knew in the heat of the moment guys would say anything.

"I'm too lucky. Damn, I love you, girl."

"I love you, too. I'm seventeen and a half weeks," she boasted.

"How long have you known, NeNe?"

Gangsta reached across the table and took her hands in his own.

"I've known for a while, but I was scared. I didn't know what you would've thought."

"I think you're wonderful, amazing, and I'm in love."

"I think you are, too, baby."

Jerry Jackson

Chapter 13

Gangsta

He was housed on the east side of the prison in Pod J, Building 2, and it was said to be the bad pod over the compound, but he feared nothing, especially not prison. When Gangsta came through the gates after visitation, people were on the yard. He walked with his head held high and he felt great. He was at Calhoun State Prison, and had been there three weeks. Gangsta knew a few of the guys at the prison, plus Atlanta niggas was deep. He liked the camp because it had a lot of females who worked there and most of the inmates at the prison stayed into wild shit.

Gangsta made a left coming up by the gym. He decided to go the long way to his pod so he could stop and holla at his detail boss, Ms. Bell, who worked in the kitchen. She had every nigga on compound gawking at her because she was young and beautiful. She paid the inmates no attention, and that was something Gangsta liked about her. Gangsta was cool with her because of his hard work and skills in the bakery. Plus, the director of the kitchen — an older lady named Ms. Smith — loved Gangsta as if he was her son.

"Say, bruh," a dude said as he caught up with Gangsta while he was walking.

Gangsta turned to see his Atlanta partna inside the fenced-in yard.

"What's up, bruh?"

"Who came to visit you?" Jay asked.

He was one laid back cat whom Gangsta respected. He'd been at Calhoun for six years. He was the man when it came to hos and drugs. Plus, Gangsta liked the way he handled business. He kept a crew of young niggas on the go.

"My lil' ho. What's up wit'cha, though?"

Gangsta stopped in front of the fence. He stuck two fingers through the gate and Jay met him with two fingers where they dapped each other up. Jay proceeded to roll up a joint to smoke. It took him a quick two minutes to get the weed twisted. He passed the joint and a lighter to Gangsta, who in return put some fire to the end. He hit it four times before passing it back.

"I'm on deck with the mid," Jay said as he hit the joint hard.

"Okay, I'ma fuck with you 'bout that on da last yard," Gangsta replied, because they weren't in the same pod.

Jay was housed in G2, where all the females worked first, second, and third shift seven days a week.

Gangsta walked off as they both noticed the lieutenant coming through the gate. He made his way around by the kitchen. When he got there, he looked through the tinted windows and spotted Tim. Tim was an old white guy who Ms. Smith also liked as much as she liked Gangsta. Gangsta waved him over.

"What's up?" he mouthed through the glass.

"Who working?" Gangsta asked while doing more hand movement than talking.

"Ms. Bell and Ms. Smith."

"Go get Ms. Smith," Gangsta said, and then he saw Tim run into the back and disappear.

The weed had already taken effect on him, so he leaned against the building and waited.

Three minutes passed, and then he heard keys in the door before it came open. Ms. Bell stepped out. She was a honey-colored, 5'2" female with a soft face. She had full, kissable lips and big brown eyes. Her body was A1 on a scale from one to ten. She was a dime, and she was no older than twenty-six years old. She had a small waist, flat stomach, and a phat ass.

"What do you want, Jackson?"

"Where Ms. Smith at?"

"She's busy, and she wants you to come make this bread 'cause Pete got locked down last night."

"Okay, I'ma come after count. My football team is finna play. Call my pod officer and let them know to send me up," Gangsta said.

"Okay, I'm 'bout to go before I lock one of these lames up," Ms. Bell said while looking over his shoulder.

He already knew a nigga had to be jacking his dick, so he just walked off and didn't look back. Gangsta knew this was part of how the chain gang went. There were niggas who did their time jackin' their dicks, niggas who fucked niggas, and niggas who acted like females.

Prison was considered a different part of the world. It had its own place of judgment, and it was a place Gangsta couldn't wait to leave.

He made his way around by G building, then passed H until he reached his pod. Ms. Riley was working the control booth while Ms. Frazher worked the floor. He hit the booth window so she could let him in.

"213," Gangsta told Ms. Frazher when he entered the pod.

She was seated up front at her mini desk. She wrote his room number down as he went straight to the TV room.

After count cleared, Gangsta signed out to the kitchen for detail. His weed high was gone and he needed something a bit more powerful than mid. He needed loud to get him going.

Officer Green, who was a very cool young officer, let him into the kitchen. He liked Ms. Bell, but she didn't give him any play either for some reason. Gangsta walked to the back where Ms. Smith was on the phone with a mean expression on her face. She pointed toward the bakery when she saw him, which made Gangsta stop and smile before doing an about face.

"Okay, Ma."

"'Bout time," she said with an attitude.

"I know, right."

He began to take off his shirt, because he was about to get down and dirty. Ms. Bell took him into the back where they got some more bread to serve for dinner, but she also wanted him to cook the pancakes for breakfast.

"Grab fourteen racks," she said.

He did as he was told and began to push them toward the exit.

She stuck the key into the lock and opened the door. Gangsta pushed past her.

Today, Gangsta just stood back and watched the other guys feed the prison as Ms. Bell directed them. She moved from inmate to inmate making sure they gave the correct amount of food and didn't overload their plates for their so-called homeboys. Every time she went to the next guy, she would cut her eyes at Gangsta. He made sure not to pay her any attention at all. Each time she looked and noticed he wasn't looking, she would make him go and grab the spoons and cups. Each time she made sure to work him. Gangsta did so with no problem. He laughed to himself each time.

After chow was served, Gangsta went out into the dining room to kick it with the other inmates and eat before they had to clean up and leave. Then Ms. Smith called his name.

"Jackson."

"Yes, ma'am."

Gangsta got up from the table.

"Ain't you cooking the pancakes?"

"Yes, ma'am."

"Well, go and get started, 'cause Ms. Bell has got to go home as early as possible," Ms. Smith said while putting her bag on her shoulder and getting ready to leave.

"Okay, I gotcha, Ma," Gangsta said and walked toward the bakery.

He saw Officer Green leaning up on the fence talking to Ms. Bell like he was getting his mack on as she smiled and pulled the flat pans out for the pancakes. Gangsta walked into the bakery while putting gloves on and turning on the oven. A few moments later, Officer Green said his goodbyes to Ms. Bell. She smiled in his face, but just as quick as he turned around to leave her smile turned into a frown and she playfully rolled her eyes.

"Stop fake kickin' it," Gangsta said with a laugh.

"Shut up."

"Where is the pancake mix?"

"The warehouse, dang."

Ms. Bell took a deep breath and shook her head, then sat down on the stool.

"You doing so much fake kickin' it yo' ass done forgot how to do ya real job, wow."

"Honey, hush."

"Let's go get it."

"I'm tired," she said.

"Yo' ass the one that's gotta go home, not me. I stay right down the road." He laughed and he walked out.

Ms. Bell tiredly got down from the stool and followed him to the warehouse. There wern't many inmates left in the kitchen, just the ones who needed to do their last minute clean up.

The next day, Gangsta signed out of his pod for pill call. He needed to meet Jay on the walk by the gym and store. He saw Jay posted, so he walked over and gave him some dap, and then the both of them walked off toward the pods as Jay lit up a joint.

"So, what's up?" he asked Gangsta and passed him the joint.

"We need to link up," Gangsta said as he hit the joint. "I can get whatever, bruh. The money ain't the issue."

"Okay, I see. Well, look, I got a ho, bruh, but she is not about to drive to Atlanta."

"That's not a problem," Gangsta replied as he passed the joint back. "What does she want, or do you handle everything?"

"Yeah, you just buy the work and drive it down here and we split whatever it is," Jay said.

"We'll try four zips each."

"Bet dat, bruh."

"She'll bring it down tomorrow."

Gangsta knew he had plenty of options to make the play happen.

"Check." Jay passed the joint, which was getting smaller, back to Gangsta. "Let me know when everything is ready."

When he got back from talking with Jay, he started making a bombay: coffee, Kool-Aid, and drink all mixed down and grinded into a smooth drink. It was a prisoner's alcohol, a drink mix almost everyone drank if they could afford it. He walked from his cell and down to the phone to call Terry to see if she was free.

"Hello," she said after she accepted the call.

"What's up, pretty?"

"Nothing much, baby. Just a little tired. I'm over my momma's house."

"Okay, good. Walk outside right quick. Look up New Road and see if Veedo is out there."

"Let me just call him," Terry replied.

"Bet."

A couple minutes later, she clicked back over and Gangsta could hear Veedo barking orders to somebody before his voice boomed through the speakers.

"What's happenin', Gangsta?"

"Shawty, what's good?"

"Man, coolin'. I'm down here in Albany making it do what it do," Veedo said, and Gangsta knew the move.

He was glad Veedo did as told and did not push the pills in the city.

"Good, so they like you down there?"

It was code for the pills.

"Boy, they adore me."

Both the guys fell out laughing.

"So, look, I need some gasoline by Friday, bruh. I need eight zones."

Zones stood for ounces.

"Ok, cool, I got that in the bricks. Terry can go grab it soon as I make the call," Veedo said.

"Bet, and what's the ticket?"

"Man, bruh, you straight."

"Nah, bruh, this bizness, and you don't owe me shit. Always keep your bizness in order," Gangsta said.

Before he turned himself in, Veedo had given him eight racks for the four pounds of purp, and all he asked for off the pills was forty racks, so as of now, Veedo's weed debt was clear.

"You right, bruh. Just give me twelve hunnid. That's what I paid. It ain't in my heart to get nothing extra from you, fam."

They both agreed to exchange the money once Terry got the product, so Gangsta ended the phone call and retired to the TV room where the guys were watching the news.

***

Veedo

Veedo was sitting on the porch of LisaPay's house counting his bankroll. They called her LisaPay because she charged for everything under the sun. She spared no one, and it was something he liked about that country girl.

LisaPay helped him by pumping the pills out of her crib. In the two weeks he'd been posted, people knew him from slanging pills in the club for eight dollars a pop. They were some of the best pills people had ever had. Veedo's name quickly elevated through Albany, Cordel, and Macon counties.

"You still riding shotgun, LisaPay?" Veedo asked once he pocketed the ten bands she just handed him.

He wanted her to help him find another spot that his customers on the other side of town would stop complaining about the drive. Veedo knew he had to stay low key, but he also wanted to get off the pills as fast as possible.

"Yup, I'ma roll wit'cha," she replied.

Veedo reached and grabbed his phone. He placed a call to his partna Chan from Bankhead Courts. He set up an eight-ounce deal and arranged for Terry to pick it up. Chan agreed, and being Bankhead born and bred, Chan knew Terry because she, too, was from the bricks.

When Veedo hung up, LisaPay was ready to leave. She had packed all her shit up in the house and locked the door. He stood up from the worn down Lazyboy that sat on her porch and walked down the few steps it took to get to his Dodge Ram F250.

Veedo climbed in, followed by LisaPay, and both of their bodies sank into the black leather seats. He cranked up the truck and adjusted the radio low so they could ride and talk.

The pills had sold very well down in Albany, and he only had sixty thousand pills left, so he knew he would need a connection on the pills fast if he wanted to keep the money flowing. Plus, Veedo was about to invest in another trap spot, so he definitely had to have more pills. He thought for a second about what he needed to do, and then he pulled off.

***

Gangsta

"Say, Mr. Green, call my pod and tell her to put me on out count," Gangsta said to the young officer.

Gangsta was going to cook the brownies for dinner that night.

When he got to the bakery, Ms. Bell was already putting butter on the pans. He noticed the brownies already mixed and ready to be laid.

"It must be finna snow, 'cause Ms. Bell is working?" Gangsta said while pulling off his state shirt and grabbing an apron.

"Don't start."

"What's up with you?"

He stood on the side of her.

"Nothing, but I've gotta get this shit done 'cause I gotta leave at six."

"Okay, let's get you out, then," Gangsta replied and started working.

He also wanted to hurry and finish up because he wanted to catch Jay on the last yard, because Jay sent word that the bomb landed. It only took a few days and the play was made. That was something Gangsta liked.

Ms. Bell and he bounced around the bakery until every pan was filled with brownie mix and most of them were already in the oven on preheat. Ms. Bell was writing on a pad as she leaned over the counter. Gangsta, who was on the opposite side of her, snatched the pen with a smile. She reached for it, but he quickly pulled way so it made her come around the counter to face him. Then he put the pen in the air. Ms. Bell decided to punch him in the stomach, but it didn't make Gangsta budge, so she just stood there looking up at him. Gangsta looked down to her, then looked up and around them before he leaned in to kiss her. She leaned back and pushed him in the chest.

"Stop," she spoke. "Give me my pen, boy."

Gangsta placed the pen in her palm. He locked eyes with her. He saw her understanding and noticed she was nervous.

"I was just joking wit' yo' scary ass," he finally said while taking a seat on the stool.

"Honey, please. If I kiss you, half the prison will talk about it." Ms. Bell said and started back writing.

"Yeah, 'cause you gonna let them see. Me, I know how to move," Gangsta replied, and he meant every word that came from his mouth.

"Yeah, right," she shot back and walked back toward him. "Plus, yo' lil' girlfriend comes to see you every weekend faithfully, I hear." Then she walked off.

***

An Hour Later

"Yard call! Yard call," Ms. Perry yelled into the pod.

Gangsta was the first one out the door.

"213," he said as he slid past her slim frame.

She had a stance like NeNe, but she wasn't nearly as pretty. She was definitely fine, though. When Gangsta made it to the yard, he was met by Jay and Nardo. They all gave each other a pound before walking off together.

"Shawty, I got mines off top," Jay spoke low enough for only Gangsta to hear.

"Cool."

"I didn't know it would be da loud," Jay smiled.

"That's all my people got, bruh," Gangsta shot back as Jay passed him a circle of loud still in a wrap.

Gangsta grabbed it and stuck it in his back pocket, and then let his long white tee hang down over his pockets.

"'Preciate it."

Gangsta walked a couple laps around the yard with Jay until he was ready to fire up some of the new loud. Gangsta decided to workout by the basketball court and stay away from the crowd. Fuck being caught up.

Anther-forty five minutes passed, and he was in his cell rewrapping the loud smelling gas. He only took out one zip and stashed the rest in his room vent.

"Gary Jackson! Gary Jackson," he heard the female officer call his name. "Room 213T."

He wondered what she wanted as he opened and stepped out of his cell.

"Yeah."

Ms. Perry looked up and then back down to her paperwork. She looked back at him again, then started walking in his direction to get closer so she didn't have to yell.

"You need to report to the kitchen," she said.

"I just got off not even two hours ago."

"The officer called for you," Ms. Perry said and walked off.

Gangsta stepped back into his cell so he could finish what he started. This time he did it with a fast pace so he could make it to the kitchen before count caught him. If Gangsta would've had some help, he could've been done, but he trusted no man to be in his business. This far he had dealt with everything solo. Plus, in prison, the less people see, the less they will have to tell. When one person peeps your move, nine times out of ten you're dead because secrets are hardly kept in prison.

As fast as he could he handled his business and sprayed his room down with bleach to kill the weed smell. Then he was walking and heading to the kitchen. He still hadn't smoked any of the new loud, but he had plans to go down through there when he got back to the pod.

When Officer Green let him into the kitchen, the time read 7:15 p.m. He had beat count by fifteen minutes. Gangsta walked into the office to find Ms. Bell at Ms. Smith's desk.

"We're missing knife #0031," she said when she looked up to see Gangsta's face as he walked in.

"I don't use them," Gangsta replied.

"I already had everyone but you checked. I gotta take you in the bakery to see if it's in there. I've already missed my homegirl's party, and I'm too mad."

"Let's go, then."

"Come on," she shot back and led the way to the warehouse.

They made it in the back and started looking around. He was on one side of the warehouse and she was on the other side looking for the knife.

"I've got it," she yelled to him.

136

"You do?" Gangsta asked and stood straight up from his bending position.

He saw her holding up the knife with a smile on her face.

"Man, your ass could've been did this." Gangsta started to walk off, but he felt her grab his shirt.

"You forgot something," she said nervously, and then looked down to the floor.

Gangsta took her hand into his.

"I forgot something?" he asked and pulled her toward him.

She willfully came into his embrace and their lips met for a quick peck.

"I don't wanna get in trouble messing with you."

"Shawty, I'm not trouble."

Gangsta allowed the hand that was holding her lower back to slide down over the curve of her butt.

"I like you," Ms. Bell spoke.

"I like you, too," Gangsta replied, and they broke from their embrace.

Ms. Bell led the way out of the warehouse while holding the knife.

Jerry Jackson

Chapter 14

Kash

Dear Big Bruh,
  What's happenin', fool? Man, me? I'm just coolin' it and keepin my head up and mind focused. I got a lot to take on when I hit the street again, so I must stay in tune. This jive won't be long. This is just something to let you know that you thought of at all times, my nigga. I will never break the code like dat sucka did us. I'm straight with money, bruh, so if you need something, then holla. Oh yeah, NeNe finna have my seed, fool. Yeah, bruh, I'm 'bout to have me two lil' soldiers. Okay, love ya, big bruh. Hit me back when you coolin'.
                                        Always,
                                        Gangsta, yo' lil' bruh.

Kash placed the letter down and took the picture that Gangsta had sent out of the envelope. He knew of two of the females from school, and the rest were pictures of Terry from Johnson Road and her friends. He saw Terry was indeed pregnant. Kash just smiled.

Kash started daydreaming about a time him and Gangsta walked the streets of Atlanta. He remembered the day he saved Gangsta's life. That was a special day for both of them. They vowed to always have each other's back and to never cross each other. The same went for their brother, Dank, who was due to get out back then.

That day Gangsta picked Kash up from the spot on Simpson in a car that was stolen, and Kash didn't care. Kash jumped off the porch once he saw Gangsta pull up.
  "What's up, shawty?"
  "What's happenin', fool?" Gangsta shot back. "I got a sucka and I'm strapped."
  Kash smiled and climbed into the car. He pulled out two bags of weed. Gangsta had a 9 mm laid across his lap as he backed out of the driveway.

"It's a nigga named Lemon from College Park, but he got the work. He got plenty of dope and money."

"How many folks he roll wit'?" Kash wanted to know.

"It's just him, bruh. Dat's it," Gangsta said with a smile, and then he pulled off.

The radio was already missing, so they both smoked and discussed the whole set up with this dude Lemon. Kash listened attentively while searching the car for anything of value.

That same day, both guys caught and robbed Lemon for some pounds of weed and some cash. The mistake was made when they did not kill Lemon. They let him seek revenge, and later that night he almost had a victory.

It was the same night of the robbery back on Simpson. Gangsta was outside talking to a freak and trying to get his dick sucked. He was leaning on the car while Kash stood across the street at the corner store with some older guys. Up the street, Kash noticed a pickup truck rolling down the block past Gangsta at a creep, and Kash notice that Gangsta wasn't paying any attention at all. Kash was locked in and ready as the pickup truck began to turn so the shooter could be on Gangsta's side. Kash jumped right into action, pulling his Beretta out, but held down by his side.

"Gangsta," he yelled to make him look up, and he also pulled his strap.

Pow! Pow! Pow!

Kash shot before anyone could react. Gangsta rolled off the hood of the car and blasted his Piston.

Pow! Pow! Pow! Pow! Pow! Pow! Pow!

The entire hood watched the exchange of gunfire. Gangsta and Kash both took off running at full speed away from the scene. Both the boys made a pact that night to forever have each other's backs, no matter what.

Later that day, Kash heard the male pod officer who worked with Ms. Jones call out for the last meal of the day.

"Chow call!"

Today was chicken day, so everybody would be going to grab their chain gang pimp except for him and a few other people. Kash slept in room 239 in G2, down the top tier. When the officer cleared the pod and closed the door, Kash peeped out of his cell to see the pod was empty. Ms. Jones stepped out as well. Kash quickly slid down to room 236, which was a short distance from his own cell.

"'Sup, nigga?"

Kash pulled the cell door closed and it locked. He pulled out a shank made from a piece of fence and sharpened down to a point. The big dude stood 6'4" easy to Kash's 5'10", 190 pounds soaking wet frame, but Kash didn't care. The big dude was lying down and started to get up, but Kash was on him with two jabs of the shank into the guy's face. The next shot hit the guy's chest, and then Kash took a step back. The big dude tried to hide his face from another blow.

"Damn, Kash, ma—"

"Pussy-ass nigga, where's that bomb at?"

He stepped back up to the big dude, who quickly sat on the bed holding his hand out.

"Here you go! Here, man."

He passed Kash a pillowcase with ounces of weed in it. Kash took it and slid out of the cell into his own. He locked the door, rinsed the shank off, and then counted six ounces of midgrade weed. He stuffed all of them into his boxer briefs, then came out of the cell and posted up on the big floor by the phone.

Kash watched as people returned from chow and waited as he noticed Pie, the nigga who's weed it was. The big dude Kash stuck was named Nut. Kash and him worked out together. Pie was from Atlanta and was considered a hard head, but Kash barred none. *Fuck these suckas,* Kash thought, because Pie ain't been fucking with the city no way.

Kash watched Pie calmly walk into Nut's cell, then quickly come back out. Pie looked around the pod until he spotted Kash. Pie walked toward the steps in a fast pace, and then down toward Kash. Kash stood there ready for whatever.

"Shawty, that's my dope you got from Nut," Pie said and stopped a few feet from Kash.

Kash was holding his banger down to his side.

"I got this in blood, nigga. Check, yo' ho's not a real nigga."

"I don't want no beef, bruh, but I ain't 'bout to let you take nothing from me, fo' real, fo' real."

"Man, fuck you, shawty."

"So, that's how we gonna rock, my nigga?" Pie asked, defeated.

"Fuckin' right, nigga. Tear it down," Kash replied and meant what he said.

After everyone got back from chow, the lieutenant and sergeant called gym call like they promised. Kash went out the door with six fresh ounces and made his way to the gym to meet up with a couple old Rydc friends who were in other pods.

He chopped it up with two partnas in the gym, ducked in a cut with his back against the wall. Kash watched Pie pull up on a couple city niggas, and they made eye contact every time. Kash was showing he was on point. He truly wasn't thinking about Pie, and he didn't care who he went to get or tell. Kash was prepared.

Gym time ended fairly quickly. Kash was the last person to enter the pod. He took in his surrounding and headed up the steps. Kash felt something wasn't right as he turned around and saw Pie coming at him with a lock on a belt. Kash got a tight grip on the railing and kicked Pie directly in the mouth. His head snapped back from the blow and his body crumbled to the ground. Before Kash could get on Pie's ass, Nut came out of cell 244 swinging a knife. Kash ducked and pushed Nut in his stomach, making him stumble back. Kash then pulled his own knife out. Officers from all over the prison rushed in as Pie started to get up. Kash swung his knife at Nut's face and caught him with it. Nut also caught Kash, but Kash didn't notice as he poked Nut at least four hard times. Nut took off running, and Kash chased him while Pie chased Kash.

***

NeNe
Three Days Later

"I'm outside, girl," her sister said over the phone.

NeNe hung up the phone, returned it to its cradle, and then grabbed her pocketbook. With the remote, she clicked the TV off and radio on, then headed out the door. She really didn't want to go out today, especially with her sister, who was creeping on Kash and doing so in his car.

Erica wanted to hook up with this guy from Bankhead Court, and NeNe just wasn't feeling her sister's actions. She didn't say anything because she didn't want to hear the million excuses why she was doing it.

NeNe made her way down the steps to Kash's Range Rover that Erica sported as if she was some down-ass bitch. Once NeNe climbed into the truck, Erica pulled off. NeNe put on her seatbelt.

"Honey boo, yo' ass takes too long," Erica said in a rush.

"Girl, I was lying down," she replied to her older sister, then put a hand on her small belly.

She listened to Erica talk while her mind was on Gangsta.

She couldn't wait until Saturday so she could see him again. That was the only time she was able to touch him, feel him, smell him, and most of all kiss him. NeNe hoped he was missing her like she was missing him.

Thirty minutes later, Erica parked by the dumpsters and texted a number on her phone.

Minutes later, NeNe spotted three guys walking toward the Range Rover. She kind of thought she recognized one of the guys, but she wasn't sure. A very, very black dude approached Erica's side of the truck and leaned in. NeNe could instantly smell the weed coming off him, and another dude approached NeNe's window while the one who looked familiar kept walking.

"Don't I know you from somewhere?" the guy asked with a heavy smell of beer on his breath.

"No, you don't."

She was about to roll up her window.

"Well, I'm PeeWee. Step out the car, ma."

He pulled at the door handle, and NeNe was glad she had it locked.

"No, I got a man."

"So? And I'ma boss," PeeWee boasted.

"Well, I don't care."

She started rolling the window up as her sister and her friend laughed. She was uncomfortable and ready to leave. She wasn't feeling this trip with Erica, and she was going to be sure to let her know.

***

Kash

The van pulled up to Macon State Prison and the big gate slid opened to let it in. It stopped to be checked by two females. Kash noticed both of the corrections officers were old and white as they checked around and under the van.

After the van was cleared, it pulled to the back of the intake building where the cert team was awaiting the new arrivals. Cert teams were elite groups of correctional officers that process inmates into any prison. They also were the ones who mainly enforced order in the prisoners.

Kash was pulled off the bus along with three more inmates.

"Who is McCants?" the sergeant of the cert team asked.

He was a big white man with a heavy voice and big chest under his black shirt, which had *cert* written across the front.

"Me, sir," Kash spoke up.

"You're going to our lockdown unit. We don't have all that stabbin' shit here," the sergeant said, then instructed everybody to go inside the intake building.

Kash had already figured he was going to lockdown because he'd been in the box at Smith three days, so he was ready to ride.

They placed Kash alone in a holding cell and locked the door. His property was outside of the cell. Kash quickly pulled five ounces out of the cuff of his nuts and stuck them under the steel bench. He stood at the door and watched the cert team strip search the other three inmates. He wondered if they would step in and search the room. He hoped not, but if they did, he knew they could not pin the weed on him.

Moments later, one of the cert team members came to the door and unlocked it.

"Step out and grab yo' property."

Kash did as the man instructed him and was elated to see the man closed the door, but didn't lock it. They did not take a long time to go through his property and to strip search him, and then they put him back into the room with his bomb and property. Kash quickly stuffed the weed in a pair of his socks that he had in his bag. Now he was more than happy to get his cell in the hole.

***

NeNe

She accepted the collect call. "Hello."

"'Sup, baby? How are you doing?" Gangsta asked.

She smiled. Her and Erica were on the highway heading back home, and she was glad to hear his voice.

"I'm making it, baby."

"How 'bout my seed. How is he or she?" he asked, and it made NeNe put her hands on her stomach.

"Everything is fine."

"I'ma see you Saturday, right?"

"Yes, if you be there. Your lawyer has you going to court in a few days. Did you not know that?"

"Nah, I didn't know that."

"Oh, yeah, that's what your mother called and told me."

"Okay," Gangsta replied.

They continued their conversation until the fifteen minutes were up, and NeNe was full of love as they hung up.

"Girl, yo' ass don't love that boy," Erica said while rolling her hazel eyes and looking at the road ahead.

"That's my baby. Anyway, just 'cause yo' ass don't got love for Kash doesn't mean I do not have love for Gary, 'cause I do."

"How do you figure I don't love Kash?"

Erica looked at her sister, and then back to the road ahead.

"Hell, you can't, 'cause you already messing around on him."

"Let me tell you something, NeNe. I do love Kash with all my heart, but he's got a life sentence. Life is life, so the boy ain't never coming home. I've got a life to live. As long as I go see him, answer his call, and shit like that, Kash will be okay."

"Well, I'm just saying, I wouldn't be messing around with nobody four months after my man goes away," NeNe replied, then added, "no matter how much time he's got."

She really meant that in her heart. No other guy mattered to her. She saw nobody else taking Gangsta's place, no matter what. She knew Erica was the type of female who jumped from man to man. She'd been doing it since NeNe could remember. Her sister only dealt with thugs and drug dealers, who somehow, someway always ended up in prison or dead. NeNe had been dealing with her sister's boyfriends for years, so it was nothing new to her. She just thought with age comes growth. She thought at twenty-nine years old, she would've grown.

***

Gangsta

Ms. Bell was doing paperwork in the front of the kitchen as Officer Green sat next to her at the table, getting his mack on. Gangsta kept going to the back, but didn't forget to throw up the deuces. He walked into the office and spoke to Ms. Smith, and then headed toward the bakery.

It'd been two weeks since Ms. Bell and he hooked up, and nobody around them knew what was up, or at least that's what he thought.

She only brought him four ounces, and she scared him when she did so because of how she panicked when she gave it to him. He'd also fucked her in the warehouse three times, and the pussy was amazing.

Gangsta was high out of his mind when he walked into the bakery. He pulled his shirt off and put on an apron. An older guy who had been locked up thirty-two years was now working with him, and he was already in his mode when Gangsta walked up.

"What's up, ol' man?" Gangsta spoke.

"What's up, young blood?"

The man looked like a young George Foreman. He had the same bald head and build. He was light-skined with thick state-issued glasses.

"Coolin'."

Gangsta began pulling pans out to warm the rolls up, and then he noticed Ms. Bell walked in holding some paperwork.

"Hey Mr. Morris. Umm, Jackson, come here a minute, please," Ms. Bell said, and Gangsta noticed something was wrong so he wasted no time walking out to her.

"What's up?" he asked as he approached.

"I'm scared."

"It's good to be scared, baby girl."

"Officer Green said he overheard the lieutenant and the sergeant talking about us."

"Fo' real?"

"Yes," she replied, walking away when the other inmates got in ear shot.

Gangsta just shook his head and went back into the bakery. He was lost in thought and wondering what was going on. He wondered how word got to the officers so fast.

When kitchen duty was over, Gangsta left without speaking to anybody. Ms. Perry signed him into the pod. He stripped down out of his clothes and took a hot shower for the next thirty minutes. He was still trying to wrap his mind around how they were exposed and who could've exposed them. All that day and well into the night Gangsta analyzed the situation and came up empty handed every time. At lockdown, Ms. Perry told him he was being transferred. He knew it was for court.

Jerry Jackson

Chapter 15

Kash
Two Weeks Later

"You need to get down and put a shirt on," the officer said.

Kash was hanging on the top rail doing pull ups and only looked at the woman. He let go and came down hard. He had sweat dripping from his body as he grabbed his shirt. He looked the woman up and down before pulling the shirt over his head. Her name was Officer Wishob, and by far she was beautiful. She was one of the best looking officers around, Kash heard through the chain gang gossip, but for some reason he didn't like her.

He's been out of the hole two weeks now, and he was already doing his thang. He liked this camp more than Smith, he just didn't like the inmates. Kash walked away from the officer and into his cell. He saw a letter on his bed from Erica. She still tried to hold him down, but the love was fake, and he saw it clearly. Most of the time when he did call her collect, he would only speak to NeNe. She kept him informed about Gangsta, who was back at Rice Street awaiting trial.

Kash's cellie was a scary white man that hardly ever came into the cell, and when he knew Kash wanted space, he stayed gone. Kash laughed to himself as he opened the fake ass letter Erica had written. Minutes later, after he read and flushed the lies on the paper, his cell door swung open and his slick partna strolled in eating a honey bun wrapped around two beef and cheese sticks.

"Fi' up, shawty."

"Roll it. It's on the table, bruh," Kash replied.

Kash's partna was tall, lanky, and slim. He was black as the night skies with a mouthful of gold teeth. His name was Blue. Blue also had a life sentence plus forty. He was from Summer Hill and had been in prison sixteen years. He worked up front in the visitation area and was one of most trusted inmates around the camp, being that he'd been in Macon ten years.

They smoked three joints of mid and made a bombay. Kash put his cup inside his locker and jumped in the shower, high out of his mind.

***

Veedo

His right-hand man and he pulled into the parking lot of Burger King on Northside Drive. Veedo parked and got out, followed by his partna, Rock. They strolled into the restaurant and noticed the two girls at a table waiting on them, so they made their way over.

"What's up?"

Veedo slid into the booth, and Rock did also. The girls both were young, but old enough to handle business.

"Hey," they both spoke in whispers.

"What happened today?" Veedo asked.

"We didn't show up," one of the girls said.

"Okay cool. 'Preciate it." Veedo reached inside his pocket and pulled out two knots of cash. "Here's ten racks each."

Gangsta had Veedo paid the two witnesses on his case not to show up to court because they were the only ones who could nail him. Veedo did not hesitate to leave Albany and help out his partna. Both girls pocketed the money.

"Now listen, we've got to be real about the whole situation, so do as the two of you agreed to do and stay ghost. If y'all need help, I can take y'all down south for a few weeks until trial is over."

Both girls looked to one another, and then back at Veedo and Rock before they agreed to go down south.

"First, how old are y'all?" Rock asked, speaking for the first time.

"I'm 18 and she 19. Why?"

"Shit, we just checking," Veedo shot back and stood up to leave.

He was followed by the two new girls, whom he had plans to put to work once they hit Albany.

***

Gangsta

"How do you feel?" his lawyer asked as he embraced Gangsta with a firm hug.

"I feel good. Now, I need you to get my parole officer to release me," Gangsta replied and waved to his mother and Terry as they left the courtroom.

The jury didn't convict him, and he was finally a free man.

"I will do it first thing tomorrow, son," the lawyer informed him.

"Okay, bet that," Gangsta said with joy in his every word.

The officers led him out of the courtroom. NeNe came to his mind, and he knew she would be overly happy. Now she could stop stressing over him getting a life sentence. His only issue now was telling both NeNe and Terry about each other. He knew it had to be done because his kids would know each other. Plus, the children's ages wouldn't be that far apart. Terry was seven months pregnant and NeNe was four or five months pregnant. Somebody was going to get their feelings hurt and both were sure to get mad at him, but he made his bed, so now he had to lie in it. Gangsta was put in the holding cell with a few more inmates who were eager to know his fate.

"What happened, homie?" one dude asked once the cell door closed.

He was one of the few inmates who Gangsta chopped it up with.

"Not guilty, fool."

"Now, that's what's up."

Everybody inside the small cell clapped their hands and showed him some love.

It wasn't long before Gangsta was shipped back to Calhoun with the bad news that his probation officer was keeping him in prison. He wanted eighteen months, and then he would clear him from probation. Gangsta rolled with it, being that he was already four months in.

He got another surprise when he got to intake and was locked down on pending investigation

"What da fuck," Gangsta said when the cert team told him to place his hand behind his back.

"Per the warden, you're on P.I.," one cool cert team member said.

"For what?"

"I don't even know, big guy. I'm just doing my job."

Gangsta couldn't believe this, but he kind of knew what it was about. It could only be one thing, so he went ahead and cuffed up, because the last thing he wanted to do was catch another charge.

He was placed in J1 until the warden came to see him. Gangsta wasn't feeling confinement, but dealt with it. He placed all his property into his locker box and made up the bunk before dropping down to his knees in a prayer of thankfulness.

***

Three Weeks Later

"New arrivals report to the counselor's area," the pod officer yelled as Gangsta was in his cell playing tunk for food with his cellie. It was his second day at Macon State Prison. He was transferred because of his relationship with Ms. Bell. The prison couldn't catch them, so they just shipped him 'cause they didn't have probable cause to fire Ms. Bell.

He paused his game and got up.

"I'll be back, pimp," he said and grabbed his state-issued shirt. Gangsta made his way to the control booth where a short, fat white woman waited for him and five more inmates to report out. He could tell she was police by her demeanor, so he humbly passed her his ID and got signed out.

Gangsta knew a couple of dudes from his first bid, so he was stopped a few times in passing, but he kept it light. He truly did not care to kick it, because his brother was on the other side of the prison and he needed to get at him. He needed to see his folks. They needed to vent, and they needed to catch up on old times.

The counselor's area was up front between the east side and west side of the prison. When all six inmates walked into the room, it was cool and clean. Everywhere Gangsta looked he saw bad bitches of all sizes and shapes. They ranged from the mailroom lady to the mental health doctor to the GP counselors. There were three standing in a group by a table assigned for the inmates. Gangsta noticed a tall black dude placing paperwork in each chair that surrounded the table. He was fresh in bright white stripes and shined black boots.

"You men can have a seat," one of the three counselors said to the group of new guys.

Gangsta took the end chair. He picked up the paperwork and sat down. One of the females started passing out pens and told the guys to start filling out the paperwork as they began their meeting.

Gangsta looked at one of the dude until they made eye contact. He nodded him over. The tall dude put the paperwork down and strolled over.

"What's up?"

"Bruh, what pod you in?" Gangsta asked.

"G2, why?"

"I'm looking for a nigga named Kash. He's from da city."

"That's my lil' partna. You talkin' 'bout shawty from Simpson," the dude boasted.

"Yeah, that's my brother. Tell shawty Gangsta down here."

"What pod you in?"

"J2."

"I can get you moved to G2, bruh. What's happenin'?" the tall dude asked.

"Shit, bet that, bruh."

"Ok, bruh, when you get back, go pack yo' shit," the dude said, and then walked off.

***

Kash

His entire workout crew was on the big yard getting it in with dirt bags, pull-ups, and pushups. Blue walked through the gate and up to the fence. He called Kash's name and he looked up. Kash figured Blue had made a move and had come up on something. He was always up to something. Most of the time it was some no-good shit, and that was one reason Kash fucked with him. Kash strolled up to the fence with sweat pouring down his body.

"What's up, fool?"

"Yo' brother down here," Blue said.

"My brother?"

Kash was instantly confused.

"Yeah, lieutenant going to get shawty now to move him over here. Nigga's name is Gangsta."

"Oh, yeah," Kash replied and was clearly excited. "Where he at?"

"Oh, he on his way, bruh. I made that move," Blue said with a smile.

"Bet, boy, it's finna go down major now. Let me finish this workout."

Kash returned to the sandbag with his crew. It was his turn on the bag. He grabbed the net bag that held a black trash bag of dirt and started to lift. His muscles swelled up every time he brought the heavy bag up to his chin. Right after he dropped the bag, he dropped down to do fifty pushups. When Kash got up from the ground, he saw Gangsta coming through the gate with the lieutenant pushing a yellow cart with his property and mat inside. It'd been a while since Kash saw his partna, and it felt good to finally lay eyes on somebody he knew was solid. Leaving his crew behind, Kash walked over to the fence with a smile on his face. Gangsta finally saw him and smiled.

"What's up, nigga?" Gangsta asked.

"Welcome to the state, baby," Kash replied, and they touched fingers through the fence.

The fence between them was the only thing stopping a much-needed hug. Kash and Gangsta walked side by side.

"This camp straight, bruh?"

"Yeah, it's okay. It's gonna be better now that I got my nigga wit' me," Kash replied.

"You got a cellie?"

"Yeah, but we'll switch him out. Go ahead and get situated, shawty. I'ma be in after yard call."

Chapter 16

Terry
Ten Months Later

Nikki was standing in the yard on Johnson Road, holding a blunt high in the sky while she danced to Eric's car system. Every now and then she would bring the blunt to her lips for a pull and inhale, and then she would turn up the wine cooler she held in her other hand.

Terry just looked at her best friend while sitting on the porch with Roxanne as a dice game was being played by the streetfull of guys.

It was Gangsta's cousin Eric's party, and everybody was out to show their love, especially his family. The kids ran around playing, the females did the cooking, and the men gambled and got high. Even the crackheads were welcome to the party today.

This was Terry's first time really hanging out since she had her daughter, Keshana. She went shopping at times, but most times she would go from gangsta's mother's house to her own mother's house. She never went out to enjoy herself because being a brand new mother proved to be much harder than she thought it would be.

"I know y'all hos ain't gonna just sit there and watch me dance, right?" Nikkie asked.

She hit her blunt and walked toward her friends seated on the porch.

"Sit yo' drunk ass down," Terry said with a smile.

"Shut up."

"Let me hit that," Terry said and reached for the blunt.

Nikki looked her friend over and then finally passed the blunt. Terry hit it twice and instantly choked while pushing it back to Nikki.

"You should've never took a break. Kids be smarter when you smoke while you're pregnant."

"Bitch, hush," Terry shouted while still choking.

The food smelled great. She couldn't wait to dig in. *Aunt Becky needs to speed up*, Terry thought while watching the kids play in the street. Every time a car would ride down the street, the kids would clear out, and when they rode past the kids would get right back to it. Terry couldn't help but wonder if her daughter would be just like the little girls she saw now who were too grown.

Terry shook her head for her own answer and said, "Hell no."

"What?" Roxanne asked, breaking her train of thought.

"Oh, nothing, I was just thinking out loud."

She refused to let her daughter get caught up by the streets. She refused to let Keshana grow up as she did. Terry focused on the loud music coming from a drop-top car riding down Johnson Road. All the kids cleared out of the way as it came through. The car pulled into the yard and she noticed Zay driving with three more guys.

It had been almost a year since the last time they saw each other, and boy was he looking good. He was decked out in gray Gucci from the sandals to the hat to his belt and buckle. Word on the streets was he had a New York connection named Bam who supplied him in Atlanta.

Everybody who was with Zay went to the dice game, but not him. Zay hung up the phone he was on, put it in his pocket, and walked toward the girls on the porch. A lump formed in Terry's throat and made it hard to swallow. *He looks better than ever before*, she thought to herself.

"What's up, y'all?" he asked all three of them.

"Let me hold somethin', rich-ass Zay," Nikki said while rolling another blunt.

He smiled. He looked down and back up, but this time he found Terry eyes.

"'Sup wit'cha?" he asked.

"Hey, Zarack."

She called his full name. She was hoping he didn't notice how nervous she was looking. She wanted to hug him.

"Come here right quick."

Terry stood up wearing some brown Prada capri pants with the shirt to match and some sandals that showed off her cute feet. Her jet-black hair was pulled back into a ponytail. The baby had given her a few extra pounds all in the correct places. She walked down the few steps into the yard toward the car Zay posted up on.

"How is the baby?" Zay asked once they stepped off.

"She's good." Terry nervously looked everywhere but at him.

She was scared because she did miss him and the times they shared together. She was confused because maybe she missed gangsta instead. Terry loved gangsta, but he wasn't there. He was never really there, and Zay always had been around. He had never left the streets, and at the same time had plenty of money.

"How you doing, though?" he asked as he reached out and took her hand. "I mean, you looking all good and shit."

"I'm good."

"Do you miss me? I miss da fuck out of you."

"No, you don't," Terry said, weakening.

"I promise I do."

"Yeah, right."

"Let's take a quick ride."

"To where?"

Now Terry pulled her hand away from him, and her heart was beating heavy in her chest.

"Let's go to Low Low's right quick," Zay replied.

"The store?"

"Yes. We'll go there and back."

Zay opened the door and Terry slid in and across the leather seat. Nikki quickly made her way over to her friend with a smile on her face.

"Bitch, you 'bout to give Zay some of that pussy!" Nikki said, drunk.

"Shut up, ho. Ain't nobody 'bout to do no shit like dat."

Zay climbed in and cranked up. Nikki tossed a rubber into the car. It fell in Zay's lap.

"No more babies," she said and walked off, laughing.

Zay pulled off and looked at Terry.

"What was that all about?"

"That bitch is just drunk," Terry replied.

She was too mad at Nikki for being so stupid. She sat back as the drop-top sped down Johnson Road and made a quick right, but not toward the store.

"Zarack, where are you going?"

"Ma's house. You know she miss you a lot, and then we going to Low Low's," Zay replied and mashed the gas a little harder.

His mother stayed on Gun Club in a small white and yellow brick house. Zay's mother always treated Terry like her own, and that alone made Terry regret not even giving her a phone call out of respect.

When Zay pulled up, Terry noticed his mother's car wasn't parked in the driveway. She started to protest, but didn't. They both got out and strolled to the door. Terry prayed that Zay's mother was there, but she had a gut feeling she wasn't.

Zay used his key to enter the crib. The beautiful living room was still the same as she remembered. She heard the door lock and instantly regretting that she ever rode with Zay. She saw in his eyes what he truly wanted. She wanted the same thing, but with Gangsta, not Zay. Terry knew if they were alone she wouldn't be strong enough to beat the urge. She loved Gangsta, but she lusted for Zay.

Terry felt him grab her waist, and he slowly turned her to face him. She loved his eyes and always had. His lips found her lips. His tongue invaded her mouth, and then she pulled back.

"No, Zarack. Uhn-uh."

"Baby, I miss you." He kissed her neck and then sucked it. He knew it was her spot. "You always been my boo."

"But, Gangsta," she moaned as he unbuttoned her pants.

"He ain't gotta know, boo."

Zay pulled her shirt over her head. Her stomach was still flat with not a mark on it. You couldn't tell she recently had a child. Her breasts were still firm, but just a little bigger as he took a nipple into his mouth.

"What if yo' mom comes home?"

Her hand held his head as he loved her breast. She missed this feeling.

"She's out of town, baby, so we good."

Zay led her to the sofa and laid her down. He pulled her pants off, and then her panties. He stepped back and pulled his own clothes off. Terry knew she was doing the wrong thing. She knew it was wrong, but it felt so good when Zay entered her wet walls.

***

Gangsta

Eight months to go was his thought daily. Eight months and he would be a free man to do as he pleased and not be told to do this or that. Not be told when to get up, when to go to sleep, or what to wear. He wouldn't have to follow any more rules or listen to any more orders. All he had were laws to abide by, and he was certain he was gonna break them.

Gangsta truly didn't have a plan. He had a stash and a few good friends, but no direction. He knew every step made by him had to be smooth and light because he escaped the grips of the courtroom. Now he was a father of two, and neither of his babies' mothers knew of the other. Both were oblivious of their children having a sister or a brother. Gangsta knew the truth had to be out in the open. His son was one month and his daughter was four. Gangsta was about to have some mad babies' mothers, no matter how he put it.

It was near chow call, and it was hamburger and hot dog day. Gangsta and Kash weren't going because they were expecting a drop to be made. Blue had convinced Ms. Wishob to mule for him, though he had no money, so Gangsta and Kash funded the entire play.

For the past ten months, the three of them linked up, made moves, and took losses. They won some, and every chance they got they tried to get at every female officer or male officer who was about the business. The trio hardly had issues, though, and Kash did most of the fighting.

Kash strolled into the cell. Gangsta and him had been cellies for the past seven months. He had just finished working out.

"What's happenin', fool?"

"Man, shit, bruh. I'm 'bout to whip one," Gangsta said, referring to the bombay.

"The ho just left outta shawty's room," Kash confirmed with a slick smile.

"Ok, cool."

"I'm finna hit dis shower." Kash kicked off his shoes. "Blue should be pulling up in the next minute or two."

Gangsta stood from the bunk and went into his locker to get the bombay material while Kash got ready for the shower. Moments later,

Blue entered the cell with a net bag and a huge smile on his face. He pulled the door closed and locked all three of them inside, and then he passed the net bag over. Gangsta sat the bombay cup down and put up a flap over the window of the cell door for added privacy.

Kash poured the contents out of the net bag. It held six phones and a half-pound of Kush that Veedo sent along with two hundred pills.

"Where's the scale?" Kash asked Gangsta.

"Gotta wait until the man gets back from chow. You know all dat shit put up," Gangsta replied while picking up one of the phones and turning on its power.

Blue grabbed the bombay cup to start whipin'. He was proud of himself for making the play happen as he promised his partnas he would.

Kash went ahead and got his shower out of the way while Blue and Gangsta began sacking up the pills and bomb. It was a Wednesday, so Gangsta hoped by the next Wednesday they would be done and ready for another bomb. The camp was dry, so it shouldn't be a problem rolling fast. The plan was that all three of the guys would keep a phone and sell the other three to pay the mule. The phones were free through Kash's connection. The guys could split all the profit from the pills and loud after paying Veedo's wholesale price.

"Go ahead and finish this, and I'm finna activate this phone," Gangsta said and stopped with the pills to pick up the phone.

"Go ahead," Blue agreed and kept his eyes focused on the task at hand.

Gangsta's mind was on breaking this heartbreaking news to Terry and NeNe. He wouldn't and couldn't continue to hide it. After about fifteen minutes, he had the phone activated. Kash was out of the shower by then and had the scale with him when he entered the cell.

Gangsta dialed Terry's number.

"Hello?" Her voice was tired and she sounded like she was sleepy.

"What's up, baby girl. Where's my seed at?"

"Sleep."

"Oh, yeah." Gangsta walked to the cell door and peeked out to see what was up in the pod, and then he closed the door. "What's up wit' you?"

160

"Tired. I gotta try to rest with her 'cause she is a handful," Terry replied.

"Well, you go ahead and get some rest. Dis my number. Just hit me when you get up, 'cause I need to talk to you."

"How did you get a phone in jail?"

"Money," Gangsta chuckled.

"Are they allowed?" Terry questioned.

"Hell no."

"So talk to me now. What you need to talk to me about?"

"I'ma call you. You just rest and hit me when you get up with Keshana," Gangsta replied.

He didn't feel comfortable about exposing his issue in front of his partnas even though they both knew the deal. Gangsta wanted to be one-on-one when he laid this news on Terry.

"Okay, well, I'll call you in 'bout an hour," Terry agreed.

"Okay, bet."

It took the three guys another hour to sack up three ounces in 25s and a couple seven gram sacks that they would sell for $175 apiece. Blue was also the put-up man, so he got all the drugs except an ounce that they would smoke on until the next drop.

With Blue gone, Gangsta decided to call NeNe. His plan wasn't to tell her that their one-month-old son had a four-month-old sister over the phone. He wanted to do it face-to-face because he was in love with her and respected her.

"Hello," she answered.

"I love you, girl. What's up?"

It was always good to hear her beautiful voice, and it showed in his tone.

"Hey, Gary. I'm feeding your son."

"This my phone, baby, so lock me in," Gary boasted.

"How'd you get a phone, boy?"

"Money."

"Baby, you 'bout to come home. Can't you get into trouble if you get caught with that thang?" NeNe wanted to know.

"Yeah, you can get sent to the hole, but that ain't nothing. I'm not getting caught, though," Gangsta assured the love of his life.

The entire time he'd been in prison he has found no flaw in her faithfulness. Her respect was genuine, whole, and full. Her intent was honest and he appreciated her and was grateful he met her when he did.

"Well, be safe, Gary."

NeNe was perfect in his eyes. Her actions to him were amazing, and he truly adored the girl for her worth as a woman. They talked a while longer until the officer came into the pod and holla'd it was count time. Gangsta ended the call with *I love you* and NeNe hung up with promises to see him that weekend.

***

Terry

Gary still hasn't returned my call, Terry thought as she fed Keshana her dinner. It was 8:00 p.m., and the last time she spoke to Gangsta the clock read 5:50 p.m. She wondered what he had to talk about, and she was hoping he didn't hear about her and Zay already. Her heart rate sped up a little when her phone finally vibrated.

"Hello," she answered.

"Can I take you out tonight?"

It was Zay. Terry closed her eyes and silently shook her head from side to side. Already she felt bad for having sex with him, and now he was calling her.

"I told you that I couldn't mess wit' you, Zay."

"So, you sayin' you don't love me?"

"I'm not saying that. I'm just sayin' that Gary is my man and he'll be home soon. I don't wanna start nothing with you, and then he pop up on—"

"Listen, listen," Zay said, cutting her off. "You left me for this nigga when I was there for you. I bossed you up and you still left me point blank at the drop of a dime for Gangsta. That was a slap in the face and hurtful, shawty," Zay pleaded his case.

"Zay, I—" she started to say, but he cut her off again.

"Please let me take you out, Terry. Let's talk over dinner."

"I don't have a babysitter," Terry gave her excuse, and she was hoping it would work.

The day she fucked Zay was a day she regretted with every heartbeat. After sex with him, she felt so nasty and low. She truly felt like a slut. Yes, there'd been many times Terry had been horny, but she could've waited.

"I'ma come to yo' crib, then. I'll bring dinner."

"No."

"Well, come to my house in Cobb County," Zay offered.

Terry closed her eyes again. *Why me?* she thought. Yes, it was evident she was lonely and eight more months was a long time, but not that long, right?

"I don't know, Zarack. If Gary finds—"

"He won't, baby. It's just dinner. Bring your daughter. I don't want sex."

"Oh, my God." Terry finally opened her eyes. "Where, Zay? Just dinner, then I'm going to leave."

Jerry Jackson

Chapter 17

Gangsta
Three Days Later

When he walked into the visitation area, he saw NeNe standing at the microwave. She wore some Apple Bottom jeans that stopped at her ankles, a pair of Air Max, and a small coat. She didn't notice Gangsta creeping up behind her.

"'Sup, baby doll?"

He pulled her by the waist toward him. NeNe turned around, smiling from ear to ear in his arms. They hugged.

"Hey, baby. How you doing?" she asked, and then pulled her head from his shoulder to look him in the eyes.

They shared a kiss. A long and much-needed kiss.

"Where's my son?" Gangsta was finally able to ask while she led him to their seats without reply to his question because he saw Erica in the next row holding his Junior. NeNe gave Gangsta the food. She walked over to her sister and took the baby from her.

"What's up, Gangsta?" Erica asked with a smile.

She was still as beautiful as ever.

"What's going on?"

Gangsta placed the food on their table, and NeNe wasted no time passing his son over. Inmates weren't allowed to hold children during visits, but Gangsta was willing to break that rule.

"How is he?"

"He's sweet. He's a sweet baby," NeNe spoke, happy to be around him, and it showed on her face.

"Do you spoil him?" Gangsta asked, not once taking his eyes off his son.

"A little."

She blushed and then opened a soda. Kash walked up minutes later. He tapped Gangsta's shoulder.

"'Sup, boy?" Kash asked.

"'Sup, fool?" Gangsta spoke in return.

They gave each other a pound, and then Kash hugged NeNe before walking to the next table where Erica was seated. Gangsta returned his attention to his son. Every now and then he'd look up to NeNe, who just sat and watched them.

The baby had put weight on her, but just a bit. It only made him wanna reach across the table. She still had those beautiful hazel eyes and that pretty face. He just missed the heck out of her. He missed everything about this woman.

"Gary, what are your plans when you come home?" NeNe asked.

It was something they never really talked about.

"I don't know," he replied while NeNe was about to take a bite of her hot wing.

She stopped and fixed him with a mean look before saying, "It's not about you anymore, Gary. You have a son to raise."

"And I am going to raise him."

"Well, get a job," NeNe put in.

"Ha ha."

"Ha, nothing. For real, baby. We both can work and come together on this."

Gangsta passed his son over to her after she put the wings down and used a baby wipe to clean her hand. The lieutenant had just entered the visiting room, so it was time to start following rules.

"Alright, I guess," Gangsta then said.

"Promise me," NeNe shot back.

Right then and there guilt hit him hard, because he needed to tell her about Keshana, but he did not want to lose his girl. She meant too much to him, but it had to be done one way or the other. He leaned over and took her free hand.

"I promise." He paused. "I promise, but listen, baby doll, 'cause I need to—" He again paused.

This is about to hurt, Gangsta thought to himself.

"What, baby?" NeNe cut in.

"This girl — no, look, NeNe, before I say anything I want you to know that I love you and I wanna spend the rest of my life with you."

"What's up, Gary?" NeNe's voice grew a bit louder and her smile vanished.

Concern was now painted across her face. It made him more nervous just looking at her.

"What girl?"

"My ex-girlfriend. This was before me and you were together. Actually, it was before we ever met. Me and her, we got.... We had sex, and she...."

"She what?" NeNe demanded.

She was confused because he wasn't making any sense.

"She had a daughter."

"She had a daughter?" NeNe repeated.

"We have a daughter."

He reached for her hand, but his sudden outburst made her pull away. She was looking at him like she did the first time they met. Gangsta saw hate flash across her face.

"A daughter? As in you're the father?"

"Yes." Gangsta felt defeated when he spoke.

"Oh, my God."

Tears formed in NeNe eyes. Gangsta reached out to her once more, but failed.

"NeNe."

"Don't touch me," NeNe yelled as she stood to her feet, holding Junior, and began to walk away.

Gangsta also stood up. He looked over to Kash and shook his head, then went after his woman.

"NeNe, wait," he said, but his pleas fell on deaf ears. He kind of jogged to catch up, and he took her arm from behind into his hand. "NeNe, baby, listen."

She turned around.

"No, you listen. How old is this daughter of yours?"

Tears fell rapidly from NeNe's beautiful eyes.

"She's almost 11 months," he replied.

"Four months older than our son. So she was pregnant as I was and you had plenty of time to tell me."

She slapped him in his face with the same arm he grabbed, and then she walked off.

After the visit, Gangsta made it back to the pod and pulled out his phone so he could make a phone call. He did not blame NeNe for her actions after he told her the truth. Hell, he expected worse. Gangsta knew he couldn't let her leave him, though. He refused to, so he quickly dialed NeNe's phone number.

"What," she said when she picked up.

"NeNe, baby, we need to talk."

"I do not wanna talk to you right now. I hate you," NeNe replied.

"I respect that, but can we talk wh—"

"Fuck, no," she yelled, cutting him off.

"When can I call then, baby? Damn, I'm try'na explain myself," Gangsta said, not knowing what else to say.

"Don't call me, Gary. I'm fo' real. I'll write you or somethin'."

With that being said, she hung up on him.

***

NeNe

NeNe, I'm hopin' with more hope than possible that this introduction finds and embraces you safe as you deserve to be. I call this an intro for reasons that I'm not the same person anymore. Not without you in my life. NeNe, nothing matters to me if I can't share life with you. You're not picking up the phone. I can't get a letter, and my whole world is crashed around my feet into tiny pieces. I love you. I love my son. I need the both of you in my life.

NeNe, I know the news of a daughter hurt you. Yet understand, it hurts me to be in this position. I never knew of my daughter until a week before I told you. I would've never held something so important like this from you. You just never gave me the chance to explain what had happened.

Baby doll, I pray you find it in yo' heart to see that my mistake happened before me and you ever met, yet it has messed the life we now share together up. NeNe, allow me to still be him. Allow me to share your life and our baby. Don't walk away, because I'm still hoping!

Always your husband,

The Streets Bleed Murder

Gangsta

NeNe read the text message, threw the phone on the bed, and then looked down at her son, who was asleep. This was at least her seventh time reading his text message since she received it three days ago.

Still hurt by the fact that her son's father had another child, NeNe couldn't bring herself to forgive him. Something wasn't right, and her heart felt it. Nothing ever lasted when she was in a relationship. It never failed that there was always something. All NeNe wanted to do was raise her son and finish school. She hated that she ever even met Gangsta because of the shit he just pulled.

Getting up from the bed, NeNe glanced down at the phone one more time, then looked to their son. *It's not gonna be the same,* she thought to herself.

For the past two days, Gangsta's mother had been calling in to check on Junior and plead her son's case, but NeNe wasn't having it. Her gut feeling said it was some sneaky shit going on. She just couldn't read between the lines. Her plan was to go see Gangsta face-to-face to tell him she would no longer deal with him. Yes, she indeed was in love with him, but he proved to be just like the rest, so just like the rest, she would get over him.

***

Veedo

"Shawty, what da fuck's going on?"

Veedo picked the phone up when he noticed Gangsta's number popped up.

"I got that check fo' ya."

"Okay, cool. Y'all niggas good down there?" Veedo asked.

He was posted up in his truck outside of the hair salon waiting on Kia and Amanda to finish up their hair and nail appointments.

"Man, we here, bruh," Gangsta shot back.

The game had been lovely to Veedo down in the country part of Georgia. He was doing more numbers than he expected and needed to expand a little more, so he and Rock got another spot. This time it was in Macon, and they planned to let the girls serve in that area with a few shooters around.

Veedo was almost out of pills, and they were one of his number one drugs. It was a good thing he had linked up with Bam, who was a New Yorker with many different connections on all types of shit.

"When da hell you bounce, bruh?"

"A few mo' months. 'Bout eight," Gangsta replied.

"Fo' sho'. These streets are sweet for the team. You know I got you when you bounce, bruh. We good out here," Veedo assured him.

"Say no mo'," Gangsta shot back.

He told Veedo he would send the money he owed him through Western Union, and then they hung up.

Veedo sat back into the leather seat of his new Porsche truck feeling like the man of the year. He was paid and loving it. He had no plans to fall off because he rocked different from most niggas. He had different visions and morals but the same goals every street nigga had, and that was to get money.

While sitting inside the truck, Veedo saw Amanda come out of the salon first with her hair braided and looking nice. She was the bad one out of the two of them and always tried to throw herself at Veedo, though he never crossed that line. The time they'd been linked with each other, Veedo kept it business at all times with both girls.

Not that she wasn't worth a fuck. She was 5'7", 152 pounds thick, and redboned just like he liked 'em. It was only money on his mind, and that's what mattered most to him. Kia came out next with her hair wrapped up in a bob, and she climbed into the truck.

"Hey, V," she said.

"What's up, pretty?" Veedo replied while cranking up.

He liked Kia's hustle and the fact she never tried to throw the pussy on him. She was all about her dollar bills. There were no ifs, ands, or buts about it. Kia was a slim female with a nice-sized booty that niggas gawked at every time she passed. She was more humble than Amanda, but was outspoken. Veedo was elated that he chose to bring both girls with him to the country. Dudes went crazy for the duo when they would step out to clubs, and this alone gave Veedo more and more customers to pump his pills and loud to, because most niggas thought with their dicks and bankrolls.

"Y'all hungry?" he asked while pulling the Porsche into traffic.

"Honey, yes," Amanda spoke up, and Kia agreed, so Veedo stopped at a soul food joint right outside of Macon County where they stuffed their faces with some good, hot food.

Veedo dropped both of the girls off at his crib before meeting up with Rock at the new spot. There were still some loose ends they had to get tightened.

"I'ma scoop y'all 'bout 10:30, so be ready." That was the last thing he told Kia and Amanda when letting them out at his crib.

"We will," Kia responded, and then Veedo pulled off.

***

Gangsta

"'Sup, Mama?"

Gangsta gave his mother a hug and kiss on the jaw, then took Keshana from Terry and pulled her to her feet so he could hug her with his free arm.

"'Sup, boo?" he asked and they kissed.

"Hey, baby," Terry replied while watching Gangsta plant kisses all over his daughter's face.

He was play-biting her tiny fingers every time she put her hand in his face. Gangsta took a seat, passed Keshana to her grandmother, and then turned his attention to Terry. Today something didn't feel right with her when they embraced and kissed. *Maybe it's just me*, Gangsta told himself while looking into her gray eyes.

Just last week he broke down and told NeNe about Keshana. Now it was time to explain to Terry about Junior, because he never got around to doing so the last. He decided it was best to do it face-to-face as well, since she visited him every Sunday with his mother. Gangsta noticed bags under her eyes and a depressed look upon her face.

"I been calling yo' butt, so where have you been?" he finally asked her.

"I've been home, but mostly over Nikki's house," Terry said.

Gangsta knew her like the back of his hand. She was his first girl and his first love, so it was easy for him to smell a lie from her a mile away. Gangsta just nodded and turned his attention to his mother, who was watching him and waiting for him to break the news to Terry. Gangsta caught the hint.

"Ma, go buy me something to eat. Warm it up, and then change Keshana," Gangsta said, because he needed a little time.

"Do you want anything, Terry?" his mother asked as she stood up.

Terry was holding her hands together and looking down while lost in thought.

She quickly looked up and smiled before saying, "Yes, a soda will be fine."

"Okay."

Gangsta's mother walked away holding Keshana in her arms.

"Where you been?" Gangsta asked once his mother left.

"I told you."

Terry looked to him, then broke their eye contact.

"I've got a son, Terry."

He found himself leaning back in the chair and resting his hands on his thighs. Terry's eyes fixed on him for a second, and she said nothing. She just stared Gangsta directly in the eyes.

"A son?"

"Yeah," Gangsta replied with a shake of his head.

"I'm just trying to figure out why you haven't told me this?"

"Because I didn't believe her. I had to get a DNA test first," he lied real quick.

"And he's yours? Our daughter has a brother? How old is he?" Terry fired her questions at him.

Gangsta could tell she was pissed. Her light gray eyes somehow became a shade darker.

"He's 7 months old," he dryly replied.

"What?"

Terry stood up and moved the table that was between them. Gangsta stood up as well, because he knew she was stupid, so the first thing he did was grab both arms. Terry tried to knee him in the nuts, but he quickly moved back.

"So yo' ass been cheating, mutha'fucka."

"Hold up, boo. Listen and just hold up. Sit down and I will—"

"No, now move," she shouted, and by then the officer walked over to see what was going on.

Gangsta assured the man that everything was okay. He slid the chair back in place under the table. Terry took her seat, and he did the same.

"Look, Terry, I was drunk. The shit happened in the club, and I don't even remember the girl, I swear," he lied again.

"Gary, you got a fucking son. A son."

"I'm sorry, baby, real talk."

"I know yo' ass is."

Terry was bouncing her knee while tears fell from her face. She had her fists balled. Gangsta reached for her hands humbly with beggin' eyes, and this time she didn't pull away.

"Forgive me, baby, please."

"Gary, you got another fuckin' kid," Terry stated in a daze, not really looking at him. "A son."

"Damn, boo, you making this shit hard."

Gangsta dropped his head in defeat. He was kind of ready to give up, though at the same time he felt a lot better now that it was in the open. He loved Terry without a doubt, but he was in love with NeNe.

He wanted the best of both worlds, but knew that it was impossible. Gangsta disliked the hurt he witnessed on Terry's face, but his mother was right when she told him to get it over with so his kids could know each other.

"Bye, Gary."

Terry pulled her hands free from his grip. She stood up and walked away. Gangsta just sat there and watched her go. He wouldn't chase anymore. The reality is he had two kids, two baby mothers, and both of them were mad.

***

Veedo

Just leaving the stash house with Rock in tow, both guys climbed into the truck. Rock pulled the Glock he carried from his back pocket and slid it under the seat before he climbed completely in.

Veedo always rode with his Beretta on his lap and ready at all time to splack the haters. Shit was good with the money count, and almost all the pills were gone, so he needed to make a move fast.

Bam fronted him the loud in as many pounds as he wanted, but Bam's pills were whack. They were nothing like Pat Man's pills, that was bangin'. Veedo had been contemplating if he should step to Pat Man. If he did, then Gangsta should know, but Gangsta had never told him about Pat Man or the bitch, and it wasn't his place to assume anything. *I gotta holla at Gangsta,* was all Veedo thought while pushing the Porsche through Albany's streets.

Rock was busy rolling a blunt from the new batch of loud that came in from Bam. Rock was the gunner of the two guys. His temper was automatic, and almost every time he got into it with someone, it ended in violence.

"Bruh, what you think about splittin' Kia and Amanda up? Keep one in Macon and one here, that way dem lil' hos don't ever try to get slick with the team," Rock said as he lit up the blunt.

"You think them hos will try us?" Veedo asked.

He wanted to know his partna's take on it, because the girls had been with them ten months and showed no signs that they'd cross them.

At the time, the two of them were being paid good money not to snitch for free.

"Fuckin' right. 'Cause them hos know the ins and outs. They know how to get around certain shit."

"Yeah, you might be right."

Veedo pulled up to LisaPay's house and saw her seated on the porch smoking a Newport with a King Kobra beer can in one hand. That was one of those two-for-a-dollar beers. He parked, but neither of them moved from the comfort of the leather seats so they could finish the blunt.

"I bet any amount of money that LisaPay is high as a bird," Veedo said with a laugh.

"Hell, I would, too."

They exited the car and walked into the yard.

LisaPay wasn't looking at either one of them when she said, "Somebody came by looking for you."

Veedo took a seat in his favorite spot on the porch, which was the second step, and Rock stood.

"Who was it?" Veedo asked.

"Who? You mean how many?" LisaPay said as she finally fixed her eyes on Veedo.

He could indeed tell she was high.

"Okay, then how many?" Veedo wanted to know.

"Four carloads." LisaPay turned up her beer can, swallowed hard, and then hit her Newport. "He said to tell you to get at him. It was some red-haired guy with gold teeth, and he left this."

She gave Veedo a card. He took it and read the name on the card. It was Pat Man's name and his phone number.

Veedo took the number, put it in his pocket, then asked, "How long has he been gone, Lisa?"

LisaPay still didn't look at him when she spoke. She took a long drink from the beer can.

"No more than 20 minutes."

Veedo gave a look to Rock and pulled out his phone. Reading from the paper, he called the given number. The phone rang a couple times, then a deep voice picked up.

"What's up?"

"Pat Man, what da move is, homie? Dis Veedo."

There was a moment of silence that seemed forever before Pat Man spoke. Veedo wasn't sure what to think.

"Ok, you must just pulled up, 'cause I just pulled off. I need to meet the man himself who got the county on lock down with my product." Pat Man paused, then continued. "With product my wife lost her life for. So tell me, where can we meet, my nigga?"

Veedo was taken aback, but he refused to show any fear. At the same time, he was confused to who could have told Pat Man he was pumping his shit.

"We can meet now, my nigga. Pull back up," Veedo said, and at the same time he motioned to Rock with his hand to get the guns.

"Ok, I'm on my way," Pat Man said, and the line disconnected.

Veedo pocketed his phone and walked into LisaPay's house followed by Rock, who asked "What dis nigga talking 'bout?"

"Talking like he know I got his shit. It wasn't no pleasant call, but I can't see how he could possibly think I got his shit."

"Well, shit, we finna see."

It only took Pat Man 15 minutes to pull up, and when he did, it only confirmed Lisa's story of how deep he was. Pat Man rolled up four cars deep, and all occupants inside jumped out. Pat Man was a redhead, freckles on his face kind of guy. He was extra fresh, and his demeanor wasn't warm.

Veedo and Rock met Pat Man in the yard while his goons stood in the streets. There was no handshake, no head nod, just Pat Man looking directly into Veedo's eyes.

"For the past month, I've had my people following your campaign, buying your pills, buying your loud, supporting your cause. Me, I'm a reasonable type guy, so I respect what you got going on, but at the same time I have my assumption that the pills you slanging is mines, so my question is who did you cop from?"

Veedo shook his head from side to side.

"Bruh, I got my own thang going on. I don't know what you tryna say."

"It's no secret that I got hit for a shitload of pills, then all of a sudden you relocated down here. You went from selling loud in Bankhead to pumping pills in over three counties. I'm far from stupid, my nigga, so don't play me like I am."

Pat Man grilled Veedo. Rock, on the other hand, was ready to pop off, 'cause it seemed the situation was about to get out of hand.

"Man, I don't know where you get your info from, but I'm not the nigga who took you off. I fucks with—"

"Bam, I know. That's my personal," Pat Man cut him off.

"Well, you should know where I get my work," Veedo shot back.

"Yeah, true, but the thing about this is me and Bam's pills are different, and these," Pat Man pulled a bag of pills out, "these are mines, and they come from you."

Veedo took the pills and examined them before passing them back with a shake of his head.

"Naw, bruh, I'm strictly getting mines from Bam." Veedo had in the past gotten some pills from Bam that were whack, so he would stick to his story.

"Well, listen, I spoke to Bam already, and he like you, my nigga. This shit ain't 'bout no pills. It's the life of my girl that got took behind this petty shit. I know you know something, but on my word to Bam I promised to approach you wit' respect. If you know anything, my nigga, then hit my line, and I got a mean award for you." Pat Man just turned around and walked away.

Later that day, Veedo drove to the city. He needed to talk with Bam face-to-face to find out what was really going on. Gangsta never told him that he hit Pat Man. Veedo just assumed so. Veedo wanted to know if it was Bam who sent Pat Man at him, or if not, then who?

Kia rode with him shotgun while Rock and Amanda held the trap down, because his plan was to be in and out.

Bam wanted to meet in a strip club, so they chose Blue Flames Veedo and Kia were checked and allowed in, then escorted to V.I.P. where Bam sat posted like the don he was.

"What's up, my boy? How you?" Bam smiled.

"I'm just here, bruh." Veedo took his seat and Kia followed. "Pat Man pulled up heavy on me today, asking me personal shit. Real deep like who my plug was. Tell me, what's up wit' *your personal*, so he say."

Bam poured up two cups of Hennessey and passed Veedo one, then Kia the other. He looked to his left and there sat Zay, a nigga Veedo knew well from Hollywood Road. Zay was a money figure. Then he saw Eric, who was Gangsta's cousin.

Veedo didn't really know Eric. He just heard he had the west side on smash.

However it went, though, Veedo wasn't there for either one of them. He wanted to know what was up with Pat Man.

Bam began to introduce them.

"Eric and Zay, I want y'all to meet Veedo, one of our team playas. He loyal, he hungry. Veedo, this is Eric and this is Zay. I know the streets talk, so you know of each other already, but what you didn't know is all y'all niggas eating off the same plate. All y'all niggas chasing the same shit, which is paper. Now, to answer your question, Veedo, I don't really know what Pat Man got going on. The kid in love, so he just acting out on what he's heard. I will calm him, though, 'cause he, too, is our team playa."

"Ok, cool, 'cause I'm not tryna be looking over my shoulder 'bout shit I don't know of. I'm just tryna get this money."

"And money you will get. Lots of it," Bam boasted. Veedo decided to mingle a while longer, then planned to feel out Zay and Eric, and both turned out to be some cool cats. He ended up trading numbers with them both. He and Kia finally hit the road, but not before stopping at his grandmother's house.

Chapter 18

Gangsta
Eight Months Later
Finally Free

He watched her from the porch as NeNe climbed out of her car with Junior in tow. Still in love, still captivated by just the mere sight of her, Gangsta stared and wished the both of them were on good terms. It'd been eight months since their breakup, and that was eight months too long. Every gesture Gangsta would make toward her she somehow blocked, no matter what. NeNe had visited him one time in those eight months and poured her heart out to him about the hurt he bestowed upon her, how disrespected she felt, and what loyalty meant to her.

Gangsta couldn't do shit but respect it, but he didn't like it. He still begged her for another chance. Gangsta knew he wasn't going to fuck up anymore once he got her back in his life, but since then the status had remained the same with them.

Gangsta watched as his mom took Junior from NeNe. That was when he began heading her way. She was looking hella good his first day home. They stood face-to-face, and then Gangsta opened his arms and NeNe walked into them.

"I love you, and I miss you." Gangsta spoke honest words.

"I'm glad you home," was NeNe's only reply, then she firmly pulled away from his embrace.

Gangsta let her go.

"Yeah, me too."

He allowed her to walk off and mingle with the crowd of people in his mother's yard. Gangsta made a mental note to deal with his relationship issues later and focused back on enjoying the party.

"Bruh!" Gangsta heard someone call him. It was Veedo approaching. "I'm 'bout to head out, bruh."

They clasped hands and pulled each other into a one-armed hug.

"Okay, foo'. Good looking, too, my nigga," Gangsta replied, referring to the conversation the two shared on the ride back from prison.

Veedo had picked him up one-on-one to give him the heads up on the visit he got from Pat Man.

Word ran through the streets that Pat Man was questioning people about Gangsta and Teyummie's dealings, so Veedo told him to be on point. It was now in his daily plan to gather up info about Pat Man, because ain't no slippin'. Gangsta walked into the house and instantly was grabbed by Terry and pulled into the hallway.

"Yo' ass sho' didn't hug me like you hugged that broke-legged bitch."

Terry pushed a finger to his face. The last thing Gangsta wanted was a fight — or a fight with her, anyway.

"Not now, Terry. Real shit, I just got home, shawty," he said while looking her directly in her eyes.

Gangsta knew through his cousin Eric that she was back fucking with Zay, and it showed in her attire, in her face, and in her new swag. Word on the street was that Zay was a major figure in the game and his plug was Bam, so Gangsta knew Terry was living the fabulous life.

"Let me catch dat bitch—"

"Terry," Gangsta's mother yelled as she walked up behind her. "Watch your mouth, girl."

Terry said not another word as Gangsta slid off and back into the crowd outside.

A lot of niggas showed love today to Gangsta. Dudes who were broke back then had a grip now thanks to Bam, who wanted to put everybody down. Bam was most known for having states on smash and his murder game.

Gangsta was worth almost four hundred racks when he touched the streets. Most of it came from Veedo and his trap spots, which Gangsta invested in. Plus, he hustled good in the chain gang, so including the seventy-five racks he had buried behind his mother's yard, it all equaled almost four hundred thousand. Without a direction, Gangsta planned to finish what he started in the streets, but this time do it better. He would smoothly get away with the actions taken.

Now that Pat Man was looking for clues or connections to him and Teyummie, Gangsta vowed to stay on top of Pat Man. There were no links to him killing Teyummie, and Gangsta doubted if Veedo exposed his hand about the pills. At the same time, Gangsta couldn't put anything past anybody, so he would just remain on point.

***

Veedo

Veedo was more than elated that Gangsta finally made it home. Veedo had a feeling shit was about to get poppin' for their team all over Georgia. Veedo hated that he had to run, but business awaited him. He strolled out of the yard and up to NeNe.

Today she wore some gray leggings and a pair of Jordans on her small feet. She was also wearing a black Baby Phat coat. Her back was to Veedo when he approached and touched her shoulder.

"NeNe," he called her name and she turned around from her conversation. "Give these to Gangsta," Veedo said and walked away.

He walked directly past the black super sport Range Rover that he picked up Gangsta in that morning. Rock was waiting for him with Kia in a Lincoln Town Car.

"That little nigga seems happy," Rock stated as he cranked up.

"Shit, he is. I'ma let y'all niggas meet in probably a few days. I told you, bruh, the realest nigga I ever met," Veedo boasted.

"So, do he like the ride?" Kia cut into the conversation between the two guys.

"He don't know it's his shit yet."

Veedo and Rock had a meeting with Pat Man and his people. Lately they'd done good business, so when Pat Man asked him to come down to sit and talk, Veedo agreed because he admired how Pat Man hustled. Veedo knew that Pat Man wanted to ask him his thoughts on Gangsta, but he knew Veedo was Gangsta's tight man. Veedo's loyalty was deep, so Pat Man never asked, but Veedo knew.

Pat Man was okay in Veedo's book, but the game had always been *safety first, play later*. From what the streets were saying, Pat Man had too much faith in Teyummie, and he slipped big time.

Veedo knew it would be hard to get him now, because everywhere he looked when Pat Man was near he had a large group of gunners with him.

It took them forty-five minutes to pull up to a brick house out in Decatur. Veedo, Rock, and Kia were searched and escorted into the crib by two of Pat Man's gunners. The three of them were led downstairs to a basement where Pat Man was seated on a sofa between two super-bad females. He smiled bright when he noticed Veedo had made it.

"Welcome, my nigga," Pat Man spoke while showing his mouthful of golds.

Veedo also saw a few cats he has done business with in the past, but most were niggas from all areas of Georgia who sold or dealt drugs and were just sitting around.

"No problem."

"Have a seat. Bam should be here in a second." Pat Man gave him a dap, and then nodded to both Rock and Kia before walking back to have a seat between the girls. "Drinks, food, and drugs are at y'all's beck 'n' call."

Veedo couldn't help but wonder what this meeting was about as he took a seat. Kia stood to his side while Rock helped himself to a drink at the bar. Pat Man was too busy to notice Veedo watching him, because something just wasn't right with this picture.

***

NeNe

NeNe hated that someone was knocking on the door, since she was just now getting into the shower.

"Hold on," she yelled over the running water while stepping out of the tub into a long beach towel.

Quickly, she walked to the door and looked through the peephole to find Gangsta and their son standing on the other side.

"Dang," she mumbled as she unlocked the door.

Gary agreed to keep Junior for that entire week, and already he was back within a few hours of him having their son. NeNe snatched the door open.

"Listen, I'll be right back to—"

Gangsta's words came to a halt when he noticed NeNe's misted body clad in a pink towel with her hair wet and dripping. She moved to the side, allowing Gangsta into the house because she was afraid of catching a cold.

"Gary, you said a week. It hasn't been a day yet."

NeNe closed the door.

"I know, I know. Look, I'ma come straight back. I promise. He asleep anyway, so he'll never know."

Gangsta laid his son down in the playpen.

NeNe silently rolled her eyes, and then reopened the door to let him out.

"Okay, fine."

"Cool, I gotta make a call at ten. Can I use yo' phone?" Gangsta asked.

The clock read 9:36 p.m. Twenty-four minutes around him was entirely too long for her to bear. NeNe wasn't ready to be around him yet. The hurt was still fresh, the pain really vivid, and the drama with his daughter's mother made it no better. It made it worse, actually.

"Gary, you already speeding. Just watch your son and enjoy being free," NeNe said.

She walked to her bedroom prepared to finish her shower, not knowing Gangsta had followed her until he said, "I'ma enjoy my freedom, my son, and his mother."

NeNe quickly turned around holding the towel to her petite frame. She pointed toward the door that Gangsta followed her through.

"Get out of my room, Gary."

"Ain't like I haven't seen you naked before."

"So," she said and stomped her feet. "Please leave. Go watch Junior while you wait to use the phone," NeNe protested, and before she knew it Gangsta was up on her.

He grabbed her arm, pulled her to his chest, and then took her by the waist.

"Come here," he spoke.

NeNe tried to pull away from him, but failed.

Fighting with him would definitely make the towel fall, so she braced herself and said, "Gary, what are you do—"

"I'm making you mines. You belong here, and I belong here."

He proceeded to try to kiss her, but NeNe swiftly moved her head.

"Stop!"

"Why, though?"

He bit down on her neck and grabbed a handful of her soft booty.

"Stop it."

NeNe was finally able to get out of his embrace.

"NeNe, I miss you."

"Gary, please leave. Let me at least get dressed," NeNe replied at almost a whisper with her head looking down.

Gangsta used two fingers under her chin to have her eyes meet his.

"After you get dressed, can we please talk? Give me five minutes, NeNe, please?"

NeNe forced herself to look away and pushed his hands from her face.

"Let me get dressed, Gary," was the only thing she said.

Gangsta stood and stared at his girl for a brief moment, and then he left the room. NeNe took a deep breath while sitting on her bed, still in a daze about what just happened. *I'll shower when he leaves*, she thought to herself, and then found some jogging pants and a t-shirt to put on so they could talk and he could leave. Right now she was uncomfortable in her own home.

After she got dressed, NeNe slid on a pair of bed slippers and walked into the living room to find Gangsta gone. He was nowhere to be found, but the baby was sound asleep.

***

Gangsta

Gangsta decided to leave NeNe's crib because he had a mission to handle tonight, and talking to her at that moment would throw him off his plan. This was a plan that would put four kilos in his stash. Gangsta wasted no time jumping on the deal, being that he just got out of prison this morning and wouldn't nobody in the world believe he would be a suspect. The plan was to execute two niggas that were in the way of his cousin Eric's major come up, and Eric's balls weren't as big as Gangsta's. When Eric told him the ins and outs of the plan and the price to do it, Gangsta jumped on the deal.

At first Eric wanted to wait and do it at a later date, but Gangsta insisted that it be done today or the next day. Any day after that he wasn't fucking with it, so Eric agreed.

The two dudes were from Hollywood Road and had every part of the complex under their direct supervision. That put a limit on Eric's cash flow, so he needed them out of the way or else Bam would soon link up with them and grant them more power. Gangsta knew his first cousin wasn't really with the gunplay, but he was a born hustler. That was one reason Gangsta decided to handle the issue. Plus, four kilos was something he hadn't owned yet, and bricks in the city were twenty racks, so all Gangsta saw were dollar signs.

One thing Gangsta knew was that he had to pave the way for him, his family, and his team. He knew not to slip at doing so, but he wouldn't pump his brakes until Kash was on the streets and his pockets were all swollen.

Gangsta pulled up to the spot Black Fred and Marko ate at almost every night. It was a hood mom and pop place that served wings, fish, and fries. It was also a place the two dudes used to wash their money, along with three more stores they basically owned on the west side of Atlanta.

Gangsta sat across the street inside his brand new Range Rover that Veedo gave him, waiting on the moment the duo would pull up so he could strike and get ghost. Gangsta silently caressed the handle of the fifteen-shot Glock. It'd been a while since he held that fire in his grip.

As expected, Gangsta saw a green van pull up to the mom and pop store. A large black dude got out, followed by a shorter light-skin dude with dreads who Gangsta knew from middle school named Marko. Gangsta felt a little remorse for being on the other side of the gun. Both guys were draped in diamonds and looking like superstars. They entered the store, and Gangsta waited another fifteen minutes so he would have enough time to case the streets for the police or people coming and going. Gangsta watched as Black Fred took his seat at a table and Marko ordered the food. After Gangsta was sure everything was clear, he slid out of the Range Rover, tucking the Glock into his back pocket, and walked toward the store.

Gangsta looked around in a normal manner for any onlookers or police from a short distance. Gangsta counted one other guy inside the store along with three workers. The closer he got to the door, Gangsta slowly pulled the ski mask over his face.

With a quick yank of the door, Gangsta was inside with the Glock spitting ammo.

Bam! Bam! Bam! Bam! Bam! Bam! Bam!

The first guy, Black Fred, caught two tips to the face. The next shots hit the shorter guy, Marko. He got two shots in the back of his head.

Gangsta ran out of the store, smoothly crossed the street, climbed inside his whip, and then he smashed out.

Gangsta made it to Riverdale in the next forty-five minute and pulled up behind Eric's cream-colored 600 Benz. Gangsta hit the lights and climbed out. It was the first time he's been to Eric's new crib, and it was nice.

"That's handled," Gangsta said as he got into the Benz with his first cousin.

It was easy to tell Eric was now major league at what he was doing. A lot had changed since Gangsta was gone. One minute Eric was a local dope boy buying nine zips and cooking up zips to slang through the hood, and the next minute he was major league. Gangsta gave Eric a pound.

"I got somebody that wants to meet you," Eric said while reaching in the backseat for the Nike gym bag with the bricks inside. "It's ninety racks in there, too, bruh. That's from me to you."

"Okay, cool, cuz, but I'm not try'na meet these niggas. I'm good, but what's up with this nigga Pat Man, though?"

"I can dig it, but my dude, he good people, and dis how I eat, shawty. He'll fuck wit' you. I'm tellin' you he good on my word, cuz.

186

And Pat Man just think you took him off and murked his bitch. Bam told him to fall back, though, 'cuz it's too much money out here for that beef shit."

"Yeah, Pat Man's best bet is to leave me alone. I don't know shit 'bout him being hit. But anyways, I got something to do tonight, real shit. I'll just fuck wit' homie tomorrow."

Gangsta opened the door and was about to get out, then he reached over to give his cousin a dap again.

"Bet, bruh, I'ma call you after three," Eric said, leanin' in for the dap.

Gangsta wasted no time going back to NeNe's crib, even though it was 12:15 a.m. Yeah, he understood it was late, but he did not care anymore. It'd been too many months, and Gangsta needed his girl back in his life. He was willing to do anything to get her.

All the lights were out as he expected them to be. Gangsta got out of the Range Rover with the bag in tow. Even though NeNe stayed in College Park, he refused to slip and let some stealing-ass nigga come up off him.

***

NeNe

She just knew the loud banging on her door was a dream. She knew who it had to be. Who in their correct mind would be at her door at this time of night but Gangsta?

The knocking seemed to grow louder as NeNe stepped out of the comfort of her bed. She wore some boy shorts and a Lakers t-shirt with her hair in a tie.

"Sorry to wake you up, but where's Junior?" Gangsta walked inside once NeNe opened the door.

"He's knocked out, Gary. Oh, my God." NeNe closed her door and walked past Gangsta back to her bedroom.

She was certain he would follow, and he did.

"I wanna talk, baby."

"You had yo' chance and you left," NeNe shot back at him.

"I told you I had to handle something."

"You said a ten o'clock phone call, but anyway, I have to be to work at six o'clock, unlike some people I know. Your son's stuff is in his room. Lock my door on the way out and please make sure it's locked," NeNe said and got back in the comfort of her bed.

Damn, Gary looks good, she thought to herself. She had to admit that. Plus, he held that little hold on her, but she refused to give in. Yes, she loved him, but once a cheater was always a cheater in NeNe's book.

She heard her bedroom door close. NeNe opened her eyes to find Gangsta taking off his shirt. He started to undo his pants, and that's when she raised up from her pillow.

"What on earth are you doing?"

Gangsta slid his pants down while kicking off his shoes, and at the same time he responded, "I'm 'bout to lie down beside my woman and son. I'm 'bout to hold y'all and talk to you until you fall asleep in my arms, and in the morning, if you still hate me, then I'ma fall back."

Gangsta pulled the covers back to find Junior balled up in his pamper and t-shirt. He moved him over and slid into the warmth of the bed.

"I miss you, NeNe."

NeNe calmly removed herself from the confines of her own bed.

"I miss you too, Gary, but I—"

"Just go to sleep." Gangsta cut her off with his words. "Get in bed."

"No, and I'm serious."

This time Gangsta sat up and looked at the woman he loved. He took a deep breath and spoke.

"NeNe, baby, listen, all I wanna do is talk. That's it, and it gives me a chance to spend my first night wit' my family."

NeNe just looked for a moment as if she was thinking about what to say. She found a chair, removed the cloths in it, then sat down facing Gangsta.

"Ok, I'm all ears."

Gangsta got up out of the bed. He knew he only had one shot, so it was do or die, and he truly wanted his woman back. He looked down to his son, then to NeNe.

"All I can say is I'm sorry. I'm sorry for not being up front from the get go with you about Terry. I'm sorry I took you through so much unecessary time wasted. Man, you the best that ever happen to me, and God knows this. I'm not finna lie to ya, me and Terry was childhood girlfriend boyfriend, nothing more. She was just my first love type shit. Now, before me and you met, I messed wit' her one time. I had just got out and shit just happened, but then I met you, and then we didn't instantly link up, and by then she was screaming she was late. But then me and you caught up, and I surely fell in love without trying. I wanted to tell you, but I wanted to be sure. I got locked up, and my beating them cases was important. However it go, I had plenty of time to tell you. I just didn't want to lose you, Nya, real talk."

"Well, it's done now, ain't no changing that," NeNe replied.

"I want another chance, NeNe. I want my family."

"You got your son, your mom, and your aunt. You have enough, but I'm sorry, Gary, I cannot and will not get back with you. I'm sorry."

The words broke him down, killed all his motivation and drive. Gangsta wasn't expecting that.

The remainder of the night, Gangsta and NeNe stayed up talking about everything. It gave the both of them the chance to truly get to know the other. Gangsta opened up to her more than he ever had to anyone in life. He put his true pain out 'bout the loss of his brother and not having a father. He told everything he had in him because he wanted his woman back. NeNe also shared with him everything she thought possible well into the wee hours of the night. Their conversation ended when Junior woke up crying.

"So, NeNe, can we at least try?" Gangsta asked while attending to his son. NeNe was already grabbing him a bottle to warm. Gangsta began to change Junior. "So, can we?"

NeNe stopped midway out the door. She turned to face the man she loved. She missed him, and he missed her.

"Let's just be parents to our son, Gary. Take care of him and teach him right." Then she walked off to fix their son some milk.

Jerry Jackson

Chapter 19

Veedo

Bam had finally arrived at the spot, and Veedo was elated because it was getting really late and he had other shit to do, plus more money to make. When Bam pulled up, it was like the nigga was the president or somebody with how niggas surrounded him coming into the crib. Alongside Bam was Zay, another money figure Veedo knew of, but never met.

Everyone who walked in with Bam stood to the side as he and Zay took seats on the sofa after pounding a few dudes. Veedo was already seated with Kia next to him.

"Ok, fellas, I'm glad all y'all could make dis trip."

Bam stood to his feet. He was the type of guy who stood at 5'8", was 170 pounds, and wore a clean bald head. Everyone could tell he worked out by his body tone. He continued talking.

"I got y'all together because it's time to elevate our game. Every one of you guys has your own spots, and maybe more. All you guys making good money, or maybe great money, but it's time to elevate."

Veedo was all ears because Bam was already on the right page. Anything dealing with money was all right with Veedo.

"If y'all niggas wanna make it in this game, we need a few good things. First, we need loyal niggas. There can be no toe-steppin' and no slick-hating. It's a team effort. We also don't need pussy in the camp or weak links, 'cause that fuckin' shit will bring us down. If you not built like Iran, then go ahead and get out the game now. Listen, I'm fucking with all you guys on consignment from this day forward. Whatever you can handle, I got it locked in. Just don't bite off more than you can chew, and please do not cross me."

"I'm wit' dat," one dude from Douglassville stated, then everybody else joined.

Eric walked into the crib and nodded to a few. He pounded Veedo up and took his seat as Bam continued his speech. Veedo made sure to pay close attention to every word said so his understanding would be clear.

Bam gave them the plan of locking down the major parts of Georgia, and everybody was down with the movement. Everyone agreed loyalty first and business next. It was 3:30 a.m. when the meeting came to an end.

Pat Man pulled Veedo to the side. Since their first encounter, the two linked up a couple times on pills, but Veedo still did not trust him. Pat Man was cool people, but he could not be trusted.

"I heard ya boy got out."

"Hell yeah, shawty home."

"You know that issue I came to you wit' months ago is dead. I can't prove shit, my nigga, and me and Gangsta always been tight, so I'm not tryna come at him sideways just 'cause the streets talking," Pat Man said and dapped Veedo up.

"I mean, bruh, me, I said back then I'm saying now. Gangsta ain't gave me shit. I been fuckin' wit' shawty his whole bid and he ain't said nothing 'bout no pills. It's too much paper out here, my nigga. We 'bout to be rich, so that's my focus," Veedo stated. They pounded again, then Veedo left feeling good about everything. One thing he knew was that Pat Man didn't want problems with Gangsta, so it was good to fall back.

Veedo got a room downtown and dropped Rock and Kia off before he drove to Summer Hill. It was a place he could forever call home. It was his grandmother's house. Everybody knew of Ms. Brown for her famous baked cookies and freeze cups that she'd been selling for over thirty years.

Grandma's house was the one spot Veedo went to for his comfort and true rest. She was his favorite person in the world. Veedo adored his granny for her warm wisdom, and no matter what the case, she always had his back.

Ms. Brown was seventy-seven, but still moved around like she was thirty-five, and not to Veedo's surprise, she was up in the living room when he used his key to enter her home.

"Hey, son," Ms. Brown spoke.

Veedo saw her seated on the sofa with a Bible opened up across her lap. She was a tiny lady, but God had her full. She wore a head full of white hair and had hardly no wrinkles on her face or on her body.

"What's up, Ma?" Veedo closed and locked the door.

"It's late. Are you in trouble or is you tired?" She knew her grandson.

"Just tired, Ma."

Veedo flopped down in his favorite chair and kicked off his shoes. The chair was his granddad's, and Ms. Brown allowed nobody but Veedo to sit in it since her husband passed in it nearly ten years ago. Veedo was the sole reason she kept the chair.

"Well, go lay your head. Breakfast will awake you," Ms. Brown replied.

"I'ma just chill right here, Ma, and kick it wit' you, 'cause I gotta peel out in a minute."

Veedo was drained from doing entirely too much the past week. His eyelids were growing heavy as he fought sleep in order to talk with his grandma, but it was proving to be an uphill battle.

"Well, I'm giving it to God right now, so you can join me or not."

Veedo admired his grandmother's relationship with God. He was raised a God-fearing man in a God-fearing household, so it was nothing to bury his thoughts in the good book with Granny.

"Take off, Grandma. I'm wit'cha."

As Veedo's grandmother read from the bible out loud, he prayed within his thoughts. See, Veedo understood there was a good side to every bad, so he prayed for protection and that the path he travelled continued to be blessed. Veedo prayed for these things and knew in his heart the game was kill-or-be-killed, hands down. He knew for sure now that he was about to be major, that people would die at his hands to get to the top.

***

Gangsta

After cooking breakfast and feeding his family, Gangsta made the phone call to his cousin, who wanted to meet at six, so it was a set date. Gangsta hung up the phone, opened the gym bag that contained the bricks and money, then pulled four fresh-wrapped bricks out of the bag and quickly slid them under the sofa, leaving the money inside the bag. Gangsta tossed it on the sofa.

He entered NeNe's bedroom. She was sitting up in bed putting Junior's clothes on. She missed work today because of staying up last night with Gangsta. They talked all night.

"Write down his sizes, too, all of 'em," Gangsta said.

"Just remember to feed him every two hours at least and make sure you change him every three hours," NeNe replied to his demands. She was looking as beautiful as ever to him, and Gangsta vowed to marry this pretty-ass woman. NeNe held a special glow about herself to him. She walked with respect and was so humble in the soul. She was so sexy that every time she passed guys, they either stared or tried to step, and Gangsta was in love like never before.

"Okay, cool, I got it."

Gangsta left shortly after NeNe got Junior dressed. He had ninety racks on him and an F/N 9 mm. Gangsta carried Junior nested in his arms to NeNe's 300C, which he decided to drive today. *I gotta upgrade her.* He took 285 and got off on Bankhead Highway, a straight shot down Bankhead and a right turn and he was on South Grand. Gangsta walked into his mother's house with Junior to find Keshana on the floor in front of the large TV. She happily jumped up when she saw her daddy.

"What I tell you 'bout sitting that close in front of that TV, huh?"

Gangsta put Junior down on his tiny feet and picked his daughter up. He kissed her candy-filled lips and stood her next to Junior.

"Ma."

"In here," he heard his mother from the kitchen.

Gangsta put the gym bag on the sofa.

"What's up, Ma? Junior in there. I'll be right back."

He kissed his mother's jaw and headed out the back door. It took him no more than twenty minutes to dig up his stash in the woods. Inside his old bedroom, Gangsta counted six more brand new guns, a bulletproof vest, and one hundred sixty-five grand, not including the eight racks he had in his safe from years ago. Gangsta put the money into the bag along with all the guns, then pushed it into the closet.

He left his mother's crib with Keshana and Junior, so he was three deep with no sleep. His only plan for the day was to kill some time with the kids, so he took them shopping and took pictures with them.

"What's Keshana's sizes?" He had to call Terry, who was acting extra to him.

"I will text it to you, and when are you bringing my baby home? Your first night home and you didn't spend it with your first-born. Had my baby waiting for your ass all night. You shacked up with that ho."

"Man, Terry, just text me the size." He wasn't hearing shit she had to say.

Gangsta enjoyed fatherhood, being that it was his first time ever being with the kids. They got all kinds of attention, and Gangsta was loving it.

Gangsta took his kids to Ebony's crib so they could meet Kash's kids. He dropped them off with promises to be back within an hour because he had to meet Eric at the club.

It'd been a while since Gangsta walked into any club, and it was his very first time in a strip club. Blue Flame was the place to be any day of the week, 'cause it hosted some super bad females from all parts of Georgia and many other states. Gangsta just didn't do clubs in his line of work, but he made this trip with exceptions. Once he paid and got frisked, Eric met him at the door.

"What's up, cousin?" They pounded fists. Eric was draped in Prada with a nice pair of Raybans on his face, and he was iced out on his neck, wrists, and ears.

"Whoa, what's hap', foo'?" Gangsta replied and followed him into the V.I.P. section of the club.

Pussy and sweat is all Gangsta smelled, along with weed and cigarettes. Music was loud, the hos were lovely — he had to approve. Inside the V.I.P. room for the first time, Gangsta laid eyes on this Bam dude, and his whole swavy spoke murder. Eric walked over and introduced them.

"Yo, Gangsta, this my nigga Bam. Bam, this cuz I'm telling you 'bout, Gangsta."

"Yo, son, have a drink, have a seat. Get comfortable. I have heard great shit 'bout you, straight up." Bam reached his iced-out hand to

Gangsta, who shook it while sitting down. "So, I hear you just came home from prison."

"Lil' eighteen months. Yeah."

"And that you wanted to make that cheddar, lots of cheese, huh?" Bam asked as he fixed Gangsta a cup of hen.

"You might've heard wrong." Gangsta looked at his cousin, then took the cup Bam handed him.

"Is that word?" Bam then looked to Eric.

"Yeah, I'm just cooling, bruh, plus I talk one-on-one. I ain't got time for co-defendants."

"Understood," Bam said, then he called the waiter and ordered up some dancers. Within one minute, a group of bad bitches walked into V.I.P. with the three guys. Gangsta grabbed an exotic-looking female.

"Hey," she spoke and stood between Gangsta's legs. His second day out and he still ain't had no pussy. He leaned back as she began to move her hips.

The girl had long, jet-black hair and a super nice body with some slanted eyes. Gangsta enjoyed a few of her dances and tipped her nicely.

"'Preciate it," he said.

"No problem. My name is Asia. What's yours?"

"I'm Gangsta."

"Why so harsh?" she wanted to know.

"Why not when we in a harsh world?"

"Well, look." Asia walked over to his ear and spoke. "I wanna hook up with you. I mean not on the sex thing. I'm talking about being cool, you know?"

"Okay, that's possible," Gangsta replied.

"Alright, I'm about to go write my info down."

And in a flash Asia was gone. Eric had walked away with some big-booty ho, so Gangsta found him at the bar.

"Man, what made you say dat you don't need no money?" Eric seemed pissed.

"'Cause I'm not try'na be down wit' no lame."

"Man, you trippin'." Eric walked away as Asia came out of nowhere. She passed Gangsta the number.

"How old are you?" Gangsta pushed the paper into his pocket and asked.

"Twenty. Why, how old are you?"

"One. I'm twenty one."

When the girl walked off, Eric pulled back up. Gangsta could tell he was kinda drunk.

"Cuz, have I ever told you anything wrong?" Eric asked, sitting at the bar with Gangsta.

"Naw, bruh, but what I did, I did for you. I'm fresh out, bruh. I'm not really tryna link up wit' new friends, feel me?"

"I feel that, but listen to me, my nigga. I'm almost rich. One more play and I'm there. You been gone, what, two years? Nigga, two years ago I was buying a quarter brick. Now I got too many of these bitches."

"I can dig that, shawty, but I'm doing my own thang. I don't need no team. Plus, most them niggas soft, shawty, they ain't built to hold that type o' paper," Gangsta said, and he meant it. Eric, on the other hand, didn't like what he was hearing, and it showed on his face.

"'Cause niggas ain't on that robbin' shit no more. It's way too much money to be risking going to jail for all the bodies taking money presents. Just hustle this shit. Lock shit down like Cool did," Eric spoke back at the same time, turning up his drink.

"I'm 'bout to push, shawty, I got to get my kids. I will fuck with you later." Gangsta and his cousin dapped and hugged at the bar before he left.

Gangsta knew Eric was telling him some good shit, but at the same time he couldn't put his trust in Bam. It was just something about the nigga Gangsta didn't like.

After picking the kids up, he decided to hit the road to make a drop for Kash and Blue at Macon. It was nothing but some phones and a half-pound of loud, so he took the kids for the trip.

"What's up, shawty?" Kash answered his phone.

"Whoa. What's hap', fool? I'm finna take shawty that pack," Gangsta said

"Okay, cool. What da mojo?" Kash asked.

"Man, shit try'na pave the way for us."

"How it feels to be free?" When Kash spoke those words, it hit Gangsta like a blow to the stomach unexpectedly, because he knew that his partna needed and wanted to be free, but he was stuck with a life sentence.

"Don't feel right wit' you left in that bitch wit' a bow, shawty." Gangsta was being honest.

The last months he and Kash were cellmates, they had grown closer like never before, and Gangsta viewed him as if he was Cool, his blood brother. It was hard for him to just leave Kash, though Gangsta vowed to fight with his partna to the end.

"It's all G, nigga. I'ma be straight," Kash answered him.

"Say no mo', fool. I got us, though," Gangsta reassured Kash.

***

The Next Day

When Gangsta pulled up at Zay and Terry's crib, he was amazed to find it gated heavily. Once cleared to go through the gate, Gangsta saw four old school cars and two Benz 600s, white and black. He knew the crib cost a grip just by the stone bricks, plus it looked to have at least seven bedrooms or better.

Gangsta parked the Range Rover. He took Keshana out of her car seat, then noticed Nikki walking toward them. She had on some tight high-ankle jeans and flip flops.

"What's up, Gangsta? Welcome home," her baby voice said.

"'Preciate it."

"You gonna stay out this time, I hope."

"Shit, I am," said Gangsta and took his daughter into the house.

Zay opened the door for him.

"What's good, bruh?"

"What's happenin' fool?" replied Gangsta, walking deeper into the nice house. Zay led him into a movie room where Terry was laid across a soft-looking chair. "I'ma get her this weekend."

Gangsta put Keshana down.

"Ok," Terry shot back without looking his way. She clearly had an attitude.

"And Terry, stop the drama you started when you see NeNe." Gangsta put her on blast in front of Zay. "You act jealous or something, shawty."

"Boy, I ain't thinking 'bout that trick," Terry got defensive.

"Why she gotta be all dat?" Gangsta and Zay both laughed 'cause they both knew Gangsta got under her skin.

"Let me holla at you a minute, bruh," Zay said once they walked out of the movie room. Zay led him to a game room that was laced. Gangsta had to tip his hat. Bam was sure enough upgrading every drug dealer in Atlanta.

"What's up, bruh, what da move is?" Gangsta asked.

"I'm just putting you on point 'cause I fucks wit' ya. Pat Man is coming at you, bruh. He feel like you killed that ho. Nigga got her phone before the police got there, got that shit traced back to you. Da nigga been on it for a minute now, and he just got the trace back last month. Bam told him to fall back, but he being slick 'bout it. He up to something, so be on your ones and twos," Zay said.

"Shawty, I sho'nuff 'preicate ya. Pat Man gon' make me fuck him up. I'm just tryin' a make it last dis time, but I will definitely give him what he wants." Gangsta was about tired of the talk.

"We all came up together on this west side, shawty. It don't need to come to that. I will holla at this nigga and see what's really going on, 'cause you family," Zay added. "Here, this your coming home gift." Zay gave Gangsta two fresh-wrapped bricks. They kicked it another 30 minutes, smoked a blunt, then Gangsta left.

Jerry Jackson

Chapter 20

Kash

Ms. Wishob was making her rounds as niggas gawked at how bad she was, plus some niggas downright stared at her to see if she was about to make a drop. Kash hated this fact, but it came with the game in prison, because if you were personally dealing either inmate or officer, somebody would peep you, and nine times out of ten somebody would say something.

Ms. Wishob had been dropping for Blue for over a year now, and niggas in H2 knew the move. There had been times Kash and Blue had to jump on a few cats for looking too hard or talking too much. Both Kash and Blue made sure to bless the pod, and the niggas were still hating.

"Shawty, you can snatch dat ho." Meco tapped Kash's shoulder when he walked up.

Meca was GF, an Atlanta gang that was most hated and feared. He was a nigga from Summer Hill who was down eight years on a body.

"Anybody can get that ho, bruh."

"I know, right."

Both guys leaned on the rail.

"Dat ho crazy, I know dat much," Kash added. Neither him nor Blue ever tried to get at Ms. Wishob, plus she liked Gangsta when he was there. Gangsta just paid no attention to her as every other nigga did.

"Where's Blue's ass at?"

"Detail," Kash said

"What's up, Kash? What's up, Meco?" Tae strolled up, a nigga from Atlanta, an old-school cat.

"GF mob shit," Meco boasted.

"Y'all wanna blow one real fast?" Kash noticed Ms. Wishob putting on her gloves.

"Shake down!" someone yelled in the pod.

Kash waited a few minutes after he saw her enter his cell. When he got downstairs, he saw her checking under this bunk, bent over. A couple niggas caught glimpses and also stopped. She was coming out of the cell moments later with a cup and spoon.

"That's the only cup I got, Ms. Wishob," Kash said while walking into his room when she walked out.

"Y'all are not allowed these." Ms. Wishob held it up and walked to another cell.

Meco and Tae walked inside the cell, too. Kash pulled out his phone as Tae began to roll up a joint to smoke. He called Gangsta, who picked up on the third ring.

"Whoa."

"What da hell going on, foo'?"

"Shit, boy, I'm on my way back to prison." Gangsta laughed, but Kash felt he was serious.

"What's up?"

"Shawty, dis shit crazy out here. All these niggas working one plug, and all these niggas eating. Pat Man, Zay, Eric, all the nobodies got that check. But peep, this nigga who plug everybody tryna fuck wit' me. Pussy-nigga crazy. Plus, Pat Man acting like he want beef. I'm just laughing at them niggas, bruh."

"Man, fuck them lames. Look, though, I can plug you with the Mexicans, foo'. I'm still good with Loco, and his folks got it."

Kash boasted Loco was the Mexican who fronted Kash the pounds of mid-grade. Kash never got the chance to cross him, so instead he kept a clean face.

"Shit, say no mo'. I gave that lil' ho that pack last night."

"Yeah, that's what's up." Kash smoked the joint with Meco and Tae while talking with Gangsta, then he ended the call.

"I'm finna shit right quick, shawty, then we'll blow one more." Kash began to line the toilet seat with tissue. Once the cell door was locked, and his two partnas was gone, Kash found the bomb in his locker box. It was ten touchscreen phones and a pound of gas. Kash put the whole bomb up, stashed in the vent inside his cell. He would move it to his hold man after count, 'cause he knew niggas was watching his every move.

***

Gangsta

Bam was parked in a black Benz truck that looked good sitting on chrome wheels when Gangsta pulled up. He noticed two black Tahoe trucks on either side of the Benz as he parked and got out.

Gangsta tucked the Glock on his hip, walking toward the Benz still wondering why Bam called him to meet. Once Gangsta was close to the Benz, two big dudes got out of one of the Tahoes. They approached Gangsta, who was on point and ready for any drama to unfold.

"Turn over yo' weapon," one of the big guys said while the other eyed Gangsta closely.

They both wore bluetooth earpieces, guns on the hip, and "Safety" written across their shirts. Gangsta pulled the Glock from his waist, handing it over to one of them while the other one patted him down, then the Benz door was opened and Gangsta was allowed to enter. He sat comfortably next to Bam and closed the door.

"So tell me, son, is this more like it?" Bam asked with a smile.

"Dis good, bruh."

"Well, look, I'ma be straight forward with you. My man Eric has sold me to you about how you a true gunner and how solid you are. I understand, and it's respected what you got going on. What I'm try'na do is build a team. A team of solid dudes who I can trust and feed at the same time."

"I can dig it," Gangsta replied.

"I need drugs to be moved. I need spots to be on lock. I need niggas bodied." Bam looked hard at Gangsta, who in return nodded his head in agreement, so Bam kept talking. "I need leadership, a quick mind, and a true hustler who adores the craft."

Bam explained the whole ordeal to Gangsta, telling him that he didn't need but one thing from Gangsta, and that was his loyalty. Bam gave Gangsta a folded-up piece of paper with six names on it. The names were some major money niggas in the city.

"What's up with these names?" Gangsta finally asked.

"These cats in our way of millions. With them out of the picture, we will become rich in no time."

Bam wanted them dead. He passed Gangsta a book bag that was heavy.

"This for the first three niggas. I got a bonus for you when the entire job done."

Gangsta didn't take the work. He didn't trust Bam. He smoothly passed the paper back.

"Naw, I'm good, homie. 'Preciate it, though."

At first Bam looked as if he couldn't believe Gangsta denied him. He smiled and took the paper back. He sat the bag on the floor.

"I'm only trying to put some money in your pockets. Eric told me you specialize in murder, so why not be paid for being so good at what you do?" Bam asked.

"Eric talk too much, for one. If I was so good at murkin' niggas, then why I had to beat all these bodies? I'm not that nigga, bruh, I'm just trying to enjoy being free, raise my seeds, and let y'all have these streets."

"Fo' sho', I can feel that, son. Well, if you ever in need and when you ready, then come fuck wit' the team. I can get you rich"

"Say no mo'," Gangsta replied and got out of the Benz. He was handed back his gun and left with plans to get at Eric. He was not trusting these niggas, and he wasn't dealing with none of the people Bam dealt with. Not on gettin' money together. Yes, they could kick it, but when it comes to the grind, Gangsta had plans to build his own team.

***

He left his truck parked in his mother's yard and jumping into the rental he asked her to get for him. Gangsta cranked up and pulled off. He needed solid information on Pat Man without anybody knowing.

Gangsta drove to Dill Avenue, one of Pat Man's main trap spots, and rode around the streets talking on his phone to NeNe about them getting back together, but NeNe wasn't hearing it. Gangsta loved his baby mama and wanted her back.

He was making sure he kept close watch on the people he saw. Gangsta spotted a dark-skin chick walking dowing the street with two kids. He made the turn on that street, then slowed the rental when he pulled up beside the girl and kids.

"Excuse me," Gangsta said and got her attention. "What's up? Where you headed?"

"Home. Why?" the girl asked.

She was cute, Gangsta noted.

"I would've took you." He smiled.

"Why thank you, but I'm already on my street." She smiled back and walked into a yard. Gangsta pulled over and spoke through the window.

"My name is Dank, and yours?"

He placed the car in park. The girl stopped walking and let the kids go toward the house. Both of the kids took off running.

"I'm Kate."

"Kate?" Gangsta got out of the rental. "So, are you single? Are them yo' kids?"

"Yes, they are," Kate replied.

Gangsta talked with her briefly and traded numbers. She seemed to be simple, and that's what he needed, somebody low key so it was easy to slide in.

Later that night, Gangsta pulled up at Veedo's condo out in Buckhead. He liked the setup and made note to check the rental price out later. When Gangsta knocked on the door, he could hear music being played and smell cocaine being cooked. The door opened up. Veedo handed Gangsta a mask and he put in on, walked into the crib, and closed the door. He saw a dude standing in the kitchen also cooking. There were piles of ounces after ounces on the dinner table, the coffee table, and both end tables. On the countertop there were piles of money and a few guns.

"You good cooking, ain't cha?"

"Bruh, this shit in high demand in Albany and Cordal," Veedo said and turned toward his partna. He introduced both guys.

Gangsta stood around and asked, after watching Veedo and Rock cook up, "What do you cook off, a whole?"

"Ten extra zips, some spending money," Veedo spoke over his shoulder.

"Bam got shit on smash, huh?"

"That's a real nigga, shawty. He just like you, bruh, I can't take nothing from that nigga. He showing love."

"So, you trust that nigga?" Gangsta asked.

"Wit' my life." Veedo pulled the mask from his mouth. "Bruh, I'm almost at a mil' ticket just fucking wit' this consignment shit. It's free paper."

"I feel that."

"He got Eric pumping heroin. This nigga went from an ounce nigga to a million dollar nigga in a couple weeks. Shit so lovely Eric hardly even hit the streets. I had to jump on his bandwagon, real talk," Veedo boasted with great pride.

Gangsta had a different sight, but didn't share it with Veedo just yet. Instead, he stayed with them until they cooked up everything, then they all hit the sports bar out in Buckhead.

***

NeNe

Junior was about to drive her crazy. He was getting on NeNe's last nerve, showing out while at the doctor's office. Everywhere else they went after that he would just act up, falling out, crying and dragging his feet when she tried to hold his hand and walk with him. NeNe whomped him twice and still got nowhere. It seems Gary Junior forgot she was his mother. The only person to contain him was his father, whom NeNe quickly called. Junior got right in line after hearing his daddy's voice.

Later that day, when they made it home, Gangsta had his daughter and Kash's two kids, also. Erica was in the living room looking at TV while Gangsta was in the bedroom texting on his phone. NeNe put Junior down and entered her bedroom after speaking to her sister.

Erica had fallen to the lowest messing with the nothing nigga she dealt with. She started using drugs and drinking while allowing her different boyfriends to make plays at her house. Erica was totally disrespecting Kash and their relationship. She stopped going to see him

206

after fucking up his money. She allowed his truck to get repoed because she didn't pay the notes, plus she had niggas driving Kash's cars.

NeNe's cries fell on deaf ears when she constantly tried to talk to Erica about the shit she was doing. Now that Erica has been to jail, NeNe was hoping this was her wake up call.

"What's up, girl?" NeNe took a seat on the sofa with her big sister.

"Nun, girl, going back and forth with Kash," Erica replied and pointed at the phone.

"Kash loves you."

"Honey boo, Kash's ass hates my guts. I messed up, NeNe."

"But he'll forgive you. Yo' butt just gotta do right, Erica, and you know these things. Go back to school, get a job. Do good, sis."

NeNe remembered when Erica was on her A-game. She was in school fulltime and worked. NeNe looked up to her sister for a lot of reasons and followed her footsteps. Now NeNe was situated with a great job, getting paid twenty-two dollars an hour working in CVS Pharmacy. She had a nice crib and could afford a car, but was so in love with her 300C she paid it no mind to buy a new one.

NeNe expected her sister to be far past her, but Erica has let these street niggas with no direction bring her down. NeNe vowed to motivate her sister back to her old self if it killed her doing so.

The kids had finally all fell asleep, and boy was she happy. Erica also dozed off, so NeNe found Gangsta in the room.

"I'm 'bout to shower. So, have you found a place to stay yet, 'cause I know you not trying to go back to your mom," she asked him because he was still fully dressed.

Gangsta was laid back on her bed with his eyes closed, but opened them to the question.

"I'm finna join you. I'm tired."

Gangsta stood up.

"No, you're not."

"Oh, so you acting like that now, huh?" Gangsta smiled at his joke.

NeNe smiled and said, "But I'm so serious."

She walked into the bathroom that was in her room.

When Gangsta entered the bathroom, NeNe was already under the water as it splashed all over her slim body. He watched in amazement as he stepped out of his clothes. It'd been years since he's been with this woman, and it showed as his dick bricked up. NeNe noticed as he stepped into the shower with her. She looked directly at his wood.

"You not getting none. I don't know what you call yourself doing."

"Man, pass me one of them rags." NeNe shook her head but did as told with a blush on her pretty face.

They bathed each other a few times and kissed a lot while they showered. Gangsta palmed her ass every chance he got, and she stroked his dick, making him harder.

"Let's get out befo' we get sick," NeNe said. Her pussy was on fire. She was about to go crazy over the dick. She was so horny they both barely dried off and made it to the bed.

Gangsta laid her down and spread her legs as he planted kisses on each of her soft thighs. He then slowly sucked her clit into his mouth when he made it to her center. NeNe arched her back and closed her eyes as Gangsta ate her out for the next ten minutes. His face covered in her love juices, Gangsta raised up, about to enter her, when she stopped him. NeNe made him lay on his back and began to give him some passionate head, licking up and down, jacking him and stroking him until he came thick, white juice that ran down her hand.

"Our daughter," NeNe joked.

She got out of bed and washed her hand, then came back into the room with a warm rag to clean her man up. After she did, they made deep, slow love well into the wee hours of the night, and NeNe enjoyed every moment.

***

Gangsta

She felt so good nested in his arms as he pushed in and out of her tight walls and hot pussy. Gangsta felt as if his dick melted entering her wetness. Gangsta sucked her tongue as he went deeper inside NeNe while she rolled her hips, one to get away from the pain and two to meet him thrust for thrust.

208

"Baby," NeNe moaned as Gangsta moved to her neck with his tongue. "Baby, I love you."

"I love you more, baby girl."

Gangsta pulled out of her and took one of her legs, pushing it over as if she was about to turn over, but still faced him, and he entered her walls. NeNe interlocked fingers with him with one hand while her free hand gripped the sheet.

Gangsta hit her in a few more good positions, and they both came good. By the time they stopped, the sun was peaking. It was their third round, and still the both of them wanted more. Their bodies just weren't willing.

***

Kash

Kash woke up when he heard the pod officer call for count time. The room was dark due to paper covering the back window, blocking the sun, and his CD player played T.I. No Mercy on low. Kash looked down from the top bunk to find his roommate still under the covers, asleep. Two fans were blowing on the floor, along with two pairs of shower shoes and two pairs of high-price sneakers. Kash looked on the table in the cell to see his bowl and cup, still half filled with Bombay, his CD player and CDs.

"Count time! Count time," he heard Ms. Berry yell, and then the doors started clicking through the pod. Kash finally sat up, legs hanging off the bed. He jumped down and walked over to the open door, where he found his shower shoes.

"Count time. You know how this ho is," Kash said to his roommate.

He then got his toothbrush and toothpaste.

It was a Monday morning coming off a major Sunday night of balling with Blue, Tae, and Meco, plus a few other city niggas. On Ms. Wishob's last day she had dropped two pounds of purp. Kash and his roommate were standing by the cell door while both officers counted. He had his operation going good at Macon. All Kash sold now were

209

ounces and front ounces. He let niggas buy for six hundred an ounce, and if he frontted it, then he wanted eight hundred. Kash didn't have a main girl, so all his money was saved by Gangsta. After count cleared, Kash pulled his phone from under the pillow on his bunk. It had a few missed calls and a couple text messages. Kash dialed Gangsta's number while rolling up a stick of purp. Gangsta picked up.

"Whoa."

"Shawty, what's up? Expected you to be knocked out."

"Nah, bruh. I'm with the kids, 'bout to hit Six Flags."

"Okay, cool. Yeah that pack official, too, shawty. I'm blowin' one now," Kash boasted.

"I'ma get to it once I duck off. I gotta focus on these children now. Yo' son is off the chain," Gangsta said.

After Kash kicked it with Gangsta a second, he walked out of his cell to go get the mop and broom. The officer on the floor was new. Her name was Ms. Berry, and boy was she stacked. She was a cool, down-to-earth female who kicked it with the inmates more than her officers, so a lot of niggas kept her name in their mouths.

Ms. Berry was standing at the booth, signing people out to details and callouts. Niggas in the pod were cleaning, getting haircuts, and shaving. Some cats ducked into their rooms to smoke before inspection started.

After the room was cleaned and inspection-ready, Kash made his way to where Ms. Berry stood. She was short and thick with a basketball booty that Kash wanted to slap.

"What's up, Ms. Berry?" he spoke, checking her out.

"Hey, McCants."

"You sho' is rocking them pants."

"Boy, hush!" Ms. Berry said with a slick blush and walked off. Kash followed.

"I'm just saluting, that's all. No hating."

"I hear ya." She stopped at the mop closet.

"Ms. Berry, if you was mine…." Kash paused and shook his head.

"What? If I was yours, what?" This time she smiled at him playfully, rolled her eyes, and walked off again.

It'd been almost three years since he'd had some pussy, and a shot of it now would be just right. Kash watched as Ms. Berry walked off and out of the pod, ass bouncing with each step she took. He knew to stay on her heels whenever she was in his pod, and when she was not, to pull up on her just to show his face.

Kash went to find Meco, who was just getting up and brushing his teeth. They pounded fists as Kash waited for his city partna to get right.

Jerry Jackson

Chapter 21

Kash
Two Weeks Later

Kash was standing on the top range with Meco when they saw the cert team come into the pod. The dudes were moving funny, looking crazy, and acting nervous.

"Lock down, everybody in yo' room," one cert member said to the pod, and that's all it took.

One thing about prison was the boys in black got their respect.

"What da fuck dis about?" Meco wanted to know, and Kash began to walk off.

"I don' know," Kash mumbled back while making his way downstairs to his room.

When the cert team had the whole pod on lockdown, two of the members stood outside of Kash's cell.

"Turn around, face the wall, get on yo' knees," one of them said as Kash followed orders.

He was already prepared for a shake down such as this. Neither he nor his roommate had a grain of drugs in the cell, plus his phone was put up. Both cert members entered the cell and cuffed him up.

"Face the wall, inmate," the cert officer said as two more walked up and started searching his cell.

Kash also saw cert officers in Blue's room. They were packing him up. Kash also saw the warden and lieutenants in the control booth with Ms. Wishob, searching around and talking to her. Kash was glad she didn't bring anything today.

The cert team searched his room top to bottom and found nothing. They uncuffed him and put him back into his room in a mess.

Kash wasn't thinking about the room. He stayed glued at the door. Looking at the booth, he saw the warden leave with Ms. Wishob and one lieutenant, and the other one took Ms. Wishob's place.

"Bruh, somebody dropped a dime," Meco stressed while holding his banger.

Tae was also on the bed while Kash sat on the sink with his feet on the toilet. Everybody was trying to figure out what happened, what went wrong, and who was the snitch. Word in prison was that Ms. Wishob had gotten walked off compound. It had everybody in the pod baffled.

"Man, somebody roll up," Kash said, because he really needed to smoke to clear his thoughts. There was a small tap on the cell door. Kash let Randy in. He was a white guy who put up Kash's phones and weed.

"'Sup, Randy?" Kash took the phone Randy handed him.

"Chillin, chillin," Randy replied, and also passed Kash a bomb of weed that reeked of loud. When the phone was powered up, a text came from Gangsta. Kash called him after reading it, but got the voicemail. It was about to be chow call, so Kash texted him back telling Gangsta the bad news.

"Shawty, dis on da mob. I think that sissy had something to do wit' it," one of Meco's GF brothers said as he walked into the cell.

"Why you say dat, shawty?" Kash asked.

"'Cause he a sissy. Plus sissy-ass nigga always hanging on the rail." Meco gave his two brothers orders to bust by sayin', "Guns up after chow."

Kash went ahead and served a few niggas and put the weed back up. He knew that once the sissy got stabbed, their pod was going on lockdown, and nine times out of ten would be shaken down the next day. He only kept out enough weed to last him and his phone, waiting on Gangsta.

***

Gangsta

It'd been two weeks since he'd been set free, and it felt good being home. NeNe was still acting stubborn despite the lovemaking. She still would not come in.

Gangsta got himself a spot in Riverdale and another spot on Holy Street off Bankhead to set up shop with the weed. He was able to link up with Loco and got some good prices on the loud. Gangsta and Loco agreed that Gangsta would buy the first two times, and after that Loco would front him whatever he could handle. Gangsta was cool with that and got 30 pounds for twelve hundred a pound. It was just something to get started, plus he still had the bricks from Eric and Zay.

Gangsta heard his phone ringing.

"Whoa." Fresh out of the shower, Gangsta was in his room when an unknown number popped up on his phone.

"May I speak with Gangsta?" The girl's voice sounded panicked.

"Who dis?"

"Amanda. I'm Veedo's peoples. The spot just got raided. The feds got Veedo and Rock. I don't know where Kia is at. I'm at Greyhound." The girl rambled off so fast Gangsta had to slow her down and have her explain it one more time, and she did.

Gangsta told her to make it to Atlanta and he'd have somebody pick her up, but to try to find Kia as well.

Damn, Veedo, Gangsta thought and got a text from Kash. Another strike of bad luck, because the mule got fired and Blue was on lock up. Gangsta decided to call Eric to see if any word was in the street about Veedo.

"Yo," Eric picked up.

"Feds snatched Veedo and his partna," Gangsta told him.

"Yeah, I heard they just got them country-town niggas. Them pigs been poppin' niggas all week."

"So, y'all straight."

"Hell yeah, I didn't really bubble wit' V on business. Bam did, and homie Gucci, he got them peoples on payroll. Our team good," Eric assured his cousin, but at the same time there was more to it than what Eric was saying. Gangsta got off the phone with his cousin and took a seat on his bed.

He wanted to know what was up with Veedo. The only people who would know were Veedo's grandma and his baby mama, April. Gangsta decided to wait until later before he contacted either.

He was glad he didn't rush into what Veedo had going on. He knew his gut feeling was right when he wouldn't fuck with Bam. Gangsta just hoped like hell that Bam didn't get Veedo fucked up, 'cause then Bam would have to pay with his life.

Gangsta finally got dressed to hit the streets. He wore his bulletproof vest under the polo shirt and packed a Glock .40 stuck down in his polo boots. He was still laying on Pat Man like he knew Pat Man was waiting to strike on him. Gangsta had already cased Pat Man's whole movement on Dill Avenue, so it was nothing to take him out for his stash. It was just hard to follow the nigga once he left Dill. Every time he and Pat Man ran into each other, it was at either the clubs or in public, and each time Pat Man would fake kick it like everything was good. Gangsta knew better, though he fake kicked out back.

***

Kash

Kash heard the doors pop open and the loud voices of niggas talking across the pod. They had been on lockdown the last couple of hours because the sissy got stabbed up for snitching. While on lockdown, Kash got the full story from Ms. Wishob. It was not the sissy who ate the cheese. It was a dude named Rabbit. He was Muslim. Rabbit was also from Atlanta and had been down fourteen years. He was an old nigga who had plenty of money and was amazingly slick. He had pressure on Ms. Wishob because he figured he could get her on his team, so Rabbit made every attempt to swindle her his way. Ms. Wishob told Kash that Rabbit had been trying to blackmail her, and when it didn't work, he went to the rat stage and wrote a statement on what she'd been doing. The warden fired her because it was too many notes on her and people talking, but no drugs or contraband were found.

Kash was heated by the sudden news. Rabbit was bigtime tripping and out of place. Kash was gonna deal with this nigga and do it fast. He saw Meco and two of his brothers coming his way.

"Let's blow one, foo'," Meco said and dapped Kash, who was looking half crazy.

"Shawty, dis bitch finna get locked back down," Kash said.

He turned around and walked back into his room.

"What's up, bruh? Who want it?" Meco asked once in the cell.

"Bruh, I talk to da ho. She said Rabbit's bitch-ass wrote the statement."

"Talkin' 'bout the Muslim nigga who be kickboxing?"

"Ok, fuck him, too, guns up."

Meco pulled his banger out.

"Let's get it."

Kash walked out and headed down a couple of cells to where Rabbit was standing with his back to Kash, talking to his brothers. Kash lifted the knife up and swung around, connecting with Rabbit's face and breaking his jaw.

"Rat-ass nigga."

He caught Rabbit again, but this time in the neck. Meco and his two GF brothers went at the other Muslims. Kash gave chase as Rabbit tried to get away, but failed as Kash stabbed him in his back and head repeatedly. Other Muslims got into the brawl, and the police also rushed in. Kash left Rabbit slumped and caught a dude charging at Meco. Soon as Kash struck the Muslim, he felt a sharp pain shoot through his shoulder, then his neck. He quickly turned toward another nigga, who swung wildly at him. Moments later, one of Meco's brothers busted the wild guy from behind.

"Who want it?"

At the same time, Kash went in with him.

"Lockdown! Lockdown!"

More and more police were running in, and niggas were going to the rooms trying to get away clean from the rumble. Most kept fighting and talking loud shit to each other as they were slammed down and cuffed up. Three Muslims and Kash were rushed to the hospital for stab wounds.

Kash awoke chained down to the bed in the ER with a nurse and two Macon State officers. Kash's head and neck were wrapped and hurting as he looked around the room.

"You finally up?" one of the officers said, standing up and grabbing his coat.

"What time is it?" Kash asked.

He remembered being rushed here, but forgot what time he fell asleep. The nurse was checking his pulse when he noticed how pretty she was.

"Time to take you back," the other officer chimed in.

"I'm wit' dat," Kash joined in.

The officers then asked the nurse how much longer she would be.

"Give me five more minutes and I will get his discharge papers." Her voice was soft and humble.

"Ok. We'll be out here, waiting," and both officers left the room.

Kash slightly sat up in bed.

"What's your name, if you don't mind my asking?"

The nurse was at the counter, getting his pain pills and other things in order.

She turned around to face him.

"Ms. Johnson."

"Okay, I'm Kash, Ms. Johnson. You look good, you know."

"Thank you. Well, take two of—"

"Write down my info," Kash cut her off.

"For what?"

She turned back to bring his pills.

"'Cause you and me need to be friends if you single."

"Well, I'm not."

Ms. Johnson passed Kash his stuff and walked out holding his paperwork.

Outside in the van, Kash overheard the officers talking about Rabbit being on life support, and Meco went straight to high max. When the van made it to Macon, the cert team was there to ship Kash and Tae to Telfair State Prison.

***

Three Weeks Later

Dear Charles,

The Streets Bleed Murder

Honey, I can't believe you acted like you did. I come to work expecting to see you and talk, but you're gone and word is out that you nearly killed that boy. What's wrong with you?

Anyway, I guess it's a good and bad thing you're gone. Good 'cause now I no longer have to hide me liking you, and I can't lose my job. Bad because I cannot see you like I would like. We never really got past go, and now I'm willing to try. I have looked you up and I fully accept your life sentence, only if you accept what comes with me. Well, I'm about to end this letter, but not my thoughts. I hope you write back soon so I can know what's on your mind. (Hope it's me.)

Always,
Yavon Berry

Kash folded the letter up from Ms. Berry. He was packed and ready to hit the compound of Telfair. It'd been three weeks since the war at Macon, and he was elated that pussy-ass Rabbit pulled through, becaue he didn't need another dead body on his hands.

They assigned him to E1. He and a few more inmates were released from the hole that Monday morning.

"What bed you in, bruh?" one inmate said when Kash walked into the small pod at Telfair State Prison.

It was another level-five prison that was bad on violence.

"134."

With both his mat and property, Kash made his way to the room. An older cat was laying down when Kash walked in. The room had a smell of oil, plus Kash spotted a prayer rug, so he knew his roommate was Muslim.

Kash put his property down and tossed his mat on the top bunk. He opened the locker box that read *Top* to inspect the cleanness of it before he unpacked.

"Bleach by the toilet if you wanna clean yo' box. They call me Roc." The older guy was the first to speak.

"Okay, I'm Kash."

He began to unpack his things. It didn't take him long to get his stuff situated. Once everything was put in place, Kash pulled a flat piece of iron with a knifepoint out of his photo album. He wrapped it for a grip and put it on his side as if it was a Glock.

"Where you come from, young blood?"

"Macon State."

"You GF?"

"Nah."

Kash cracked the door open. Now he was ready to smoke one and chill, because he was physically tired already of prison.

"Oh, so you from Atlanta?" this new roommate asked.

"Yeah."

"Well, yeah. You got a lot of homeboys here."

"Check," Kash said while stepping out of the cell into a brand new environment with new faces.

When he did step out, it seemed as if every eye in the pod was on Kash, bar none. Each nigga he caught looking at him, Kash stared him down.

The TV was on, but turned in another direction so the booth officer couldn't see that it was on. Small yard was also going, so Kash stepped out to see what was what.

It wasn't long before he heard that Dank was in the next building, D building, and he was GF, one of the Capo's. It didn't surprise Kash to know if niggas rolled with Dank, he would have rank, because he wasn't no ho. He was about his issue. But to Kash, he was a ho-nigga, because people didn't know the other side. Niggas didn't know that the 6'4", hard-body GF member was a rat, and Kash vowed to expose him and everything he had going on.

After the yard ended, Kash made a phone call to Gangsta to let him know where he was and to inform him that Dank was at the same prison in the next pod.

"What?" Gangsta laughed. "You seen 'im yet?"

"Hell naw, bruh. We ain't went to chow yet," Kash replied.

They talked five more minutes and ended the call 'cause he was using somebody's cell phone.

***

Gangsta

Gangsta couldn't believe the state fucked around and put Kash and Dank together at the same camp. He knew for certain Kash would kill Dank first chance he got, so he knew Kash wouldn't be at Telfair long at all.

Gangsta pulled his Range Rover up in Hollywood Brooks on Hollywood Road, the west side of Atlanta. It was a spot Eric now ran with an iron fist, slanging crack from nicks to bricks. You could get it in Hollywood Brooks. He parked next to an ivory-white Benz Coupe, which confirmed Eric was there as expected. Gangsta jumped out holding a brand new Glock 19 clutched in his fist. It was either be on point or get murked at this time of the night in Atlanta, and Gangsta was ready to do the murking, 'cause he refuse to go out bad.

When he made it to the door, Gangsta put the Glock in his back pocket. He was let in after he knocked to find Eric on the sofa with a gun next to him, smoking a blunt.

"What's happenin' fool?"

"Boy, the feds snatched up two of my partnas."

Eric hit the blunt hard.

"Shit."

"Yeah, that's what I said. What's up, though?"

"I need you to cook these bricks up for me."

Gangsta remained standing.

"I don't know, cuz, I shut down Johnson Road and even here. I'ma duck off befo' them feds start watching me. I got enough paper to relax."

"Nigga, you just said yo' team was good. I thought you was straight?" Gangsta couldn't help but ask.

"I don't know. I'm just being on point. I will cook it for you, cuz, but not tonight."

Eric looked stressed, like the feds already had him. One thing for certain, Gangsta had to get off Hollywood Road and had to do it fast, because he felt a sweep.

"Shawty, get ghost if you feel like that."

"You right, cuz, that's what I'm gonna do. Just lay low," Eric said while looking into space.

Gangsta scooped Keshana up from his mother's house on South Grand when he left Eric, then drove to College Park to pick up his son from NeNe. There was nothing in the streets but some jailtime, so he would much rather spend his time with his kids.

He called NeNe's phone and got no answer. He dialed her house and still got no answer, and he wondered why as he drove down Camp Creek Parkway. She had been off work and knew ahead of time he was coming to get Junior, so what was the issue?

Gangsta called two more times and got the same thing. He made it to NeNe's three-bedroom house and saw her car parked, which pissed him off, 'cause now he knew for certain she was being funny. Gangsta got out, then took Keshana out of her car seat. He carried her to the door and his heart dropped from his chest when he saw the door had been kicked in, but somebody closed it back.

Instantly Gangsta backed off the porch and quickly put his daughter back in the car. He got his gun out and proceeded to the door.

He did not hesitate going right in, and the house was a wreck. The living room was a mess, and he rushed from room to room to see the same thing. His heart felt heavy when he got to his son's room. Gangsta wanted to break down, but he had to think first, and the first person who came to mind was Pat Man.

Gangsta didn't want to call the police or try to figure out what was going on himself. After a quick look around, he rushed back outside to his daughter. She was safe. He got in and pulled off with murder on his mind.

***

Kash

"Chow call! Chow call! Make sure you're state dressed before leaving the pod," the female officer yelled over the intercom.

The Streets Bleed Murder

Kash made sure to wear three shirts and a sweater under his state shirt, dressed with the banger in his boots. The extra clothes were for protection from being stabbed.

When he stepped out, he saw a group of GF's gangsters awaiting the rest of their members. Kash proceeded to walk solo, because he was on a mission and didn't wanna chat with the new faces right now. Kash knew Dank's building was next to come up, so he took a seat after grabbing his tray.

"Say, bruh, I got cookies for yo' main," some dude said to Kash.

"I'm straight," Kash bluntly spoke and watched the pod start to fill up in the chow hall.

It took at least ten minutes for the lieutenant and sergeant to run E1 and E2, but Kash waited until Dank's pod was let out and headed up the walk. Kash had slid the knife from his boot and now held it in his fist tightly as he watched carefully.

Dank walked into the chow hall with a small group of GF members. Kash wasted not another second running up on the group. Dank's eyes got big when he saw Kash and the knife he held. He swung at Dank's face. He ducked from the first blow, but quickly caught the second one wildly in the back with three deep shots. Somehow Dank got loose and pulled his own banger as two more of his GF partnas did the same, and all three worked on Kash.

Kash didn't feel the stabs on his side, his back, and one blow to his face. He was focused on Dank, who he wet up really good. When it was all said and done, Dank got hit seventeen times by Kash, and Kash took nine that sent him back to the hospital, and from there he was headed to super max at Jackson State Prison.

One of Kash's lungs collapsed on the way to the hospital, so he was kept when he arrived and doctors got to him. Everybody involved went to high max except Dank. Kash was cool with that. *Fuck it,* he thought while lying back in the bed. The only good thing to come out of this was he was stuck with the same nurse, Ms. Johnson.

Every chance he got, Kash would tell her how pretty she was to him and how he wanted to get to know her. He would do it in a slick manner, a respectful gesture, but he was pressing good. So good she finally responded.

"Now, you know I can't talk to you."

"Why?" Kash asked.

The officer with Kash was a old white man who loved coffee and stood outside the door at all times.

"'Cause you locked up."

"You not the police. You work just like my momma work, my sister work. Hell, you got the freedom to do what you wanna do. You grown, ain't cha?" Kash didn't give her time to respond. "I know you is, I'm just say'n. You beautiful and seem to me from your personality that you wifey type."

"Wifey type?"

"Like fo' real, though." Kash looked her in the eyes. "Everybody I know done crossed me 'cept one nigga, Ms. Johnson. I need true love, and something telling me I can get it from you."

"I don't know," Ms. Johnson mumbled while doing her daily check.

Kash stayed at the hospital four days and went straight to high max. He never got an answer from the nurse, but for those four days he did not stop his press game. He continued to go at her. Ms. Johnson did let her guard down at one time, telling her age and name and that she had a daughter, but that was the only info he needed. Kash was released from the hospital on her day off, so she did not see him leave, and Kash tried to stay a while longer 'cause he felt like she was breaking.

Chapter 22

Terry

She stood up to leave, pissed off at Zay and even madder at herself for becoming pregnant. Terry was pissed because Zay was yet to say anything about the baby. Keshana was almost two years old. Terry had no business getting pregnant. Yeah, it was a true fact Zay had enough money to take care of her and both the kids, but Terry had stuff she wanted to do herself, like go back and finish college and own her own salon and spa.

Tonight Zay had her in the club, and boy was he full of drink, 'cause he was talking shit and fucking with everybody. He thought everything he did deserved a laugh. Terry cursed herself for even coming out with him after telling him about the baby and he brushed it off with plans for the club. She should've known not to go anywhere with him.

"Come on, I'm ready to leave, Zarack." Terry had on some Prada leggings with a sheer top, white and yellow to match, also by Prada.

She stood looking down at him acting out, and she was tired of it.

"Just chill, baby," Zay slurred.

Terry was elated they had a driver, 'cause Zay was for sure drunk and she wasn't feeling him acting like a fool, but this was her boyfriend, so she stuck around as long as possible. Now it was over.

"No! Let's go." Terry walked off knowing Zay would follow her or he was sure to get left behind.

Just as Terry thought, he was out of the club with a crew of gunners, where he joined Terry in his S550 black Benz.

At times, Terry wished for the normal life how Gangsta lived. He wasn't flashy or loud, nor did he do clubs, but Zay needed the attention. He was loving the bright lights and money-throwing.

Terry enjoyed the benefits of being Zay's girl. He went over and beyond for her and Keshana. Whatever she wanted, Zay got, no questions asked, and that was the good part about him. Once inside the car, Zay started feeling on her roughly, not knowing he was out of line until she slapped his hand with a scowl on her pretty face.

"Yo' ass still have not said two words about this baby growing inside me, and you try'na fuck."

"What you want me to say? Shit, I'm happy, baby, but I'm horny, too."

Neither Terry nor Zay noticed Gangsta's range rover until he blocked the Benz in from pulling off. Terry saw Gangsta jump out with a look she had never seen on his face.

He snatched the door open, gun in hand.

"Terry, get in my truck, take Keshana somewhere safe. Zay, me and you gotta ride."

Zay sat up, and Terry did the same.

"What's going on, bruh?" Zay asked, visibly shaken by the gun Gangsta held.

"Somebody kicked in NeNe's door. My son missing, she missing, the crib is a mess, and Zay, me and you know who the number one suspect is," Gangsta said as Terry got out.

"Man, I swear, whatever it is that's going on ain't got nothing to do with me, bruh. I would never do no shit like that," Zay said. He had quickly sobered up, and Gangsta had his full attention.

"I'm not saying you, Zay. I'm saying you know who it is, though, and where to find this bitch-nigga." Gangsta got inside the Benz. "So, what you gon' do?"

"Shit, bruh, I'm with you. I don't know dis shit, but this your son involved," Zay said, then told his driver to drive.

Terry pulled off when she saw them pull off. Her heart went out to NeNe and Junior. No matter if she liked the bitch or not, she didn't want anything to happen to her and Gangsta's son. Terry silently prayed for those involved, because the streets were about to get ugly.

***

Gangsta

Gangsta felt his phone vibrate and saw it was NeNe's number. He quickly picked up.

"Nya!"

"Fuck, nigga, dis ain't no NeNe."

Gangsta couldn't recognize the voice.

"Ok, where is she and my son?"

"For the right price, you just might see them again. So, check this out, nigga. How do it feel to be on the other side the gun?"

"My nigga, what's the price? Fuck all that shit you talking. I'm not 'bout to put up no fight. My son and his mom don't got shit to do with what I got going on," Gangsta stressed. He was hoping his family was ok.

"Well, since you put it that way, let's just say I need a million bucks, pussy-nigga," the caller said. Gangsta still could not put a face with the voice. Zay sat on the passenger side listening to the voice, also.

"Give me a minute. I'm 'bout to make two calls." Gangsta didn't have that type of money, but between Zay and Eric, he knew he could come up with it.

"They die if you put the police in it," the caller said, then hung up.

Gangsta called Eric, who told him to come pick up 300 racks. It was all the money he had. Zay also offered 200, which was all he claimed to have on him. Gangsta had 300 saved himself. He called NeNe's phone back.

"Yeah, nigga, what's up?" the caller answered.

"I got 850 and four bricks," Gangsta said with panic in his voice. All he wanted was his family back.

He had figured Eric and Zay were flexing about being rich. Though they had money, Gangsta knew it wasn't like that.

"I will call you wit' directions in a second." Then the line went dead.

Gangsta wanted to break down, but knew he needed to be strong for his son and NeNe.

Zay's driver finally made it to Pat Man's house. He lived in Forrest Park in a nice house surrounded by an iron fence. When Gangsta and Zay got out in the driveway, they were met by two of Pat Man's partnas.

Instantly Gangsta pulled his gun and pointed at the one closer to him.

"Where Pat Man's bitch-ass at?" Both of the dudes put their hands up in the air.

"Feds got him yesterday at the mall."

"Nigga, where is my son?" Gangsta couldn't help but ask.

"Man, we don't know what's going on. I'm just coming over here doing like Pat Man ask us to do and make sure nothing was in the crib, 'cause the feds coming to clean house," the guy said.

Gangsta looked at Zay, then said, "Call the county, make sure Pat Man locked up. And if not, I'm gonna murk both of you niggas right here, I promise." He looked to both guys.

It took Zay five minutes to confirm Pat Man was indeed locked up. Gangsta let both the guys go.

He and Zay rode to Bam's spot, which was an hour away. He also texted NeNe's number for the dude to call him back, and within minutes the phone rang. Gangsta picked up.

"What's up, tell me something."

"Bring the money to the graveyard across from Hollywood Courts. Go all the way to the back, and when you see a box, put the money in it."

"Where's my family?" Gangsta wanted to know.

"When I know the money good, then your folks will be seconds behind, so don't be late. I'm waiting on you," the caller said and laughed a little before hanging up.

"I need dat money, Zay," was all Gangsta could say.

***

Terry

She couldn't believe someone actually kidnapped NeNe and her son. It scared Terry to know a person was capable of such acts. It had her not ever wanting Keshana anywhere but with her.

Gangsta also had too much going on for this to all of a sudden happen. He just got out of prison not even a month ago and already was into something.

Terry was at the house with Roxanne and their other best friend, Nikki. All three girls sat in the living room trying to figure out what was going on in the streets. Word had traveled that the feds kicked in Eric's mom's door looking for him.

"Girl, this shit, it's crazy. Somebody snitching they ass off. Nineteen niggas from Hollywood Brooks, Johnson Road and Bankhead got snatched by the feds. I had a gut feeling they was coming at Eric, anyways," Nikki spoke and hit the blunt they were smoking

Terry was in deep thought when something hit her that Zay mentioned while they pillowtalked through the night. She remembered Zay saying something about Bam being caught up in DC some months ago with a lot of drugs, and then got out the next few days.

"Come to think about it, girl, Bam's ass might be the nigga, 'cause tell me what type of nigga get knocked with so many bricks and get out so soon?" Terry shared with her friends. The statement made Roxanne sit up.

"When did Bam get locked up? I never heard 'bout this one," Roxanne said

"Yeah, 'cause it's been months ago, Zay said. He just said he felt strange about the whole situation. Zay really don't say too much, but that conversation I didn't forget. It have me watching Bam every time I see him."

"That will be messed up if that boy set everyone up like that. Nigga from out of town come down here, trick everyone with a lil' money, and then bust they heads," Nikki spoke with a shake of her head, and then Roxanne added, "And them niggas ain't got no money like dat Bam taxed on them bricks, I heard."

"Girl, I know for a fact that Zay got a few millions, and Eric for sure. I just don't understand whoever's telling — what's their reason?" Terry questioned herself.

Everyone's heads turned when car lights pulled into the driveway. All three girls rushed to the window. Terry was happy to see it was Zay's Benz. He and Gangsta climbed out and headed to the house. The girls all took their seats as the door came open.

Neither Gangsta nor Zay looked at the girls. They walked directly into the movie room. Terry followed after telling her friends to wait.

"Bruh, this all the money I got on me now, 'cause I just spent it with Bam," Zay said and opened a safe that was hidden under one of the big movie chairs. Terry looked at Gangsta and never saw him so helpless and lost.

"Thank you, my nigga. I got you soon as this shit is over."

Gangsta gave Zay a pounded fist. Terry stopped Gangsta before he left. Zay went up to get a change of cloths.

"Feds are looking for your cousin. You ok?"

Gangsta had defeat in his eyes when he looked at her. It looked as if he was about to cry at any moment.

"Yeah, just want them safe, Terry. These fuck-niggas got my son."

"What do they want?"

"A mill."

Zay walked back downstairs, which stopped the conversation. Terry was confused, because if all the people wanted was a million, then why would Zay give Gangsta the dummy stash designed for robbers?

Gangsta left to go meet Eric for the other money. Terry's heart felt bad, and now she felt some kind of way, 'cause Zay could have given Gangsta the money. It was some fishy shit going on. Terry wasn't stupid.

Chapter 23

Veedo

Rice Street held him on lockdown along with a lot of other cats. There were 43 niggas the feds snatched up, and half snitched on each other. Veedo knew with statements from Kia and Amanda he was for sure done, plus Bam was working with the Feds, so Veedo took it like a champ awaiting his fate.

Veedo still hadn't reached out to anybody because too much was going on. Not even worried about a lawyer, he just kept it real with himself by accepting the fact that FBI meant prison time. Niggas didn't get away once the feds snatched them up.

The person who most shocked Veedo was his right-hand man, Rock. Months before the sweep, Rock had gotten popped with three bricks and quickly gave up Veedo, though when he mentioned Bam's name, the FBI knew they were dealing with a drug ring. Veedo didn't expect that blow from Rock, not at all. It hurt when he thought how bad Rock did him. Veedo sat up many nights and wondered what was going to happen from here. He was still caked up, minus the stash at LisaPay's house. He had paper put up with family, so no matter what, they wouldn't get that. But what would he do once he was free from prison?

It did not surprise Veedo that Kia and Amanda turned state on him. Hell, he paid them not to snitch, and you cannot just buy loyalty on the streets. Veedo hated this, but had to deal with the outcome of the situation.

Bam was out on the streets tricking every drug dealer he could. Veedo should have known something was wrong when Bam asked him to come up front with a half-million dollars. Just weeks ago he stated he would front whatever.

Later that day, at feed off, Veedo received a kite from one of the jail trustees. It was a kite from Pat Man. He quickly opened it and began to read.

Say, Veedo, I don't know if you on point or not, but that nigga Bam is a snake. He set all of us up. I got all the statements and wire taps in my cell from my lawyer. The nigga got popped, him and Zay, in DC. The folks let Zay go, but booked Bam. Couple days later he got out. How ironic, huh? Yeah, the feds been on us two months watching our every move. I also got statements from them two lil' hos you was working with. Everybody locked up except Zay and Bam. Bruh, it don't take a rocket scientist. Get word to yo' boy to fall back.

***

Gangsta

It was his third time calling Eric, and still he couldn't get an answer, so Gangsta called his aunt. All he had on him was 600 thousand and four bricks. He badly needed the other 200 grand.

"Hello."

"Aunt, where is Eric?"

"Baby, the feds just picked him up on 285 with a trunk full of money. They kicked my door in two hours ago. Gotta get a new one soon," his aunt said, which broke Gangsta's spirit.

"Ok, aunt, let me know what's up with Eric when you find out."

"You be careful, too, Gary, alright?"

Gangsta didn't know what to do. All he could think about was his family. He knew he needed 200 grand more or the deal would be off. He considered calling the cops, but decided against it. Gangsta would never forgive himself if something happened to his family.

He called NeNe's phone back, but didn't get an answer. Panic started to set in as he rode down the highway. He wondered why that girl Amanda didn't call back. So much shit was going on, and he couldn't put his finger on any of it.

Gangsta made a call to Loco, the Mexican he recently hooked up with. Loco agreed to meet him downtown, where they both sat inside Loco's Bentley right outside the Best Western.

Loco was a short, skinny Mexican, one of the first Mexicans Gangsta met who didn't have tattoos and didn't do drugs, plus Loco was young and already a boss.

He greeted Gangsta with a handshake, then asked, "What can I help you with?"

"Loco, man, my son and baby mama been kidnapped, and I don't have all the paperwork to pay these niggas."

"Damn, man, what kind of beef you got in these streets? Who are those that got your family?"

"That's what I'm trying to find out now, man. But what I need is the loan, man, and I get my family back," Gangsta replied.

"Ok, man, so what do you need?" Loco asked.

"200 grand."

"No problem, man. Do you need me and my people to go with you to have your back?"

"I think I need to roll up solo on this one, man."

Gangsta felt better about the situation already. He made the call again to NeNe's phone, and it was picked up, but this time it wasn't the dude. It was a female.

"Hello." Gangsta's heart dropped.

"Who is this? Erica?"

"Yes, Gangsta, we are safe...."

The phone was snatched from Erica and the dude got on.

"You got 20 minutes 'til time is up. I'd be at that graveyard fast if I was you." The phone hung up. Gangsta just stared at the phone until Loco broke his train of thought.

"Was that them, man?"

"Yeah. I got to get going. You ready to give me that loan? I'm trying to make this shit happen."

Loco went to the trunk of the Bentley and counted out the money. He and Gangsta dapped before they departed.

Gangsta wasted not another second going to Hollywood Road to get this situation over with.

It took him no less than 15 minutes to make it to Hollywood Road. Gangsta parked at the store next to the graveyard. He got out with the money and bricks, a glock hidden under his shirt, and his bulletproof vest.

It was dark and hardly anybody was out in the streets as he made his way through the graveyard, going to the back as directed. Gangsta scanned the entire graveyard and saw not a soul. He kept walking to the back until he saw a brown box next to a tombstone. It was now or never, Gangsta thought, and put the bag he held inside the box. Gangsta pulled his phone out and called NeNe's number. The phone rang and went to voicemail. He called again, but stopped when he heard leaves crunching under someone's footsteps. Gangsta quickly turned around, and that's all he remembered as he was knocked out cold by the butt of a gun.

To Be Continued...
The Street Bleed Murder 2
Available Now!

Stay Connected with Us!

Text **LOCKDOWN** to 22828 to stay
up-to-date with new releases, sneak peaks,
contests and more…

Thank you!

Submission Guideline.

Submit the first three chapters of your completed manuscript to ldpsubmissions@gmail.com, subject line: Your book's title. The manuscript must be in a .doc file and sent as an attachment. Document should be in Times New Roman, double spaced and in size 12 font. Also, provide your synopsis and full contact information. If sending multiple submissions, they must each be in a separate email.

Have a story but no way to send it electronically? You can still submit to LDP/Ca$h Presents. Send in the first three chapters, written or typed, of your completed manuscript to:

LDP: Submissions Dept
Po Box 870494
Mesquite, Tx 75187

DO NOT send original manuscript. Must be a duplicate.

Provide your synopsis and a cover letter containing your full contact information.

Thanks for considering LDP and Ca$h Presents.

Coming Soon from Lock Down Publications/Ca$h Presents

BOW DOWN TO MY GANGSTA

By **Ca$h**

TORN BETWEEN TWO

By **Coffee**

BLOOD STAINS OF A SHOTTA **II**

By **Jamaica**

WHEN THE STREETS CLAP BACK **II**

By **Jibril Williams**

STEADY MOBBIN

By **Marcellus Allen**

BLOOD OF A BOSS **V**

By **Askari**

BRIDE OF A HUSTLA **III**

By **Destiny Skai**

WHEN A GOOD GIRL GOES BAD **II**

By **Adrienne**

LOVE & CHASIN' PAPER **II**

By **Qay Crockett**

THE HEART OF A GANGSTA **III**

By **Jerry Jackson**

LOYAL TO THE GAME **IV**

By **T.J. & Jelissa**

A DOPEBOY'S PRAYER **II**

By **Eddie "Wolf" Lee**

IF LOVING YOU IS WRONG... **III**

Jerry Jackson

By **Jelissa**
BLOODY COMMAS **III**
SKI MASK CARTEL II
By **T.J. Edwards**
BLAST FOR ME **II**
RAISED AS A GOON V
BRED BY THE SLUMS
By **Ghost**
A DISTINGUISHED THUG STOLE MY HEART **III**
By **Meesha**
ADDICTIED TO THE DRAMA **II**
By **Jamila Mathis**
LIPSTICK KILLAH II
By **Mimi**
THE BOSSMAN'S DAUGHTERS 4
By **Aryanna**

<u>Available Now</u>
<u>RESTRAINING ORDER</u> **I & II**
By **CA$H & Coffee**
<u>LOVE KNOWS NO BOUNDARIES</u> **I II & III**
By **Coffee**
<u>RAISED AS A GOON I, II, III & IV</u>
By **Ghost**
<u>LAY IT DOWN</u> **I & II**
<u>LAST OF A DYING BREED</u>
<u>BLOOD STAINS OF A SHOTTA</u>

The Streets Bleed Murder

By **Jamaica**

LOYAL TO THE GAME

LOYAL TO THE GAME II

LOYAL TO THE GAME III

By **TJ & Jelissa**

BLOODY COMMAS I & II

SKI MASK CARTEL

By **T.J. Edwards**

IF LOVING HIM IS WRONG…I & II

By **Jelissa**

WHEN THE STREETS CLAP BACK

By **Jibril Williams**

A DISTINGUISHED THUG STOLE MY HEART I & II

By **Meesha**

PUSH IT TO THE LIMIT

By **Bre' Hayes**

BLOOD OF A BOSS **I, II, III & IV**

By **Askari**

THE STREETS BLEED MURDER **I, II & III**

THE HEART OF A GANGSTA I & II

By **Jerry Jackson**

CUM FOR ME

CUM FOR ME 2

CUM FOR ME 3

An **LDP Erotica Collaboration**

BRIDE OF A HUSTLA **I & II**

THE FETTI GIRLS **I, II& III**

Jerry Jackson

By **Destiny Skai**

WHEN A GOOD GIRL GOES BAD

By **Adrienne**

A GANGSTER'S REVENGE **I II III & IV**

THE BOSS MAN'S DAUGHTERS

THE BOSS MAN'S DAUGHTERS II

THE BOSSMAN'S DAUGHTERS III

A SAVAGE LOVE **I & II**

BAE BELONGS TO ME

A HUSTLER'S DECEIT I, II

By **Aryanna**

A KINGPIN'S AMBITON

A KINGPIN'S AMBITION **II**

I MURDER FOR THE DOUGH

By **Ambitious**

TRUE SAVAGE

TRUE SAVAGE II

TRUE SAVAGE **III**

By **Chris Green**

A DOPEBOY'S PRAYER

By **Eddie "Wolf" Lee**

THE KING CARTEL **I, II & III**

By **Frank Gresham**

THESE NIGGAS AIN'T LOYAL **I, II & III**

By **Nikki Tee**

GANGSTA SHYT **I II &III**

By **CATO**

240

THE ULTIMATE BETRAYAL

By **Phoenix**

BOSS'N UP **I , II & III**

By **Royal Nicole**

I LOVE YOU TO DEATH

By Destiny J

I RIDE FOR MY HITTA

I STILL RIDE FOR MY HITTA

By **Misty Holt**

LOVE & CHASIN' PAPER

By **Qay Crockett**

TO DIE IN VAIN

By **ASAD**

BROOKLYN HUSTLAZ

By **Boogsy Morina**

BROOKLYN ON LOCK I & II

By **Sonovia**

GANGSTA CITY

By **Teddy Duke**

A DRUG KING AND HIS DIAMOND

A DOPEMAN'S RICHES

By Nicole Goosby

Jerry Jackson

<u>BOOKS BY LDP'S CEO, CA$H</u>

<u>TRUST IN NO MAN</u>

<u>TRUST IN NO MAN 2</u>

<u>TRUST IN NO MAN 3</u>

<u>BONDED BY BLOOD</u>

<u>SHORTY GOT A THUG</u>

<u>THUGS CRY</u>

<u>THUGS CRY 2</u>

<u>THUGS CRY 3</u>

<u>TRUST NO BITCH</u>

<u>TRUST NO BITCH 2</u>

<u>TRUST NO BITCH 3</u>

<u>TIL MY CASKET DROPS</u>

<u>RESTRAINING ORDER</u>

<u>RESTRAINING ORDER 2</u>

<u>IN LOVE WITH A CONVICT</u>

<u>Coming Soon</u>

BONDED BY BLOOD 2

BOW DOWN TO MY GANGSTA

Jerry Jackson